PICKLE

By JJ Knight

USA Today bestselling author of

Single Dad on Top
The Accidental Harem
Big Pickle
Hot Pickle
Spicy Pickle
Uncaged Love
Fight for Her
Reckless Attraction

Want to make sure you don't miss a release?
Join JJ's email or text list.

LIBRARY OF
CONGRESS
SURPLUS
DUPLICATE

ABOUT THE PICKLE SERIES

★★★★★
"OMG I was snort laughing by page 2!" ~ Judy Ann Loves Books Blog

★★★★★
"It's laugh-out-loud, snort-your-drink, absolutely-do-not-read-this-book-in-public hilarious, with this crafty writer's clever wit creatively showcased on every page." ~ Book Addict Book Blog

★★★★★
"The poster child for how a romantic comedy should be written. I dare you to try and not laugh or fall in love with this book!" ~ Dog-Eared Daydreams

★★★★★
"Hilarious cute read full of pickle puns." ~ Cool Moms who Read

★★★★★
"You know you are in for a whole lot of fun." ~ Life, Books, and More Blog

★★★★★
"The puns, the innuendos, the hot pickles...I loved it all!" ~ Kay Reads Romance

★★★★★
"This series has so much hilarity that I can't stop laughing about it." ~ Southern Chics Lit

★★★ SPICY PICKLE ★★★

First, she tampered with my pickle.
Then, she got us both kicked off a cooking show.
Now, we're fake engaged.
Sit back, friends, this is one crazy tale of treachery and pickle juice.

Anthony:

All right. Here's how it went.
My pickle went viral.
Millions saw it. Thousands ate it.

Hold up, pervs. Let me backtrack.

I invented a very spicy pickle made with ghost peppers. One bite and you'll swear someone stuffed a hot coal in your mouth. It's extremely popular in pranks.

I'm in the middle of filming with a prominent cooking show when in walks Little Miss Perfect Pants from a rival deli to insist she has improvements for my pickle.

It all goes downhill from there.

———
Magnolia:

Read the reviews and weep, Anthony Pickle.

I got the best of you on reality TV.
You got me back with a very public kiss.

After your new deli poached on my territory, I swore to
hate you. But every time those smoky eyes meet mine, I
melt a little.

Cheesy, right?

By the time you kiss me, I already know I'm in deep.
But then you propose?

How am I supposed to keep faking it when every swoon
is real?

Copyright © 2021 by JJ Knight All rights reserved.

No part of this publication may be reproduced, distributed, or transmitted in any form or by any means, including photocopying, recording, or other electronic or mechanical methods, without the prior written permission of the publisher, except in the case of brief quotations embodied in reviews, fan-made graphics, and certain other noncommercial uses permitted by copyright law.

This is a work of fiction. Names, characters, businesses, places, events and incidents are either the products of the author's imagination or used in a fictitious manner. Any resemblance to actual persons, living or dead, or actual events is purely coincidental.

Edition 1.2

Casey Shay Press
PO Box 160116
Austin, TX 78716
www.jjknight.com

Paperback ISBN: 9781938150920

1

ANTHONY

I'm about to show my pickle on television.

I have to admit, I'm anxious.

It's not that no one's seen this pickle. Thousands of people have.

In fact, thousands of people have *eaten* this pickle.

But never on television.

Wait.

You seemed confused.

Whoa, whoa.

No, it's not *that* kind of show.

Heh, heh.

Let me try this again.

I've made myself a new pickle.

Nope. That's worse.

One more try.

I'm about to go on a cooking show with a spicy pickle recipe.

Now it's starting to make sense.

My delicatessen, Boulder Pickle, got some fame after

a challenge daring people to eat one of my ghost pepper pickles went viral on TikTok.

There are thousands of videos of men crying, women spitting out pickle bits, people running in circles, and diners dumping water on their heads.

We got so many take-out orders for the pickle that I had to hire two extra people to meet demand.

When the series coordinator for *America's Spiciest Chef* calls asking to film a segment about the pickle in their traveling test kitchen, I know I'm about to get my fifteen minutes of fame.

With my pickle, of course.

Okay, maybe I *like* saying it.

Right now, I'm on the set, arranging the spices I need to teach viewers how to make their own ghost pepper pickles.

From the front, I appear to be standing in an ordinary kitchen with a sink, stove, and chopping block. Behind me is a wall with a double oven, a refrigerator, and shelves filled with aesthetically pleasing dishes.

But beyond the counter, a line of cameras, light operators, and runners zip around to prepare for the segment. Assistants move around me, setting up props. I fiddle with a set of clear bowls that hold my ingredients, trying to calm my nerves.

To be honest, I'd prefer anyone else from the Pickle family be on the show to represent our chain. Jason, the oldest, is pure charisma and the camera loves him. My middle brother Max is used to media attention, since he's a sports figure.

But I'm just me. Third brother. Culinary chef. Not particularly smooth.

I tried to pawn this gig off. I really did. But in the end, Dad put his foot down. I'm the leader of the chain. I invented the pickle that went viral. It has to be me.

I have lots of reasons to feel concern. The show's host Milton Creed is a polarizing figure in the culinary world. Everyone wants to be on his program, because it's popular and sure to bring attention to a restaurant.

But the man himself is rather unpredictable. He can be funny and generous with some guests, then turn on a dime to be caustic and condescending to others. You never know what version of Milton you're going to get.

I shift the bowl of garlic two millimeters to the left. Like it matters.

"All set?" A young woman with a mop of black curls pauses as she shines the last gleaming ring on the stove top.

"I'm moving things out of nerves at this point."

She nods. "We have to make it perfect for Mr. Creed."

"He's a stickler, then?"

"Totally." She lifts each clear plate in a stack to examine. "I've only been here for three recording sessions, and that's longer than half the stage crew."

Wow. "That bad?"

She leans in and whispers, "Worse than you can imagine. He leaves a swath of disgruntled ex-employees in his wake."

"Yikes." I shift my collar away from my neck. I

didn't think I could get more nervous, but this has done it. "How is he today?"

"Haven't seen him yet. But he generally hates Tuesdays." She adjusts a kitchen towel on a metal hook. "Good luck."

Then she's gone, leaving me wondering why anyone would hate Tuesdays.

But that's one question answered. I had a feeling Milton Creed might be a tyrant to his crew. I haven't met him yet. His "people" have done all the contact—the phone calls, the segment coordination, and even the rehearsal.

I'm tempted to run. But Jason insisted the show would be excellent publicity for our family chain. Dad said he couldn't be prouder.

A friendly man in all black approaches. "Mic time," he says. "Don't think about where it is or try to talk into it. Just act natural." He clips the tiny bit of metal to the edge of my apron and runs the wire to a pack on the back of my belt. "This is going to be a fun one."

"Because of the spicy pickle?"

"Maybe?" He gives me a wink, and I wonder what he means. My nerves kick up another notch.

A round, red-faced man with a headset crosses in front of the mock kitchen. "Places everyone. Milton is coming in." He turns to me. "Don't worry about the cameras. Just respond to Milton."

I fumble with my hands, setting them on the counter, then hooking my thumbs in my apron pockets, then dropping them by my sides. The spotlights all focus on the right side of the set.

The opening music to the show blares from the speakers, and then, there he is, Milton Creed.

He's shorter than he looks on television, thinning hair spiked out, pale face remarkably smooth. That's a *lot* of makeup.

Milton waves to the camera. "Welcome to *America's Spiciest Chef.* I'm your host, Milton Creed."

He heads my way. "Today we have the young owner of one of America's finest family delicatessen franchises. Say hello to Anthony Pickle!"

I sense cameras turning in my direction. "Thanks, Milton," I say. "Glad to be here."

So far, so good.

Milton shakes my hand. I realize he's standing on a small step to be closer to my height.

He turns back to the camera. "If you're on TikTok, you couldn't miss Anthony's ghost pepper pickle challenge, which went viral in a big way. Let's take a look at some of those great pickle moments."

A screen lights up on one side. Several of the pickle challenges are shown in quick succession. My shoulders start to relax. It's unfolding like the rehearsal. After the video, I'll show the ghost peppers, cut some up, mix the brine, and reveal the finished product, which is already waiting behind us in the refrigerator.

But when the attention is back on us, Milton says something we didn't rehearse. "Now we all love a little healthy competition. So, when we put together the show about the spiciest pickle, we decided to find other enterprising deli owners who might blow our socks off."

I turn to him in surprise. "What?"

He ignores me. "So, on this special pickle edition of *America's Spiciest Chef*, you're not going to see just *one* spicy pickle, but *two*."

I spot my astonished face on a monitor and straighten my expression. The last thing I need is to become a viral meme. *Shock-face Pickle.*

Milton keeps going. "In our *own* special challenge, we will be tasting not only Anthony's viral ghost pepper pickle, but one by another young chef. She says *her* fiery pickle will put Anthony's to shame. Everyone, welcome the genius behind the Tasty Pepper, Magnolia Boudreaux."

He's got to be kidding me.

A young woman strides through the set door and into the light. She's dressed in a bright green dress with a white apron. I want to seethe. Green and white are *my* deli's colors.

Now I understand why my apron is black. I'm the bad guy in this situation. Magnolia's long blond hair flows down her back, pulled away from her face with a ribbon to give her a fresh, innocent look.

I've never met Magnolia, but I know who she is. Her father owns the other family deli in Boulder. They completely resented me opening a restaurant in their market, even though Boulder is more than big enough for both of us.

And now his daughter has invaded *my* pickle segment.

Magnolia turns to me and extends a hand. "Hello, Anthony." Her big sky-blue eyes are fringed with curled lashes. She looks like an American Girl doll. The viewers are going to love her, an angelic princess next to the big bad wolf who raided her forest.

I can barely say her name through my gritted teeth as I shake her hand. "Hello, Magnolia."

"Ho ho!" Milton says, and the gleam in his eye tells me he hopes we go at each other's throats. "Do I sense a rivalry here?"

"Of course," Magnolia says, her voice simperingly sweet. "My family has been a Boulder tradition since 1958. How long has your deli been open, Anthony?"

I clamp my jaw again. "Four years."

Her laugh is melodious, but each peal sets me on edge. "Such a newcomer." She elbows me in the ribs. "But I'm sure you have nothing to worry about. How could I possibly dethrone the spiciest pickle in Colorado?"

Milton puts a hand on her shoulder. "Things are heating up in *America's Spiciest Kitchen*!" he says, his glee apparent. "Let's get to work on some fiery dishes!"

Magnolia's smile is as innocent as a lamb as she says, "May the best pickle win."

2

MAGNOLIA

Anthony Pickle's expression is priceless. Shock has taken over every feature. Those thick eyebrows lift to his hairline, his smoky eyes wide. His mouth is an open *O*.

Got him.

It's about time I made some inroads on this rivalry. My family has owned the Tasty Pepper for six decades. Then a few years ago, here comes this Pickle brother with his ridiculous bread names and monthly pickle flavors, poaching on our territory.

And he's the one who goes viral!

But he hasn't won today. My family pitched this show to Milton Creed a few weeks ago, as soon as we saw the pickle challenge go bonkers on TikTok. Wouldn't Milton like a viral segment to match?

My father told him to let us put our spin on that ghost pepper pickle, and we'd have a culinary moment to rival Gordon Ramsey challenging his own mother.

Milton bought it.

And here we are. Anthony has *no* idea this pickle competition was *my* family's brainchild. I love the element of surprise. I just wish I wasn't the one on camera. I'm having to fake every bit of confidence. To be honest, I'm petrified.

Milton pats Anthony on the shoulder. "What do you think?"

Anthony pauses a moment, looking from Milton and back to me.

He faces the cameras. His voice is low, rich, and resonant as he speaks directly to the viewer. "I'll put my pickle up against what she's got any time."

Oh, my. My face flares hot.

Milton Creed snorts so hard that the director calls for a cut, and the crew collapses with laughter.

Anthony's surprised face tells me he didn't intend to be shocking. He whips around to face me. "I'm sorry. I didn't mean —"

"Forget it," I say. "It's fine."

But he's upset. "No. Really. It wasn't until the words came out of my mouth that I realized what they would sound like."

I wave my hand. "It's fine. Payback for me showing up."

"No! God! I was talking about pickles. Jesus! I should not be representing my family on this show."

Now I'm amused. So, he really *is* that awkward.

"It's fine, Anthony. I doubt the comment will make the show."

Truth is. I'm totally as poise-challenged as him. I might come from a long line of deli connoisseurs, but my magic is in accounting. I do the books for the Tasty Pepper, not the cooking. I don't serve customers. I hide in the back with my spreadsheets and financials.

I have no aspirations to be the spokesperson for the family. I'm only here because I drew the short straw and got stuck being the one who went on stage.

While the techs get their spotlights back in line and a makeup artist rushes on set to refresh Milton's pancaked face, I glance down at Anthony's artfully arranged assortment of spices, oils, and pepper. Our real head chef Dan has promised me that what I'm doing will work. I simply have to stay poised and confident while I do exactly what he taught me.

When the director has the cameras rolling again, Milton turns to me.

"Magnolia, tell us how you're going to *beat* the hottest pickle in America."

The double entendres are off and running. Milton is not awkward like Anthony. He's doing it on purpose.

I'd like to smash a ghost pepper in his face. But instead, I open my eyes wide as if I haven't the faintest notion that *beating a pickle* might mean anything other than winning this contest. My family's deli is on the line, so I have *bigger* pickles to beat.

"Well, Milton, I have a secret weapon right here." I pat the lump in my apron pocket. "But I think we should let Anthony demonstrate how to make his modest pickle before I improve it."

Anthony isn't laughing. "Magnolia, there isn't anything hotter than the ghost pepper. It's at the top of the Scoville scale."

I anticipated this answer. "There's Carolina Reapers, remember."

"We're making food, not pepper spray. Is that what's in your pocket?" He looks genuinely flummoxed.

Milton can't resist that one. "Or is she happy to see you?"

Whew, boy. I should have known this would happen. Milton has a reputation. But I'm here, and I have to see this through.

I bat my eyelashes exactly the way my sister taught me in our lessons before I came on the air. I'm not the least bit ditzy, flirty, or doe-eyed normally. I stick pencils in my hair to hold it out of my way when I'm working, and my coke-bottle glasses have a coating to protect me from blue light and eye strain while I run figures.

But today I have a blowout, contacts, and look like a Swedish pretzel girl. It's for a good cause. Our deli means everything to my family, and I'm going to fight fire with fire.

I tilt my head. "You'll have to wait to find out what I've got in my pocket."

Milton is eating this up. "Getting cold feet, Anthony?" He nudges the taller man's ribs. "Afraid this porcelain princess will do it better?"

Porcelain princess? This is too much. I contemplate stomping his Italian leather shoe. But I simply paste on the fake smile I've practiced all week.

Anthony shakes his head. "Not at all. I'm dying to find out."

He picks up one of the bright red peppers. "The ghost pepper has a rating of one million on the Scoville scale, which rates the heat level of food," he says. "And while it is dangerously potent…" He meets my eye. "…it's also a beautiful flavor on your tongue."

My neck blossoms with heat. Maybe he's not as awkward as I thought. I feel off balance, like I'm not sure of anything anymore.

Milton fans himself with a potholder. "Is it getting warm in here?"

"It's about to," Anthony says. He picks up a wicked knife and tosses it into the air. It spins above our heads, the light winking on the blade. He catches it easily on the handle, and even I have to gasp.

"It's fun to eat dangerously," he says.

Anthony wields the knife like a master swordsman in a duel. *Whack, whack, swish, swish, chop.* The pepper falls into neat, even pieces, its sharp aroma bringing tears to my eyes.

Okay, pause.

I have a confession to make.

I've never eaten anything with ghost pepper. I'm a spice wimp. Just the thought of it makes my eyes water.

No matter what happens on the show, I have to avoid tasting Anthony's pickle *or* mine. Smoke will come out of my ears.

I'm not here to embarrass the Boudreaux name. No one can know about my weakness.

So, *shhhh.*

Milton tugs a checked handkerchief from his breast pocket and waves it over the peppers as if to ward off the burn. "I can't believe people eat this!"

Anthony slides the knife along his palm, leaving

behind a bright line of red. I inhale sharply, thinking he's cut himself. The rest of the crew must think so, too, because there's a collective gasp.

"Just the pepper," he assures us, tapping the blade until four perfectly square bits of red are revealed, starkly bright against his skin.

He can manage a blade, that's for sure.

He lifts his hand close to my nose. "Always make sure you don't have any knicks or cuts, or you are in for the burn of your life."

I can only nod. He blows lightly over the pepper, and the fire in the aroma burns my nostrils. When I lift my hand to block the vapors, he grins and rinses his hand. "Always be aware when you've touched the pepper juice. Whatever you touch next will get a good dose. Don't let it be your eye." He gives me a grin that makes my belly flip. "Or anything else sensitive."

Okay, never mind. He's not the least bit awkward.

Everything in my body is already stirring.

Between his knife work and his cleverness, he's got everyone mesmerized. A tendril of doubt unfurls in my gut. Can I get the better of this man?

"Show us how it all comes together," Milton says. He's switched allegiances, I can tell. I must wrestle this show back to my favor.

"There's more to a pickle than *pain*," I interject, crossing my arms over my apron front.

"But the pain is what people want," Anthony says easily, rapidly mincing a few more bits of pepper and sliding them into a clear glass jar. He moves on to a clove of garlic. "An ordinary pickle wouldn't inspire people to challenge friends and foes to upload videos."

I'm losing here. I have to do something.

"What if it was both painful *and* delicious?" It's too soon, but I have to play my hand.

His knife goes still. "You can do that?"

I stand straighter. "I can."

"There you have it!" Milton cries. "The gauntlet has been thrown. Will Magnolia's adjustment to the famed Pickle family recipe make it better?"

Anthony quickly adds the rest of his spices to the jar and fills it with vinegar and oil. He tugs a girthy cucumber from a basket and slips it inside the glass. "And now it's ready to cure." He screws on the lid.

"How long should it remain there?" Milton asks.

"Seven days," Anthony says.

Milton lifts the jar and examines the cucumber. "So, Magnolia, should your addition to the recipe also sit for a week?"

"No, Milton," I say. "Simply add it to the mix and wait about two hours."

"Did you already do this?" Milton asks.

"Yes," I say. "I stole one of the jars of Anthony's pickles from your very own fridge."

Milton's hands smack on the counter as if he's shocked, but it's only theatrics. This was always the plan. "You tampered with the set?"

"I did."

"Well, show us your secret weapon!"

I slip the jar from my pocket. The clear glass reveals the pale green sauce inside. I pass it to Milton.

He opens the lid and sniffs. "Does it make it spicier?"

"It amplifies the flavor by opening your taste buds," I tell him.

Anthony snatches the jar. He passes it beneath his nose. "Tomatillo?"

I nod. "Betcha didn't even think of that."

"I didn't. It's brilliant." His eyes meet mine. "It will do everything you say."

My breath halts. He's looking at me like I'm a genius, the one true thing he's always looked for.

"It will?" I shouldn't ask the question. On this show, I'm the chef, the one who will win the pickle war.

Not an accountant who picks peppers off pizza.

But Milton frowns. "We won't know until we taste it! Who will win this family rivalry? The longstanding Boudreaux family whose title as the favored deli of Boulder has gone unrivaled for sixty years? Or this upstart with his tawdry pickle, all bite and no flavor?"

Crap. Milton's right. This is war.

I shake myself to ward off the spell Anthony's somehow put on me.

"Prepare to go down," I say.

Anthony's eyes hold mine as he gets in the zinger.

"With relish."

3

ANTHONY

I'm way out of my comfort zone with Magnolia.

The first double entendre was an accident. *Put my pickle against what she's got.*

The second was all the show's host. *Beat his pickle.*

But I'd thrown propane on the grill with *going down with relish.*

And it was all recorded for posterity.

Hello, meme-ville. I'm your latest resident.

I'll have to go into hiding when this segment airs. My brothers are going to have a field day.

Magnolia turns to the refrigerator and pulls out two jars.

Ah. This is why I was told to bring a spare. So she could doctor one.

I've been played.

The tomatillo sauce has clearly been added. Instead of the pinkish brine of my ghost pepper jar, hers is grayish green. It looks pretty gross, the shriveled cucumber sunk into the cloudy oil and vinegar.

In fact, Milton looks like he's about to say something nasty about it. I get in a word first. "So, two hours in the tomatillo will do it?"

I hold up her sauce jar next to the cucumber jar so it's clear that the green sauce is what caused the odd color. Otherwise, it looks like snot, bits of loose tomatillo floating around the pickle.

"I'm sure we could play with the timing for optimum flavor," she says. "But two is enough."

She's wrong, I think, because the spices take time to penetrate the cucumber and should all be placed together at the same time. But I don't think she's here about the purity of the recipe.

It's revenge.

She's on this show to make me suffer for entering the deli market.

This is my fault. I should have reached out and asked for a Tasty Pepper item to expand the TikTok challenge. But the truth is, I had no control over what happened. I was so blindsided by the whole thing that I barely kept up with demand. Ghost peppers aren't common, and I depleted my suppliers. I could barely keep my head above water as this played out.

Involving other delis never even occurred to me.

Milton takes both jars. "Should we give them a whirl?"

There's no telling whose allegiance he'll land on. If it was so important to Magnolia to be here that she challenged me, then something's forcing her hand at her deli.

But it's not my show, and it's not even about me. It

never was. Magnolia is about to reap the reward or the doom of what she's done.

"You definitely want to try hers before mine," I say. "It can take your taste buds a while to recover from a ghost pepper if you're not used to that level of burn."

"So, ladies first?" Milton winks.

"She's the chef to beat," I say.

This doesn't placate Magnolia. In fact, I sense a tremble in her hand, fisted by her side. She's nervous. She shouldn't be. The tomatillo is a brilliant choice. I wish I'd thought of it.

I steal a look at her face, and I see it. Beneath that upturned chin, that defiant stance, is pure fear. Why? Is there that much riding on her pickle beating mine?

An urge to protect her rushes through me. Who is putting pressure on her? Her father? The family? Are they in money trouble like my brother Jason was for a while with his deli? Restaurant margins can be thin.

Milton opens both jars and reaches for a fork to stab one of the pickles.

"I'll do the honors," I say quickly. I remove both pickles and place them on the cutting board, careful to keep plenty of tomatillo juice on Magnolia's. It hasn't had time to cure, so keeping the sauce on the slice will help her case.

I make a big show of sliding knives across each other and spinning the blades. Then I chop both pickles so quickly that only a slow-motion replay would reveal how they fell apart.

I can totally nerd out with knives.

"Now that's a show," Milton says, and I realize I've

pulled him back to Team Anthony. That's not what I'm after.

I step back to allow Magnolia access to the cutting board. "Would you like to do the plating?"

She gazes up at me with those blue eyes that could bring a man to his knees. "You're the showman."

"And you're the chef." I pick up one of the clear plates and slide a pickle slice on it. I take care to keep it well coated with tomatillo.

I pass the plate to Milton, and he holds it up to the camera. One of the operators pulls in close. "Magnolia's tomatillo-enhanced ghost pepper pickle!" he says.

I place my own slice on a second plate.

"And Anthony's original viral spicy pickle!" Now both plates are aloft.

"Magnolia's first," I remind him.

Milton sets both plates on the counter in front of him. "You sure are pushy about that." He sends his gaze to the camera, as if he's talking to the viewers. "I think Anthony has something up his sleeve. Perhaps it's to his advantage if I do his last."

He stabs my pink-tinged pickle. "I say Anthony's first."

Damn. I can't stop him. I hope he's used to fire, because if my ghost pepper burns his taste buds to dust, he won't even taste the difference between Magnolia's version and mine.

"Here comes the burn!" Milton says, then pops my pickle in his mouth.

His eyes go wide. "Oh no," he says, removing the fork with the pickle still attached. "Cut! Cut! Cut!"

He falls off his step and pushes me out of the way to make it to the sink, blasting the water and leaning under the faucet. I step back, close to Magnolia, as he turns his head sideways to run the water directly into his mouth.

His heavy makeup begins to melt onto the stainless steel. I glance over at Magnolia. She's grimacing and when our gazes clash, she shrugs.

A woman in a crisp, tan suit hurries forward. "Milton? Are you all right?" It's Shelby, his assistant. She showed me around earlier today.

Milton leans against the counter, breathing hard. "Cameras off!" he rasps, then sticks his head back in the flow.

"Cameras off!" Shelby calls. A flurry of activity ensues off stage. One by one, the red lights on the cameras wink out.

Two more crew members rush onto the set. "Mr. Creed? What can we do for you?"

I step forward. "Do you have some milk? Cheese? Something high fat?"

The curly-haired prop woman says, "I think so, in the green room."

"That will calm it the fastest," I tell her.

She takes off running.

Milton pulls back from the spray again, lapels soaked, hair dripping, his face streaked with makeup. He looks like a mannequin that's been dunked in acid.

Magnolia and I edge away until we reach the end of the counter. I don't know what will happen to the segment. I thought Milton knew what he was getting into. We had just watched the videos of people running in a panic after biting one of my pickles. Maybe he thought they were pretending.

I'm glad he tried mine first. I wouldn't want Magnolia to take the blame for this.

Shelby pulls a kitchen towel from the rack and places it around Milton's neck. "We'll get you some cheese. It will be all right."

"Should I turn this off?" Another crew member reaches for the gleaming faucet.

Milton smacks his hand away and sticks his mouth in the flow a third time. Everyone watches as he gargles the water and spews it into the sink. Then he shuts it off and leans forward over the counter, his forehead resting on his hand.

Shelby turns to me, her face contorted with anger. "What did you do to that pickle? Are you *trying* to embarrass the head of *America's Spiciest Chef*?"

"No. It's—it's the same as all the ones I make." But then, I hesitate. What if Magnolia tampered with mine when she doctored the other jar? Did she set me up?

Her eyes are wide and innocent when I turn to her. My anger flares, and I lunge for the cutting board. I snatch my knife with such a fury that several crew members jump back.

I stab another slice of my ghost pepper pickle and lift it with the blade.

Milton seems to know what I'm thinking and raises his head to watch. The curly-haired woman arrives with a plate of cheese.

He snatches a piece and shoves it in his mouth,

visible relief on his face as the burn eases. "Eat it," he rasps at me. "I want to know."

I was born with a spicy pepper in my mouth, so unless something has gone terribly wrong, the pickle will be fine for me. Hot, sure. But fine.

I slide the slice off the knife with my teeth, feeling the burn on my lips from the pepper juice.

But when I bite down—good Lord. I cough, sending the pickle slice into the sink. My mouth burns like I've tried to extinguish a hot coal inside it.

A murmur slides through the room.

The prop woman moves the cheese closer to me. I take a piece and bite down, sliding it to the part of my mouth that hurts the most. Someone did this to my pickles. And there could only be one culprit.

I turn to Magnolia. "What did you do?"

Her face drains of color. "Nothing! I just added tomatillo! I was escorted by a crew member. She can vouch that I only changed one jar!"

Shelby glances around. "Amber! Where are you?"

A tall, slender figure emerges from the gloom into the light of the set. "Yes, Ms. Shelby?"

"Did you leave Magnolia alone with the jars?"

Magnolia lets out an indignant *harrumph*, but Shelby silences her with an upturned hand.

Amber's chin trembles. "No—no, of course not. We came on set. Opened the fridge. She took out one jar and added the green sauce. We didn't move the other."

Shelby taps her cheek with a long, red-painted nail. "Did you escort her in and out?"

Amber wrings her hands. "We were together the whole time. I never took my eyes off her."

Milton wipes his forehead with the towel. "You're fired anyway. Get off the property. Where is the security guard who let this woman in?"

Another man steps up to the corner. "He's by the door."

"Bring him here."

Amber sniffles, and when Milton sees she hasn't moved, he shouts. "Get off my set!"

Amber jumps and hurries away from the kitchen.

Milton whirls around to face us. It's hard to look at him, half of his makeup rinsed off, a strange brown color leaching from the roots of his hair.

"Let's figure this out, shall we?" He picks up the plate with Magnolia's slice. "If it was Magnolia who tampered with Anthony's pickle, would she also do it to her own?" His pink tongue angles toward the plate, touching only the barest edge of the pickle.

He flings the plate down, cracking the glass. "Horrible. Just horrible." He snatches another piece of cheese. "Get both of these shysters off my set."

I hold out my hands. "Whoa, whoa. You don't think I would ruin my own pickle, do you? I didn't even know Magnolia was going to be here until you surprised me with it."

Magnolia pushes past me. "I don't like your accusation! I improved his pickle! I can't help that he did something so terribly wrong to his recipe that it became inedible!"

Milton looks back and forth between the two of us.

"All I know is that you two have ruined my segment. I've got the cost of the crew, and the rental of this facility, and I will have nothing to show for it."

Shelby pats his back. "We'll find a way to salvage something. Talk about this rivalry gone bad. We'll make them look like raging infighters."

"You can't do that!" I yell.

"I can if I want! You signed a waiver!" he shouts back. "You could have killed someone with those pickles!"

"I doubt that." But even as I say it, I know I need to think. Whatever was in those pickle jars was not food. It was a chemical. Something no one should eat, ever.

And Milton eating *my* pickle was recorded. If he airs this footage, my deli could be ruined. I glance out at the crew. The red lights on all the cameras are off. But I see something that gives me pause. A telltale glow of a cell-phone held aloft.

Shelby sees me staring and turns to follow my gaze. Her expression darkens as she realizes what it is. "Who is that?" she shouts.

The cell phone goes dark.

"Get that person!" she calls out. "They've recorded this!" There's a shuffle of feet, then the bright white of an exterior door opening.

Several crew members take up the chase.

Shelby turns to me and Magnolia. "Do not forget you signed a non-disclosure," she says. "One word of this, and we'll sue you to oblivion."

She takes off after the others.

The portly security guard in a blue uniform arrives,

and Milton orders him to escort us out.

He takes both of our arms, but I shake him off and break his hold on Magnolia. "Don't treat us like this. We're leaving."

He gives us a beady glare.

When we're out the back door, there's no sign of what might be happening on the other side of the building.

The cold wind whips my hair, and Magnolia wraps her arms around herself. "My coat and things are inside," she says.

"Mine too," I say.

"I can't drive my car until someone fetches them."

"And I don't have my phone. We had to surrender them." I glance back at the door.

"I guess we go back in?" she says.

"I'll do it." I step toward the door, but Magnolia holds out a hand. "Wait. I want to say something."

I turn to her, my anger pounding in my temples. "What?"

"I didn't tamper with the pickles. Well, no more than to put tomatillo in one."

"I didn't either."

Her teeth chatter. "Did you make them the way you usually do?"

"Yes."

"And nobody else had access to them?"

I stare at the ground. "A ton of people did. I pickled these a week ago."

"Does someone have it in for you?" she asks.

I let out a long breath. "I don't think so. My crew is

loyal."

"But you can't be sure."

She stands in the afternoon sun, her blond hair almost white as it blows wildly in the wind. It's freezing out, and a shiver runs through her body. Even though she's clearly the enemy, I have to resist the urge to draw her close to keep her warm.

"That crew member with the cheese told me they all pretty much hate him. One of his people could have done it."

"And dragged us down in the process." She presses her lips together, her eyes shining with emotion. "This segment was supposed to help my family's deli, not ruin it."

I sigh. "Nothing's happened yet."

"Yet."

The curly-haired crew member appears from the back door, holding a bundle of coats.

"Oh, thank God," Magnolia says, rushing toward her.

The woman hands off Magnolia's purse and jacket, then brings me mine. "Figured you'd be needing these."

I check that my keys and phone are in my pocket. "What's going on in there?"

She shakes her head. "I shouldn't talk to you two at all."

"But we're getting blamed."

She glances back at the building, but she says quickly, "Hell has broken loose. Somebody probably recorded the chaos. If they sell it, Mr. Creed will go on the warpath."

Magnolia and I glance at each other. "Was it someone on your crew?" she asks.

The woman starts backing away. "Nobody knows yet. They're trying to figure out who had a cell phone. We check ours at the stage door."

"Someone could have snuck one in," I say. "Had a spare on them."

"Maybe. I better get back before they think it's me." She turns to hurry inside.

Magnolia stuffs her arms into her puffy white coat. She looks even more like an angel than before.

"Do you think whoever videoed it also wrecked the pickles?" I ask.

She shrugs. "Sounds like it won't be our problem."

I nod. "I guess the best scenario is they scrap the whole thing."

"What a waste," she says.

"Better than them using any of it."

Magnolia nods, her face grim. "Of course. See you around."

"I *am* sorry," I say.

"For what? That I didn't succeed in my pickle coup?" Her blue-eyed gaze penetrates me.

"Just sorry in general."

She shakes her head and speed walks to her car.

I stand there another moment, looking at the rear exit of the building. This was supposed to be a big triumph for the Pickle family, positive publicity to keep us going.

Clearly Magnolia hoped for the same.

And it all went south.

4

MAGNOLIA

As I drive away from Anthony and our disaster, I don't know where I want to go.

It's time for the lunch run at the Tasty Pepper, so I could probably slip in the back door and hide in my office without anyone noticing me.

But given that I currently look like an Instagram influencer wannabe, maybe I should revert to normal Magnolia mode before dealing with my dad's questions about the segment.

I head toward the apartment I share with my sister. Havannah should have left for the deli hours ago. This will give me time to think about what I'm going to say to them both about the show.

I have no idea what Milton Creed is going to do. His manager seemed to have ideas for how to salvage some of the content.

Would he throw Anthony under the bus? Me? Both of us? Milton would never air any footage with his makeup melting under the faucet. So that means the only usable footage is through the moment that he tastes the pickle.

My mind whirls as I park my car and stomp to my front door. Has my whole plan to elevate the Tasty Pepper backfired spectacularly? Are we ruined?

I imagine the worst. Mass protests in front of the deli. Foreclosure. A sheriff padlocking the front doors.

Then a man's voice says, "Heya."

I glance up. It's my neighbor Hank in running gear. He's a workout junkie who's never deemed me worthy of speaking to before. He blocks my path up the sidewalk, so I step into the dead, frozen grass to avoid him.

"Hey, hey, hey!" he says, holding out an arm. "You new here?" His magazine-worthy face is full of interest.

Great.

Of course he likes me dolled up. I've seen a whole parade of beautiful women walk the path to his apartment in the two years I've lived here.

I dash aside to avoid his touch or meet his eyes, aiming for my door.

Unfortunately, this seems to be exactly the challenge he's looking for.

He sidesteps in front of me. "I'm Hank. I would love to show you around. Give you the *lay* of the land."

Oh. My. God. Is that seriously one of his lines?

I stare him down. Surely, he recognizes me now. I'm right in front of him.

But his expression holds.

Unbelievable. Did I change that much? Or did he never take a good look at mousy me?

"I'm busy," I say.

He leaps back as if he's been electrically shocked. "Magnolia? Is that you?"

Yeah, he knows my voice. Figures.

"Same as always." I circle him and shove my key in the lock.

"Have you always looked like this?" he asks. Clearly, I've frazzled his limited brainpower.

"No time for this, Hank. Later."

I push the door open, and only when I'm leaning against it, the steel barrier between me and Hank, do I let out a breath.

This day is a disaster. A complete catastrophe.

Maybe I won't go to the deli at all. Maybe I can hole up here forever. Never show my face again.

At least I'm alone. I glance around at our small living room. The floral sofa, a hand-me-down from Grandmama. The TV. Oh, the TV. Maybe I'll spend all day watching Netflix and forget what happened today.

"Magnolia? Are you back?"

Oh no.

Havannah emerges from the hallway wearing a natty pink robe. She looks like hell, much worse than when she did my makeup this morning.

"What are you doing here?" I toss my coat and bag on the sofa.

"Wasn't up to snuff." She clears her throat. "Thought I'd have a bit of a lie-down."

She's been watching reruns of the *Great British Bake Off* again. I always know because she starts using their expressions after a binge. We both do.

"What is it? Stomach? Head? Fever?" If she's sick, I

can claim to have caught it, too. We can hide here with pints of cherry ice cream and forget everything. Claim to be contagious. I could get a good two or three days of peace out of it.

"Breakfast didn't agree with me. I'm fine now. About to clean up and head in." She pushes her mat of golden hair back from her face.

Phooey.

"How'd it go?" she asks.

I guess I might as well practice the story on her first. She can help me prepare answers for Dad. "Dreadful. Let me get this makeup off and I'll tell you."

Havannah follows me to the bathroom. I stare at myself a moment. Nothing about my appearance is remotely how I normally look. Long lashes. Honey smooth skin. Pink lips. It's all an illusion made by my sister. Her dress, too. I never wear them.

"You sure you want to take it off? You look so pretty." Havannah lifts a section of my hair. "You should blow it out more often."

"Hardly. It took forever." I wet a washcloth and press it to my face. The icy water bites my skin.

"There's a cream in here that will get that." Havannah opens a drawer and sets a jar on the counter. I ignore it. I'm done with beauty products for the day.

My makeup bag is sparse. I have a maroon-tinted lip balm I bought by accident. A blue eyeliner I wore for an 80s party. And an aging mascara I sometimes use when stress causes too many eyelashes to fall out.

Which is bound to happen any moment.

After a good hard scrub, I drop the washcloth and

peer into the mirror. What? I'm almost as doll-like as before. Are these products made of actual paint?

Havannah pushes the cream toward me. "It's the setting spray," she says. "I wanted to make sure you didn't sweat it off in the lights."

"Right." I open the jar and smear the cream on my cheeks.

"Let me." Havannah lifts the cloth and starts working on my face. "Good thing I'm here, I guess. I thought you'd head into work. Dad will want a report."

I lean against the cabinet, closing my eyes. Havannah is two years older than me and goddess-level beautiful. Even though we have the same hair color, the comparison stops there.

Havannah is confident, stylish, and superlatively involved with clothes and makeup. She was a cheerleader, a dancer, and always had her pick of boyfriends.

We had a real fight about who would go on the show with Milton. I said she was the natural choice—perfect and beautiful and used to being looked at.

But she'd refused to do it and wouldn't say why.

Dad made us draw straws. Obviously, I lost.

Havannah moves to my cheeks and lips, so I open my eyes to look at her. Something is wrong. She's not made up, and her hair's a disaster. I'm pretty sure that robe harkens back to high school.

But still, jealousy bites me at her poise, even when looking like she does right now. The comparison between us has never gotten easier, even though we're in our mid-twenties. The more beautiful she got, the more I retreated into my work.

She got a degree in hospitality, and I went into accounting. We roomed together once we both graduated, even though it's meant I have to endure the revolving door of her boyfriends. Neither of us thought we'd be back at the deli after college, but the economy has been crap for new grads, so here we are. Failures to launch.

"Done." Havannah turns to the sink, and I steal a glance in the mirror. My face is blotchy but back to being mine. I release the green ribbon in my hair and hastily fasten the heavy strands into a ponytail.

"Let me change, and I'll tell you everything," I say, heading toward the hall. "I'm going to need a game plan for handling Dad."

"That makes two of us," she murmurs as I leave.

What does that mean? Who knows? Havannah has always been dramatic.

When I've switched into a more typical outfit for me, gray dress pants and a white button-down, Havannah has left the bathroom.

I follow the clattering sound to find her in the kitchen, peeling back the top of a yogurt container.

"I thought you said breakfast made you sick."

"I'm better."

Something is definitely up with her. "What's going on?"

She shoves a scoop of yogurt in her mouth and shrugs.

When I stand in front of her, my sisterly attitude face on, she says, "Really, Mags, it's a conversation for another time. Besides, what happened on *America's Spiciest Chef?*"

I plunk down in a chair by the bright yellow breakfast table. Havannah always complains that it looks like a sun exploded in here, but it makes me feel more cheerful. Except maybe today.

"I don't think the segment's going to air," I say.

Havannah's mouth falls open, revealing a glob of watery white yogurt.

I hold up a hand to block the view. "Havannah, for real."

She swallows the yogurt and sets the container on the cabinet. "Payback for the thousand times you did it."

"When I was four!"

"Still. Payback. What happened?"

There's no sense delaying any longer. "Everything was fine. Anthony came out. Milton announced that there would be a pickle challenge. I came out. I said I had improved upon the recipe."

I hesitate, trying to determine how to explain the next part.

"And then?"

"Something was wrong with the pickles. Both jars. Milton tried to eat one and practically doused himself with water after. Anthony tasted them and said there was some chemical on them to make them burn."

"Oh my God! Did you taste them? Are you hurt?" Havannah races to sit in a chair next to me.

"No. I didn't get a chance. Everything happened fast. The crew came running. They accused me of tampering with the jars."

"Seriously?"

"I accused Anthony of botching the recipe."

"Yikes." Havannah sits back in her chair, crossing her arms over her robe. "I bet he didn't like that."

"No. But then Milton kicked both of us out. And on top of that, somebody recorded the whole thing, so the footage is out there."

"The cameras were still rolling?"

"Not the official ones. Somebody sneaked a cell phone in, then ran. Milton is in a rage. He could bury both of us if he airs any of this on his show. Or if any of this information leaks from the rogue recording. I don't know how to respond if it does get out. I don't know anything!"

I try to suck in a breath, but it's like my chest is made of concrete. I press my hand to my heart. "Havannah?"

She kneels next to me. "You need to breathe. You're going to give yourself a panic attack."

I fight with my lungs. I can't take a breath.

"Blow out first. All the way. Empty everything." Havannah grips my hand.

I work on it, holding on to her and trying to exhale.

"Now take it back in slowly. Don't suck it in."

When I've managed two normal breaths, Havannah heads to the refrigerator and pulls out a carton of milk.

"I'm going to make some hot cocoa like Mom used to do. We'll drink it slowly and think this through." As she fills a pan and rummages in the cabinet for the cocoa, I focus on my breath to avoid another panic.

It's hitting me all the different ways that this day

could blow up in my face. In Dad's. I'd seen what happens to small family restaurants that get caught up in a viral social media mob. They can tank your reviews everywhere. They can get you delisted from places that send business your way. They can make life hell.

I think maybe I just ruined everything.

5

ANTHONY

When I finally enter the back door of Boulder Pickle, the lunch run is in full swing. Kennedy, my line manager, barely spares me a glance as he rushes out of the stainless-steel walk-in fridge with refilled cheese bins, his green apron strings flying behind him.

Dru, who does most of the prep work, empties a vat of onions on the cutting board. His dark forehead creases with concentration as he chops madly to keep up.

I head to my office to drop off my coat and keys, switching out the black apron for a bright green Boulder Pickle one.

By the time I cross the kitchen again, my manager, Marie, is waiting by the door to the dining room, her plastic-gloved hands clasped tightly in front of her matronly chest.

"The lunch rush is underway, as you can see," she says. "But I wanted to ask about the show."

"A disaster. I'll brief everybody later. Let's get through lunch."

She nods curtly and lets me by. I lose myself in the work for an hour. I fill in wherever I'm needed, manning the register, clearing tables, or fetching ice for the over-burdened drink machine.

Only when the steady stream of customers has reduced to a trickle do I head back to my office. The incessant buzzing in my pocket is no doubt my family, wanting to know how my segment went.

Time to deal with it.

I scroll through the notifications. Texts from my brothers Max and Jason. Two from dad. One from Grammy Alma.

I set the phone down. I haven't taken time to compose myself and figure out what to say.

There's no telling what Milton Creed might do. I'm not sure if I should warn everyone or downplay the possibilities.

I wish I had someone who could feed me informa-tion about what happened after we left. Hopefully they caught whoever took the cell phone footage. Probably the best scenario is if it's an inside job, they catch the culprit, and everything is kept quiet.

I'm about to start replying to everyone, but I remember the pickles. They were tampered with, and Magnolia suggested it happened here. I have no doubt that a disgruntled member of the show's crew is to blame, but I ought to make sure before I talk to everyone.

In the kitchen, several staffers load the mountain of

plates and plastic cups from lunch into the dishwasher. I slip into the industrial walk-in refrigerator unnoticed.

The back right corner is devoted to pickles. In addition to jarring the original flavors for this location, my staff also provides the specialty pickle of the month to the other three franchises, Jason's in Austin, Max's in L.A., and Dad's in New York. Well, I guess the New York one is mine now, but it's hard to think of it that way. It was always Dad's.

Each shelf is carefully marked with the flavor and date of pickling. I locate the rows of ghost pepper pickles. Boulder is the only deli offering it right now. I didn't want to burden the others with the complications of that flavor going viral, plus I wasn't sure we could even find enough ghost pepper to keep all four delis stocked.

The jars that I took to the show early this morning were pickled last Wednesday. This particular batch I did myself, knowing I would be using them on air.

I pull one out. The seal makes a bright *pop* as I turn the lid.

I sniff it first, wishing I had taken a moment to examine the tampered one more carefully. There might've been a chemical trace if I hadn't been under too much stress on the set to sense it.

These smell the way they always do. The rosewater looks perfect. There are no utensils in here, so I take the jar out into the kitchen and pull a fork from the bin.

A few staffers glance my way as I stab the pickle and place it on one of the cutting boards.

Dru pauses as he chops sweet gherkins at the other

end, prepping relish for the dinner run. "Everything okay, boss?"

"I don't know," I say. "Probably."

I tug a knife from the magnetic strip at the end of the metal table and cut several slices from the pickle. Nothing looks awry.

I tentatively place the slice in my mouth.

The fire of the ghost pepper sears my taste buds, but it's nothing like the burning sensation I had this morning.

This pickle is fine.

My shoulders relax. It wasn't me. I quickly slice the rest of the pickle and place it in the bin to go out on the line. Dru pauses beside me on his way back to the fridge. "I'm going to slice a lot more of those. We went through more than expected today. That TikTok challenge is going strong."

"Thanks for handling it."

I head to my office and close the door. It's time to talk to my family.

Two o'clock in Boulder is one in L.A., three in Austin, and four in New York. We've got every time zone covered.

I fire up my video chat and send invitations to my dad and brothers.

Dad shows up first, pulling his apron off over his gray head. "Anthony! I've been dying to know how it went this morning. How was Milton Creed?"

"It was a mixed bag," I say. That's the truth.

Jason pops on next, his feet up on the desk in his

office. "The famous bro," he says. "Tell me all the ways you screwed this up."

He has no idea how close he is to the truth. "Enough to make you happy."

His face flickers. "Really?"

Now Dad looks concerned. "Did something go wrong?"

I wait a moment to see if Max will pop in. It could still be the lunch rush there. When he doesn't show, I decide to get it over with.

"The pickles were chemically altered, and they burned Milton's mouth. We're not sure who did it."

Both Dad and Jason start talking at once, and I can't make out what either one is saying as the chat switches from one to the other in rapid succession, leaving both voices garbled.

I wait until they both pause. "Only one of you can berate me at a time," I say.

Dad goes next. "I'm getting our lawyer on the line." His gaze drops to his phone.

"This sucks," Jason says. "Although, watching Milton in pain might have been gratifying to all the people he's crossed."

"That part will never air. He had the cameras shut off."

My screen pings with the join request from Lance, our family's lawyer since I was a kid. I patch him through.

"So, what happened?" Lance asks.

Dad speaks up. "Someone doctored the pickles and burned the host."

Lance's expression shifts to astonishment. "Is he going to sue? Have we heard from anyone on his team?"

"Let me go back a step," I say. "There's more you need to know. I wasn't the only one on the show. They brought in Magnolia Boudreaux."

"Who's that?" Jason asks.

I picture Magnolia's perfect face. She was something. "The daughter of John Paul Boudreaux, who owns a family deli here in Boulder."

Dad nods. "I know him."

The lawyer chimes in. "Do we have a good relationship with him?"

"Not particularly," Dad says. "The family was not thrilled when we opened in their territory, but that's where Anthony wanted to stay. There was no other place to put his restaurant."

"How did she end up on the show?" Jason asks.

"It appears that featuring both of us was the plan all along. She added tomatillo sauce to my ghost pepper pickle to make it more flavorful, so the show was in on it. They wanted a challenge between our two pickles."

Jason looks incredulous. "How did she get access to your pickle to add tomatillo?"

"Apparently someone escorted her in, and she took the spare from the refrigerator. I was the only one who was clueless."

The lawyer scrawls a note on a yellow pad. "Should I reach out to Milton's legal team?"

I shrug. "Maybe? Because to add the fun, someone took some rogue footage on their cell phone and may have escaped with it. They kicked me and

Magnolia out of the set before we knew what happened with that."

"Dayum," Jason says. "What *didn't* happen today?"

Dad rubs his eyes with the heel of his hand. "So where did we leave things?"

"I checked the pickles when I got back. They are fine. Clearly someone tampered with them on the set."

Jason perks up. "Was it old man Boudreaux, then?"

"His daughter insists she didn't. And she had an escort who claims Magnolia only doctored her own jar."

"So somebody set both of you up," the lawyer says. "Did Milton express his thoughts?"

"He's blaming me and Magnolia. He thinks we tried to embarrass him. But I got word from the crew that he can't keep staff. He's a tyrant. It makes sense to me that someone took an opportunity to get back at him and recorded the whole thing."

"Sure sounds like it," Dad says.

I nod. "I think it's an inside job. We were collateral damage."

The lawyer sets down his pen. "I would recommend hiring a social media cleanup team. We should have them on retainer in case this blows up."

"Agreed," Dad says. "Anthony, did you get any indication from the Boudreaux clan what they were going to do about this?"

"I spoke to Magnolia briefly in the parking lot."

"Is she hot?" Jason asks.

"Not relevant," Dad says.

But Magnolia invades my thoughts again, her blond hair blowing in the wind outside the studio.

"Ah ha," Jason says. "Look at baby bro. She's hot."

I lift an eyebrow to make him shut his trap. Not that it's ever worked before. "She's concerned, but we both felt Milton would cover it up. He does have a lot of footage of us, though. And we signed agreements that he could use it however he liked."

The lawyer frowns. "I told you guys to insist on prior approval of the segment."

"He wouldn't do it," Dad says. "You know that. He would have walked on the whole deal."

Lance makes another note. "At this point, the best-case scenario is that they don't use anything at all."

That makes everyone somber.

Dad sighs. "I'm sorry you had to go through this, son. The whole business can be unpredictable. Milton was a crapshoot. We knew that going in."

I nod.

Max's request to join the meeting pops up.

His face is eager for news. "How's my famous brother?"

I sink into my chair. "Trying not to become infamous."

As the days pass, I assume the whole thing is over.

But I'm wrong.

The day the pickle hits the fan, Marie and I are working on a new bread to send out to the other Pickle delis. The stainless-steel counter is covered in flour. She and I are both wrist-deep in dough.

There's a commotion in the dining room, which is odd, since it's normally dead mid-afternoon. Marie and I look up to spot Kennedy dashing through the door from the dining room, his mini dreads flying behind him.

"Anthony, you gotta get out here. People with news vans and cameras are camped on the sidewalk out front."

I peel off my gloves. "Marie, would you mind getting on my computer and doing a quick check of *America's Spiciest Chef's* social media? See if anything's gone down referencing the show I did."

It's been almost a week since the recording session. I never told the staff everything that happened, only that the taping had not gone well, and I wasn't sure they were going to air any of it.

Marie hurries toward my office. I untie the flour-encrusted apron and set it on the counter. "Stick to your duties, everyone. Don't talk to anyone if they come in. I'll handle this."

In the dining room, two of my employees stand near the windows, peering out the blinds. The only exterior view is through the glass door, but I don't see anything from my current angle.

"What's happening?" I ask.

My cashier Michelle lets go of the blinds. "Two news vans. Three miscellaneous photographers. Looks like they're setting up to do an interview."

"Are the doors unlocked?" I ask.

Michelle's eyes grow big beneath her fringe of black bangs. "Should I lock them?"

"No. I was curious if they could waltz in here."

"They seem happy to set up outside. Nobody's approached the door."

I glance around the room. Two tables have diners, all craning their heads to watch us. I don't want them to think a crime is happening.

"I was recently on a cooking show," I say. "This is probably to do with that."

They relax and return to their sandwiches.

I pinch the collar of my green Boulder Pickle polo to make sure it's straight. I'm about to approach the door when Marie hurtles into the room. "Anthony, you'll want to see this before you go out there!"

She thrusts a phone in my face. "It's a brand-new Twitter account, and this is the only post."

The video is vertical, like a cell phone makes. The still frame shows the set of Milton's show. All three of us are there, Milton, me, and Magnolia.

This is it. It's out there.

I press play.

Milton says, "You sure are pushy about that."

So it's skipping to the good part.

He puts the pickle slice in his mouth. The footage zooms in, although the quality isn't great. But you can make out that Milton is in distress as he yells, "Cut, cut, cut!"

Unlike the official cameras, which all stopped at this point, the cell phone footage goes right on showing him blasting water on his face under the faucet.

I watch it all the way. It goes through the accusations, first me suggesting that Magnolia had done it.

Then her saying that I had screwed up both jars. It doesn't cut off until Shelby shouts, "Who is that?" and the footage blurs for a second before blacking out.

It's only been up for a few hours, but the comments are racking up quickly. There are already over three thousand.

I glance up at the rest of the staff, who are glued to their phones. "So, what's everyone saying? Positive? Negative?"

Michelle swipes her finger along her screen. "It's starting to be called the Battle of the Pickles," she says. "All the entertainment sites are picking it up. They think you two hate each other, and Milton got caught in the middle of your feud."

I've heard enough. "Lock the door."

"We're closing?" Michelle's face is full of shock. "We have six more hours!"

"You'll get paid," I assure her. "I need to talk to my family. Our lawyer. I don't think I should speak with reporters until I know what to do."

Lance said last week that we should hire a social media expert in case something happened. Had Dad done that? I had no idea. Technically, I'm in charge.

I pat my pocket and realize I don't have my phone on me. I must've left it in my office. I hurry through the dining room. "Let the diners out the back door when they're done," I call. "Don't let anybody in the front door."

By the time I get my phone, it's already buzzing.

I've missed a call from my dad. The current one is from Lance. I greedily pick it up.

I skip the greeting and go straight to, "What do I do?"

"There's a live broadcast in front of your restaurant," Lance says calmly. "Have you talked to anyone?"

"No. We locked the door and shut down the deli."

"That's probably the wisest course for now. I'm going to patch you through to a social media person. Her name is Charity. She'll coach you through a prepared statement. Are you ready?"

I nod, realize I'm on the phone, and say, "Yes. Thank you."

A cheery female voice comes on. "Anthony Pickle?"

"That's me." I sink into my chair. I don't like that my deli is closed. Or that there are news vans outside. I don't like any of this. "What do I do?"

She laughs, and the fact that she can be amused in the face of my disaster makes anger rise in me. This isn't funny.

"First, don't worry. We can help you through this. We will turn this all around so that it's a positive experience for your business. I've done this a long time. You're in good hands."

My heart slows down a notch. It *is* good to have an expert on board.

As I drag a notepad across my desk to take notes on Charity's talking points, I think for second on Magnolia.

I wonder how she's holding up.

She seemed more poised on camera than I did. She's obviously not easy to rattle.

6

MAGNOLIA

The Tasty Pepper is deathly quiet this afternoon. Mom and Dad left to meet with a distributor about supplies for the upcoming holiday season.

The manager is in the kitchen with the crew, finishing the lunch cleanup and prepping for dinner. My line manager Shane is manning the sandwich station alone.

The only customers in the dining room at this hour are an elderly couple, quietly talking in the back corner. I decide to take a moment to do some inventory of the paper goods stored in the cabinets beneath the drinking station. It's impossible to do any other time of day, and I don't want to stay after closing.

Shane comes up behind me. "Can I help?"

I bang my head on the way out. "Ouch."

Shane stands above me, tall and lanky with an overly bright expression. I suspect he has a crush on me. But he's still in college, a good five years younger.

"I'm good, Shane. It's just inventory."

He gets down on one knee. "I can count them for you."

"That's sweet, but——"

The door jingles. I'm saved.

"You'll want to get the customer," I add.

He nods and moves to the sandwich line.

I duck into the cabinet. Sixteen packages, although a few are squashed. I start reloading them, then realize a pair of ankle-breaking black heels are directly by my knees. Did she order already?

I'm blocking the soda fountain. "Just a sec. I'll get out of your way."

Her voice is like a purr. "I'm here to see you."

Great. It's probably somebody here to peddle a new coffee or try to sell cleaning supplies. With my parents out, I'll have to handle her.

I bang my head a second time, strands of hair falling over my face as I extricate myself from the counter.

The woman doesn't look like any sales rep I've ever seen. She has perfectly coiffed black hair and a red suit with a pencil skirt that fits her like it was custom-made.

Her face is perfect, and her expression can only be described as the cat that ate the canary.

"Magnolia Boudreaux?"

My whole body goes on alert. Sales reps don't usually know my name, only my dad's.

In fact, this woman looks like someone from Milton's camp. I've been waiting for a shoe to drop since the filming.

God, I hope this woman *is* a sales rep. I'll buy her coffee all day long.

I quickly shove the rest of the napkin packs inside the cabinet and stand up. My shirt is wrinkled, and my knees picked up dirt from the floor. I brush them off. "Can I help you?"

Her smile sets me on edge. "I was hoping to ask you a few questions about your segment with *America's Spiciest Chef.*"

I knew it. "Who are you?"

She tugs a laminated badge from the depths of her cleavage. "Amelia Little. You've probably seen me on the local news."

So, she's *not* one of Milton's people. I glance at the pass. "Nope."

"Well, I'm a reporter. I understand you filmed a segment with Milton Creed last week."

"How do you know about that?"

Her eyebrows arch in a way I've only seen in makeup ads. "I guess you haven't seen the footage that was just released?"

My heart thuds. "What footage?"

"It's trending on Twitter." She reaches into that ample décolletage a second time to extract a phone. "It's right here." She turns the screen to me.

It's the rogue footage all right. Vertical and shaky, but definitely showing the moment when Milton spit out the pickle.

"The taping was recorded by someone with an illegal cell phone in the studio," I say. That seems a safe thing to admit, since the evidence is right before us.

"That's right. I take it you haven't been on the Internet today."

I slowly shake my head.

"I stopped by the Boulder Pickle and several news vans were already set up there. It seems I'm the first one to make it to you."

Of course they would go for Anthony first. He's the star chef.

And I'm an *accountant*. I have to be careful or they'll figure out I can't cook. The last thing we need right now is a double scandal.

Amelia tilts her head. "You look different from your segment."

My hands fly to my hair in a twist with a pencil stuck through it. I'm not wearing any makeup. No cute dress. I'm a mess.

At least she doesn't have a camera. Not in here. I desperately want to see outside, but the windows in our 1950s building are high. I can't see outside without going to the door.

"It's a working day." I gesture to the cabinet. "I'm doing inventory."

She nods. "I think they'll love you even more looking like an everyday girl."

That is code for you'll be a perfect *How It Started/How It's Going* meme. Anthony will dazzle them with knife work, and I'll be the butt of the joke.

Her smile is as fake as a Stepford wife. "We'd like to interview you. I have a camera crew set up outside."

I suck in a breath. "I can't do that. I don't have anything to say. No comment!" I take several steps back, but she walks forward like we're doing some terrible predatory dance.

"It's only a few quick questions. Everyone is dying to know if there's a rivalry between you and Anthony Pickle. Did you or him, or the two of you together, doctor the pickles to make Milton Creed look bad? No one would blame you. Milton has his share of enemies."

She's baiting me. The negative press could be tremendous.

"No!" I say, "we're closed. Please leave right now."

Amelia is unfazed. "Your hours are posted on the door."

I continue walking backward, away from her. "We reserve the right to refuse service!"

Shane stands by the sandwich line, his mouth open in shock.

"It's just a few questions, Magnolia. We would like to hear your side of the story."

"There is no story! We did a segment. Something went wrong! I didn't have anything to do with it!" My butt rams a table, and the metal legs screech on the floor.

"I assure you Anthony will tell his side of the story. You don't want your version to go untold."

Her smile is glossy. I shudder as I walk backwards to the kitchen. There are other people there. Maybe someone can get this vulture off me. Shane seems frozen in horror.

"I'm going to the staff kitchen. Customers aren't allowed back there."

"Magnolia, it's just a few questions." She's getting perturbed, speaking through gritted teeth.

My shoulder smacks against the kitchen door. I'm

about to push through, terrified Amelia will follow me, when the elderly man from the corner takes the reporter's arm.

Amelia turns to him with daggers in her eyes. "What are you doing?"

"Magnolia said no one is to go back there other than staff. I'll call the cops if you don't back off."

His wife comes up behind him, holding her finger over her cell phone screen with all the menace a curly gray-haired woman can possess. "Don't make me hit the green button!"

I realize they are long-time regulars. They've got my back.

"Thank you," I say and turn to race through the kitchen.

The staffers whip their heads around as I hurtle by. "No one talk to the press!" I don't stop until I'm in my office and the door is closed and locked.

I sink into my chair. *What is happening? What will I do?*

I sit for a moment, taking deep breaths. I don't know what's going on out there. I keep thinking someone will bang on my door.

When several long minutes pass, I shakily pick up my cell phone to text Sakura, our manager. *Is she gone?*

Sakura answers quickly. *She left but the crew is still outside. Should we shut down the deli?*

Yes. Lock all the doors, front and back.

I send a quick text to Dad saying footage from the show has gotten out and that reporters are starting to arrive. Then I send one to my sister.

While I wait for responses, I Google my name.

The hits line up, one after the other. Entertainment shows. Cooking blogs. The Twitter link that has the original footage. Thousands and thousands of comments.

It's happening. The cat is out of the bag.

As I scroll through all the coverage, I wonder how Anthony is doing. The reporter said there were news vans at the Boulder Pickle. At least he's confident in front of a camera.

They'll have to slide food under my door from now on.

Because I am never leaving my office again.

I hole up for two hours before a timid knock that could only be Sakura.

Our manager can be tough on the staff, particularly when it comes to the quality of the food. But with our family, she's like a doting aunt.

"Magnolia?" she says through the door. "There's someone here to see you."

Surely, she hasn't let a reporter back here.

"Who is it?" I ask.

I do not expect the voice I hear coming through the door. "It's Anthony Pickle. I wanted to see how you are doing with the reporters. My deli got invaded, and I figured you were getting the same."

I press my hands to the door. "Anthony?"

I can almost hear the smile in his voice. "The one and only."

"I'll leave you two to it!" Sakura says brightly. I swear I hear the matchmaking in her tone. As if. Anthony owns the deli that could bring down ours!

My hand moves toward the doorknob when I suddenly realize, oh no, my hair is in a bun. I don't have any makeup on. My pants are dusty. My shirt is wrinkled.

I don't look anything like the girl he saw at the filming.

"Go away," I say.

"Are you okay?"

"I'm fine. I just—I just don't want you."

"I'm here on business. We need to talk about how to manage all this."

He sounds determined to talk to me. I turn to search around the room. There's no makeup. Nothing for my hair. No sister to help me. God.

I don't know why this is so critical. I'm happy being me. The accountant. The back-of-the-building daughter.

But something resists. Anthony saw something else. Something almost magical about me. I don't want to spoil it.

He goes on. "I wanted to make sure we were on the same page about the publicity." His voice is low and rich enough that I can feel the vibration in my belly. I press my hand to my stomach. If you could get pregnant from a voice, I'd totally be knocked up.

"What do you mean?"

"We hired a social media coordinator. We felt we

needed to control the message, at least until we can react to whatever Milton Creed is going to do."

I lean my forehead on the door. "He's not going to be happy the footage got out."

"I bet not." Anthony's laugh makes my skin tingle. "Do you want to review notes? Come up with a plan?"

"I didn't talk to anyone," I say. "And I don't intend to."

"That's certainly a strategy."

"What did you say to them?"

"I mainly put them off. Said that there had been a mishap on the set, and we were waiting for a full investigation."

"You sound like a politician."

"The words came straight from the social media company."

"You can't think of your own statement? Something that reflects the values of your family business?"

There's an edge to his voice when he speaks again. "I'm trying to *protect* my family business. Our chain has to support all of us."

I step back from the door. "Right. Poor you with all your fancy branches. I'll have you know that this one restaurant supports my grandmother, my parents, and me and my sister. We have a lot to lose."

"I get it," he says. "That's why we hired someone to spin this."

My frustration peaks. "There's nothing to spin! Someone who hates Milton decided to screw him over. I thought we decided this."

"Maybe so, but we can't accuse his crew. We don't have proof."

"Well, how do we get it? If we don't figure out who did this, then *we* go down."

He's quiet for a minute, and I assume he's pondering the wisdom of my words.

"Can you come out, so we can talk this over?"

No, no, no, no.

"I'm already late for something," I say. "Can you call me tomorrow?"

"I'm here now. You're impossible to get a hold of. You have the restaurant on automatic voicemail."

I *had* done that in a panic when I first holed up in the office. "Are you saying you want my number?"

"It might be useful." He's starting to sound perturbed.

I press my back to the door and frantically glance around my office for something to help me.

Grandmama's gigantic wraparound sunglasses sit on a shelf where she keeps some personal things. I snatch them up and stick them on my face.

I have my white coat. It's long enough that you can't tell what I'm wearing underneath it, especially if I zip it up all the way.

I pull it on.

Somewhere, I have a knit hat one of the staffers made for me last Christmas.

I open a drawer or two and finally find it under a pile of mismatched gloves. It's thick and deep purple.

I jerk the pencil from my hair and let it fall. With the hat pulled down low, my blond hair spills out without revealing there is no styling to it. The sunglasses hide the fact that I have no eye makeup on.

I bite my lips and pinch my cheeks, remembering the scene from *Gone with the Wind* where Scarlett tries to heighten her color. I snatch up my purse.

Here goes.

I open the door.

Anthony Pickle stands in the hallway between my dad's office and mine. Despite the half-dark due to the sunglasses, I can see that he's exactly as I remember. Tall, handsome, friendly.

I try to maintain my disdain in the face of his absolute adorableness. There's no apron today, just a fitted black jacket over a green polo that probably has his deli's logo on the pocket. His jeans fit the way jeans were invented to do.

In any other circumstance, I'd be drooling.

But we are soldiers in a bitter war, finding ourselves reluctantly on the same side against a common enemy.

"Give me your phone," I say.

His eyebrows lift at my order, but he unlocks it and passes it to me.

"This is only if something happens where we need to communicate about Milton Creed." I punch in my numbers. "No hanky-panky."

"Oh, but I love to hanky-panky. Especially in texts."

I glare up at him. His impish smile is bright and endearing. I have to harden my resolve. "You're not taking this seriously at all. It could be the ruin of both of our businesses."

He takes his phone back and pockets it. "All right.

I'll be serious. No cat videos or pickle memes." He's still grinning, though.

I brush past him to enter the kitchen, then push my way out the back door. He follows close behind.

"You're not going to speak to the reporters?" he asks. "They're aggressive."

"Not a one."

"Good luck with that. Let me know if it gets to be too much for you."

Ugh. Typical man. Thinks he can solve my problems. "For what? So you can send your social media coordinator to tell me what to say?"

"I want to help. We're in this together."

That makes me stop. "Anthony, I went on that show specifically to get publicity for my deli. To steal it from *you*. There's no reason for you to feel like we need to team up over this crazy mess we've found ourselves in."

"You really want to take me down, don't you?"

Now that we are out in the sunlight, I can see him better. His face is scruffy, but it's the right amount of stubble to look sexy. He's nice. Earnest. I should like him.

But I can't. I can't afford to.

"We all do what we have to do," I say. "If that means we have to work together for something, then I will do it. But generally speaking, the better your deli does, the worse it is for me."

I try to turn away, but he holds out a hand to stop me. "You truly believe that don't you? You don't think there's room enough in Boulder for both of us?"

He doesn't get it. "Your pickle chain expands aggressively. You don't even look at what damage you might cause small businesses without your money and power. That New York branch is a powerhouse that propels you into the limelight in ways little guys like us can't compete with."

"You shouldn't have to," he says. "There's plenty of sandwich lovers in Boulder."

"Wake up, Anthony Pickle. My demographic is loyal but becoming elderly. You're cornering the market on the young. My family can't afford to lose."

I jerk open my car door and thrust myself inside.

Only when I've slammed the door, silencing my conversation with Anthony, do I start to question what I've said to him. It's not his fault his deli is bright, attractive, and youthful. That TikTok made it a wild success.

We don't even have a TikTok for the Tasty Pepper. I wouldn't know the first thing about what to put on it. Mom manages the Facebook page. It's her speed.

I realize I haven't started the car. And Anthony Pickle hasn't moved.

He's watching me like he's trying to figure me out.

Fat chance of that. He doesn't even know what I normally look like.

We have a stare-off through the glass for a full thirty seconds.

I break it by honking, startling him.

He gives a wave and walks away.

All right, readers. I know you're judging me.

Don't throw the book at the wall. It's just I don't know what to do. I'm scared as hell. When I told Dad about what happened at the taping, he assured me that the Tasty Pepper's customers are loyal. That they'd see us through.

But there's a reason my sister and I live together in an apartment. Our restaurant doesn't support all of us. Our customer base tends to dwindle, not expand. Almost everybody who walks in is over fifty.

At some point, Havannah and I will want a life. Our own houses. We need the Tasty Pepper to do better than it is.

To be honest, I've been trying to find a way to open a second branch. Scrimping, saving, moving money around as I do the books. We need another store, a second round of monthly profit.

But now there's Boulder Pickle and Anthony's obvious prowess in running it. He knows how to get publicity, to be clever with his specials and flavors. And he has the backing of a chain to help them through a difficult publicity problem.

He has all the advantages.

We just can't win.

7

ANTHONY

Everything hits the fan again on Saturday night.

I'm sitting in my condo, waiting for my friend, Sebastian, to come by for an evening of pizza and killing zombies, when my phone starts buzzing like crazy.

There's a text from Charity, the social media coordinator, asking to call her.

One from Max, saying, "What are you gonna do about it?"

My cousin Sunny has sent a link with a thousand exclamation marks.

I click on it right as Sebastian knocks on the door.

I walk over absently and open it, my eyes on the phone.

"Hey," Sebastian says, smelling of sausage and jalapeno from the box he carries in his arms. "What's got you all up in your apps?"

I don't look up as I kick the door closed. "Something's happening again."

"From that cooking thing you did?"

"I'm getting texts from every direction."

The website Sunny sent must be getting hit like crazy, because it won't load. Sebastian retreats to the kitchen, his long black ponytail swinging. People say he looks like Lin-Manuel Miranda. I can see it.

"There's beer in the fridge," I call. I refresh the link to see if it will open. Meanwhile, two texts come through from my brother Jason.

What fresh hell is this?

Dad is gonna freak.

God. Why can they see this, and I can't?

Sebastian returns with two open bottles. He holds one out to me. "Looks like you're gonna need this."

I take it and head to the corner desk for my laptop. "I think the zombies might have to wait." Sebastian's a good friend, so he won't care. "Feel free to start on the pizza."

"I had no intention of waiting." He plunks down into a seat in front of the box.

I type my name in a search box and a whole host of links line up. Most of them are from when the footage leaked, so I switch to the news tab. And immediately groan.

"What's up?" Sebastian mumbles around his bite of pizza.

I read him the headlines.

"Prominent TV host accuses chefs of malicious prank. Milton Creed lashes out at chefs who tricked him. *America's Spiciest Chef* host promises retribution for pickle prank."

"Oh, shit," Sebastian says.

"Shit is right." I click on the first link.

Prominent TV host Milton Creed has accused two guests on his popular cooking show of a horrifying prank. In the shaky cell phone recording, Creed is shown in clear distress after tasting a pickle recipe by Boulder Colorado deli owner Anthony Pickle.

I let out a long gust of air. Yeah, he's totally blaming us.

The article goes on to talk about the pickle challenge and has quotes by members of Milton's crew backing up the accusations that Magnolia and I pulled a stunt to embarrass him.

I click through to other articles, but they are the same.

"This is bad. Really bad. Why did nobody call to ask our side of the story?"

Sebastian slides another slice of pizza out of the box. "It's not like they have your cell. They're probably calling the deli."

The deli. Boulder Pickle closes early on Saturdays, because we discovered that no one wants sandwiches past about seven-thirty on a weekend. The crew is still there closing up, though. "I'm sorry, I need to call over there," I tell Sebastian.

He waves me away. "Just don't expect this pizza to be completely intact when you're done."

"Have at it."

I pace the living room as I dial my manager's cell.

The deli phones will have switched to closed mode, so they won't even ring at this hour.

Marie picks up. "Everything okay, Anthony?"

"Have we had calls from reporters on the deli line?"

"I haven't checked. But you know, Angelina did say that she got a few weird calls toward the end of the day, but nobody left a name or number."

"Can you check the voicemail?"

"Sure. Is this about the show again?"

"Yeah, Milton Creed finally spoke up about the footage."

"Oh, dear. You want to stay on the line, or should I text you anything I get?"

"Just text me. I need to deal with family. Thank you."

While I wait to hear back from Marie, I quickly text both my brothers, my dad, and Charity. Charity asks if I want to take a call, but I say not yet. I want to talk to Magnolia first.

Charity advises me not to be too open with the other deli owner, in case I'm being recorded, or my text could be screenshot.

Would Magnolia do that?

I dial the number Magnolia put in my phone when I visited her last week. It rings several times, then switches to voice mail.

I leave a message. "This is Anthony. I'm assuming you've seen all the press Milton is stirring up accusing us of pulling a prank on him. Just checking to see if you wanted to join forces on this one. Let me know."

I sink into the sofa. What a mess.

Text messages start to come in from Marie.

"The voicemail is hopping. Two bloggers from some cooking sites. A local news reporter. And a scheduler from *Mornings with Eileen*."

I sit up at that. *Mornings with Eileen* is one of the highest-rated talk shows in the world. It's up there with *Oprah*.

I ring Marie back. "What did Eileen's people say?"

"That they want you on the show. To call back."

"What's the number?"

She gives me the digits.

Holy crap, this is big.

I call Charity. "*Mornings with Eileen* called."

I think she'll give a little whoop or something, but her voice has the same calm quality when she says, "Excellent. You'll have the opportunity to get your side of the story out."

"So, you think I should do it?"

"Given the velocity of this news story putting you in a negative light, I think you have no choice. Did they invite Magnolia?"

"I have no idea."

"Find out. Then we can prep you alone or the two of you together."

I picture Magnolia stomping out to her car after our last interaction. "Is that a good idea?"

"You two are hostile?"

"Maybe a little."

"Hmm. Well, let's see if she's even in play. I work for you, Mr. Pickle. But if she's going on, it's far better for you two to have a united front than to bicker with each other."

She's right about that.

"You want me to contact her?" Charity asks.

"No," I say quickly, probably too quickly. "I already left her a message."

"Keep me posted. I'm on twenty-four-hour retainer for your family."

Damn. "Thanks."

Sebastian drops onto the sofa next to me. "Your life is crazy, Pickle. What now?"

"I left a message for Magnolia, but I really need to get in touch with her."

"That hottie blonde?"

"Yeah."

"You gonna go see her again?"

"I don't know. We didn't end well last time."

Sebastian picks up his game controller. "I'll be here killing shit until you're ready to jump in."

"Let me text her and I'll hop on." There's not much else I can do.

Instead of calling again, I quickly tap out a message. *I'm going on Mornings with Eileen. You in?*

And to ease the anxiety of waiting, I start killing zombies.

8

MAGNOLIA

I'm completely surprised when I come home after closing down the Tasty Pepper on Saturday night and find my extrovert sister sitting on the sofa in sweatpants, eating ice cream straight from the carton.

I flop down next to her. "Did your date cancel? Is Tinder down? Have all possible avenues for getting a date tonight been obliterated?"

She shoves the spoon in the empty carton and dips her chin, giving me an unblinking stare that would unnerve the hell out of me when we were young.

I hold up my hand to block her gaze. "Stop with the eyeball voodoo. What's going on?"

She shrugs. "Wasn't into it tonight. Thought I'd catch up on some sappy Hallmark movies."

"You know they all have the exact same plot, right? A woman goes back to her hometown, meets some single guy, then they fall in love while saving her cupcake shop. The end."

Havannah smiles. "I know. That's why love them so much."

She has a point.

But to be honest, they make me sad. Dating is nothing like a Hallmark movie. I know, because I've tried it. Many, many times. Even though I am the epitome of a girl with a home-spun business in need of a perfect man, I don't appeal to a guy for more than three dates. They ghost.

I've read self-help books. I've endured many lectures from my sister.

Something about me doesn't inspire them to pursue a relationship.

This does not mean I'm a virgin at twenty-five. I am not. I've tried initiating a relationship in every way. Kissing. No kissing. Banging. No banging. Start slow. Burn fast.

My timing is somehow always off.

So, reader, it's definitely me.

"Watch the movie with me?" Havannah asks.

There's a tone to her voice that concerns me. Havannah is the bubbliest person I've ever met. She's always happy. Well, except for the hours of six to eight a.m., or later if she hasn't had coffee. Then, she's a shrew.

But otherwise, she's like a life coach, a cheerleader. She always sees the bright side of things. The glass half-full. Silver lining in the cloud.

I'm the practical one. I look for solutions, not saviors. Structure, not spontaneity.

But today, something is up with her.

"You've twisted my arm." I peer into her carton. "Even though you ate all the ice cream."

"No worries. There are four more in the freezer."

I jump up. "Really?"

"I stocked up. Bring me another one when you come back, please."

I check out the freezer. Sure enough, four more pints are shoved in there.

"Cherry or Chunky Monkey?" I call out.

"Chunky Monkey, please!"

I take cherry for myself, grab a spoon, and head back to the living room. Havannah has already queued up a snowy Christmas Hallmark movie. The holidays are a couple of months away, but the weather fits.

I snuggle in next to her and steal half of her blanket. "We haven't done this in forever."

"I know. It'll be good."

My phone buzzes. It's an actual phone call. I dig it out from my purse.

I don't recognize the number. Whatever. I send it to voice mail.

We eat and watch in silence right up to the point, which happens in every Hallmark movie, where the woman gets a little something on her cheek, dirt or frosting or cake batter. You know the scene. The hero wipes it off for her, and they share the *meaningful look*.

Havannah picks up the remote and presses pause. "Look at that," she says. "That's the moment that gets you."

"It's the pivotal scene in every Hallmark movie."

"No. I mean in real life. That's the look that gets you in trouble." Her voice breaks.

Whoa. This isn't Havannah at all. She's the swooning kind when she watches movies like this.

I set my ice cream down. "What's wrong, H? I haven't seen you like this since your high school boyfriend left for Oxford."

She sniffs. "Don't remind me. I'm hormonal enough as it is."

Oh. I get it. Why she's weepy *and* why she's home. "Having one of those cycles that are extra emotional?"

"If only," she breathes.

I start to get a terrible suspicion. She was sick the morning of my show, but better later. She's been reducing her hours at the deli, which isn't normal. She likes to be the person who greets customers when they come in.

And so much ice cream. So much. Normally, Havannah is on a perpetual diet.

I don't want to say what I'm thinking, though. If I'm wrong, she will never let me live it down.

"You going to tell me what's up?"

Havannah stares into her ice cream container. She hasn't eaten much of the second one. "You're bound to figure it out. Promise you won't tell our parents?"

Uh oh. "Please tell me it's not what I'm thinking."

Her watery eyes meet mine. "I only found out a week ago. I was late, so I took a test."

Holy crap, it's true. "Who's the father?"

At that question, she's suddenly animated, pushing

back the blanket. She sets the ice cream down so forcefully that it almost topples. I lunge forward to catch it.

She paces the room. "That's the problem."

"Don't tell me you don't know."

Havannah smooths her perfect hair away from her face. "I've been reading all over the Internet, trying to narrow down exactly when it happened. Eggs. Sperm. Ovulation. I'm hoping that when I see the doctor, they can tell me the date of conception so I can figure it out."

Oh, my. "How many contenders are there?"

"Only two, I think. Possibly three."

"Havannah! That's a lot, even for you!"

"I should never have watched all three *Fifty Shades* movies in a row!" she cries. "It did something weird to me. I just *had* to go find someone willing. Let me tell you, if you get on Blendr, you can find people fast."

"Do you know their actual names?"

She walks in circles around a chair, her face all pink with emotion. "Kind of."

"That means no."

"I can probably find them."

Now I'm the one off the sofa. "How are you going to find them if all you have is some username?"

"I'm not a complete idiot, Mags." Her perfectly arched eyebrows angle toward her nose, the angriest expression she possesses. It's still stupidly cute.

"And what does that mean?"

"It means I pay attention to their credit cards. I write down their names."

I relax a little. "So, you *do* know their names."

"Well, I know *first* names." She bites her lip. "Two of them paid for dinner with cash."

I'm about to say something, but she holds up her hand to stop me. "I met one of them at a hotel, and I can probably find a way to get the front desk to give me information. I'll have to be crafty."

I sink back down on a chair. "Oh, Havannah. What are you going to do?"

"I guess I'm going to have a baby. I know I don't have to, but...I am. I will."

"You have a job. A supportive family."

She whirls around to face me. "You think so? Are Mom and Dad going to freak? What about Grandmama?"

I don't know. My expression must concern Havannah, because she kneels in front of me. "Do any of them ever say anything about me? Things like I'm too loose? That I date too much?"

I shake my head. "You know our family. They're not ones to say negative things about either of us. Even if they are thinking it."

Her eyes plead with mine. "Do you think they're thinking it?"

"Of course not. I know you're a wild one. But you've done plenty of long relationships. It's just in between you get a little crazy."

Havannah stands back up. "If only I hadn't broken up with Brad. This would have happened with him. We could have gotten married. He wanted to do that."

"But you didn't, remember? He was too boring for you. You weren't ready to settle down."

Havannah raises her hands to the ceiling. "And look where it got me!"

"Would he take you back? Would he be willing to resume even if you're pregnant?"

"With someone else's kid? I don't think so." She sinks onto the sofa. "Besides, he's dating someone else now. I don't want to bust them up."

"So, what happened exactly? Aren't you on the pill or something?"

She buries her head in the cushion for a moment, then finally turns her face out. "I was. But I wanted to switch. So, while was dating Brad, I got off, and we were using condoms. It was only supposed to be until I started the new thing."

"So you were using condoms with these guys."

"I was. But apparently eighty percent effective really does mean only eighty percent effective. That's one in five, Magnolia. I had a one in five chance of getting pregnant." She hides her face again. She looks a mess, her sweatpants all askew, her hair snarled.

"Okay," I say. "I'll help you find these guys."

Her voice is muffled as she says, "Once I see the doctor I can narrow it down. Two were on different weekends, and one was mid-week. Hopefully, they are far enough apart to know without DNA testing them all."

"That sounds good. I'll help you once we get there."

She lifts her head from the cushion, and her crazy tangle of hair reminds me of when we were young, dashing all over the playground. We've always been close, even when I am standing in her shadow.

"I need a plan," she says. "I don't want to go to whoever-he-is begging to be supported or whatever." She looks around the apartment. "I'm gonna need to support myself *and* a baby. We'll need something bigger, or I'll have to get my own place. We're not pulling enough money to do that."

I know what she means. I personally take out the minimum I can from the deli to cover the apartment. We're paying off college loans while supporting three households off profits. It's a lot to ask of one deli.

"Have you thought more about opening a second branch?" she asks. "Maybe you and I could run that one. That way the original one can support Mom and Dad and Grandmama, and then we can take on the risk of the new one."

"I have," I say. "Part of the reason I did that stupid show was to get more interest in us so we could open a branch that appeals to younger people."

She perks up immediately. "So you think we can do it? Is it a matter of getting a loan? Can we use the original deli as collateral?"

"Probably."

It's a big risk. We would have to get our parents on board. It's their risk, too. But I don't say that right now. She needs this moment.

Thank goodness that terrible Milton Creed problem is behind us. Even if my plan hadn't helped our business, at least I hadn't hurt it.

Havannah rolls off the sofa and comes over to wrap her arms around my shoulders. "I know this is gonna work, Mags. It has to. I need to be on my own, stronger than I was before." Tears fill her eyes.

Her crying always makes me cry, too. "I'll help you," I say. "I'm happy to live with you and the baby. We will need those extra savings to get by until the new restaurant takes off."

She nods against my shoulder "I think I'm really tired." She kisses my cheek. "We'll talk more about it in the morning. And maybe come up with a plan on how to tell Mom and Dad."

I squeeze her arm. "Absolutely. I'm here."

"I'm so grateful," she says. "And for the record, I take back every single thing I ever said about not wanting a baby sister. You're the best thing that's ever happened to me."

I give her another hug. "Me too, H. Go get some sleep."

After she's disappeared down the hall, I pick up the softening ice cream and return it to the freezer.

I've been optimistic with her, but to be honest, I don't see any way we could open a new branch and support the two of us easily. We'd be leaving Mom and Dad with two positions they'd need to hire for. We'd have to buy or lease a place and fix it up. The loan payments would happen right away.

Unless we were a success straight out of the box, both the new branch as well as the original would be at risk while we built. We don't have the capital lying around.

It's been my goal for years to do this, but the Tasty

Pepper has resisted growth. We never seem to do well enough to warrant a second franchise.

I head back to the living room for my phone. There's a voice mail notification. Probably spam.

I read the transcription of the message, and my belly drops.

It's Anthony Pickle. He says Milton Creed is coming after us for our so-called prank. It's hitting the news everywhere.

I do a quick search. No, no, no. This could not come at a worse time. If support for our deli erodes rather than grows, then nothing will work. We wouldn't be able to open a second branch, and we might not even be able to support Havannah and me with the current one. And the baby.

My brain flashes to having to move back in with our parents. Moving Grandmama out of the retirement village she loves and in with the rest of us.

Or worse. The deli failing completely. Everyone having to get jobs.

I press my hand to my chest, my breath wheezing. Nope. I can't go down that path. *Get control, Magnolia.*

There's a text, too.

Mornings with Eileen contacted Anthony.

It's a huge show. He's asking if I'm in.

Was I invited, too? I quickly call into the deli's voice-mail and check the messages.

Sure enough, there it is. The booking agent for the show has left me a message asking if I would like to tell my side of the story.

Everything opens up.

Maybe I screwed up when I was on *America's Spiciest Chef*.

The world has given me a second chance.

I can get on the show, impress everyone, maybe even announce the new branch.

It will work.

It *has* to work.

All I have to do is not blow it.

9

ANTHONY

I get a distinct sense of déjà vu as a young woman with a headset over her pixie cut leads me through the guts of the studio to wait in a green room for my turn on stage.

I'm wearing normal clothes this time, not a black apron and, theoretically, I'm not going to be put forth as the bad guy. But walking the halls behind the stage at Eileen's show feels the same as Milton's.

I'm sure as hell just as nervous.

The flight from Boulder to L.A. was mercifully short. At first, I wondered if this was a terrible time to leave the deli, but Marie assured me everything would be fine. Reporters still show up every once in a while, but with both me and Magnolia refusing to give them more ammunition for Milton Creed, they are hunting other stories.

My brother Max picked me up from the airport. I'm staying with him and Camryn while I'm here. He dropped me off at the studio with stars in his eyes. I think for the first time in my life, I've made my hotshot brother jealous.

"Are you nervous?" the pixie cut woman asks as we pass crew members talking in hushed voices, some leading other guests for today's recording.

"Not too much," I say. "You'd tell us if Eileen had also invited Milton Creed, right? I don't need any more surprises."

The young woman's laugh is melodious and bright. "I certainly haven't seen him around. Based on my show notes, it's just you and Miss Boudreaux."

When we step into the green room, which is outfitted with a long table of snacks and several leather sofas, Magnolia is the only one there.

She's chosen a similar look as Milton's show, long blond hair pulled back from her face, fringed eyelashes, and perfect pink lips. This time her dress is a deep blue, cute sparkly silver ballet slippers on her feet. Otherworldly beautiful. I have to force my gaze away.

Magnolia didn't answer any of my texts or calls. I didn't know she would also be on the show until I saw her name with mine on a promo that aired a few days ago.

In the week since Milton made his claims against us, the idea that we tricked him has taken hold in the general public.

The original ghost pepper pickle challenge, which started this whole mess, has morphed into prank videos where you fool someone into thinking they're eating something they like, but you give them something horrible. The hilarity is in their shock.

Charity has advised me not to comment on the change other than a statement about how popular TikTok challenges are always evolving.

She says it is only a matter of time before someone poisons somebody on one of those TikToks, and I don't want to be anywhere near the headlines when that happens.

Going viral isn't everything it's cracked up to be.

The pixie cut woman is apparently assigned to us until we go on stage. She sits down next to Magnolia.

"Is it time?" Magnolia asks.

"About ten minutes," the woman answers. "I'll be with you until we walk down."

I head to the snack table and pick up a bottle of water. My throat feels ridiculously dry. I was nervous on *America's Spiciest Chef*, but now I'm a wreck.

Magnolia folds her hands primly in her lap. If she's nervous, I can't see it. "Will Eileen stick to the questions she had us prepare?" she asks the woman.

"Not entirely," the woman says. "She may have follow-up questions based on the energy she feels in the audience when you answer. She doesn't want the whole interview to feel scripted."

Magnolia's foot begins to wiggle. So, she *is* nervous.

The woman's phone buzzes, and she pulls it out. "Excuse me one second."

I sit at the far end of the sofa from Magnolia. We might as well get used to breathing the same air.

She glances at me, so I say, "I asked her straight out if she was going to surprise us with Milton."

"So did I," Magnolia says, and relief washes over me

that she's talking to me. I'm completely in the dark as to why she's avoided me since that day I came to visit her deli.

I turn my water bottle over in my hands. "I had hoped we could review our answers, but from the rehearsal, it sounds like we're mostly on the same page."

Her face tilts to me slowly, almost menacingly. "Some of us speak from the heart, not from a professional spin doctor."

I meet her gaze. "Some of us are afraid of screwing everything up. Again."

She glances down at her hands.

The woman returns. "They're ready for you in sound."

I stand, brushing the knees of my charcoal dress pants out of habit. I'm used to being in the kitchen, not in front of cameras twice in two weeks.

Once in the sound room, a friendly pink-cheeked technician takes my water bottle, my cell phone, and my keys. "Any change in your pockets that will jingle? We don't want anything making noise or falling out on stage."

"I'm all clear," I say.

She also takes Magnolia's purse. "I'll get this back to you the moment you come off stage. No extra cell phones on you, right?" She winks.

I manage a short grunting laugh.

"There's no pickle to poison," Magnolia says dryly, and I turn to her in surprise. So, she does have a sense of humor.

We're led to the wings of the stage, and I sense

Magnolia shifting nervously beside me in the half-dark. There's a studio audience this time. There will be no stopping the cameras to redo anything.

I lean closer to Magnolia and whisper, "Break a leg." She continues to stare ahead.

When we're led on stage, I kick back on the sofa, one ankle crossed over my knee. Magnolia remains primly upright and attentive. She clearly wants to get everything right.

She plays the opening questions straight, reiterating that she was escorted by a staff member to add a single ingredient to one of the pickle jars.

I explain that I placed the jars in the refrigerator early that morning, and that after the disaster, I tested the rest of the batch to confirm that my ghost pickle peppers had been fine when they arrived at the set.

"This is quite the mystery," Eileen says. "And Milton insists that his own investigation into the matter shows that no one could have possibly tampered with the pickles after they were placed on set."

"I don't think he knows his crew that well," I say, then chide myself. This was not on the list of safe responses that Charity made me memorize.

Eileen's eyes light up. We've gone off track.

"Did you notice any animosity on the set when you were there?" she asks.

I ponder what to do. Eileen is a warm figure in the talk show circuit. Even when she asks the hard questions, you never feel like it's anything more than a friendly aunt trying to help. I glance at Magnolia to see if she is going to answer. She sits perfectly still, her eyes unwaveringly on Eileen.

I guess it's on me. I stick with the facts. "He fired someone right in front of us."

Eileen leans forward. "Did he, now?"

I sense the audience is also on the edge of their seats. This is the exact moment the woman who led us here talked about. Eileen will dig because everyone's interest has been piqued.

I choose my words very carefully. "I'm sure he's got employees with an ax to grind. It happens even in my deli."

Magnolia snaps her gaze to me. "Is that how your deli works? Because there is no infighting at my deli. We are a friendly family who lifts each other up."

Eileen's eyebrows raise even more. "So there really is a rivalry between you two."

That took a turn. I have to get us back on track.

"If there's a rivalry, it was stoked by Milton himself, when he put us both on the show to pit our pickles against each other. Boulder is a restaurant-friendly city, and many of the owners of the local eateries get along beautifully."

My speech makes Magnolia snort. *Uh-oh.*

"When have you and I ever spoken?" she asks. "Because if we had, you would learn that your arrival decimated our family's plans."

Eileen is eager to hear more. "How was that, Magnolia?"

"We were planning to expand. We'd done our

85

research. We knew where to place a new deli to maximize business."

"Did Anthony take your spot?" Eileen asks.

Magnolia's face lights up with anger. "He did! Right from under us!"

This is all news to me. I tug on my tie. "You were the other bidder?"

Her face falls. "There was another one?"

"Yes. We outbid them. It wasn't you?"

Her chin quivers a bit. "We weren't quite ready to bid."

A rush of protectiveness like the one I felt on Milton's show washes over me.

Eileen plucks a tissue from a box and passes it to Magnolia. "So Anthony's ambition ruined your family's hopes and dreams?"

Oh God, this is going south in a hurry.

Magnolia squeezes the tissue to her chest. She's either genuinely upset or a very, very good actress.

"My grandparents, and then my parents, have run the Tasty Pepper for sixty years. My sister and I would like to ensure we will always have our deli as their legacy."

I expect Eileen to keep sympathizing with her, making me out to be the bad guy, but she surprises me. "Isn't that how business works? You have to beat the competition."

Magnolia's jaw drops. "He didn't have to open precisely where we wanted to expand!" she snapped. "He was a college kid who had no idea what he was doing!"

"And yet he's here, beating you at your sixty-year game," Eileen says.

Magnolia lets out a yelp of anger. "Who do you want to support? A family institution that has kept people lovingly employed for six decades, or a tawdry upstart with an inedible pickle?"

The crowd bursts into applause.

Magnolia is activated now. She sits tall, talking as if Eileen and I aren't even here. "You won't burn your taste buds right out of your mouth at the Tasty Pepper! You'll get homestyle bread and time-proven recipes made by a staff who doesn't care what's viral on TikTok. They want to make you feel like home."

More applause.

Eileen nods in agreement, but it's clear she wants her show to shift back to its original intent. "Anthony, how would you like to see this situation resolved? Should Milton Creed stand down?"

"Absolutely," I say, glad I can divert the attention from Magnolia's rousing speech. "He's damaging the reputation of our restaurants with these wild accusations."

Eileen tilts her head, her glossy black hair touching one shoulder." It's my understanding that you thought the segment would be about you, and Milton surprised you by bringing a rival on the show."

Where did she get that information? It was nowhere in the prepared questions, and the viral footage begins after that announcement. I choose my words carefully, "He was trying to stir up interest in the show, give it a little punch." I hesitate. "Sort of like you're doing right now."

"Hey!" Eileen says with a laugh. "I *resemble* that remark!" She turns to the audience. "There you have it. Anthony Pickle and Magnolia Boudreaux have knocked the ball right back into Milton's court. Maybe the case of the poisoned pickle will remain unsolved."

She goes on to promo the next guest, and I feel my shoulders relax. We're done.

As we're escorted off the stage, Magnolia storms ahead of me in a huff. "You played right into that," she says over her shoulder.

"Played into what?" I rush to catch up with her, pausing only when the sound guy angles us toward the room to remove our equipment.

Her voice is a hiss. "Now everyone's going to talk about our rivalry."

"You were the one going on about family values!"

The man unclips the mic pack from the back of Magnolia's dress, and she quickly expands the distance between us. "I had to make a good impression, Anthony. I have to open a second branch."

"So open the second branch!"

"How can I do that when at every turn, you're there messing things up for me?"

I have no idea what she means. "How did I mess things up?"

"By being you!"

The woman with our personal items approaches and passes Magnolia's bag to her. "Your coats are at the checkout as you leave," she says. "I'm happy to take you there and call a car if you need one."

"I need to leave," Magnolia says. She dashes down the hall. The mic man and the woman shrug at each other, then turn to me.

"Apparently I can't do anything right." I accept my phone and keys and take off slowly down the hall to avoid catching up to Magnolia.

I have a terrible suspicion that this problem just got bigger.

10

MAGNOLIA

When Dad picks me up at the airport, he's so excited about my big triumph that he decides to host an early-morning viewing party in the private dining room of the deli.

I'm nervous. I don't know how I'll end up looking on the show. I can only hope my heartfelt speech about our family business will help our cause.

All the Tasty Pepper staff members are invited, and to avoid making anyone having to do extra work for the party, he orders a spread of pastries and breakfast fare from a bakery down the street.

He dresses up for the occasion with a blue button-down shirt and black slacks instead of his usual jeans and Tasty Pepper polo. He greets staff members as they pass, ever the host, funneling them toward the food table festooned with green and red balloons to match our deli's colors. He's brought his own TV, set up on a serving table for the occasion.

Mom arrives only a little ahead of air-time, leading Grandmama through the back door.

Grandmama is perfectly put together as always with elegantly coiffed gray hair, regal stature, and a monochromatic pastel blue suit. When I was in elementary school, I used to think she and Queen Elizabeth were the same person.

The two of them take seats next to me. Grandmama places her hand over mine. "I can't believe you're about to be on my favorite morning talk show!"

"So exciting," Mom says. "They flew her there and put her up in a hotel and everything."

The rest of the staff starts to settle in their seats. Everyone is here. Our manager Sakura beams at me from a table over. The early morning staff, the afternoon staff. All the full-timers and most of the part-timers. The room is bursting.

"Can I get you anything, Grandmama?" I ask. "There's lots of lovely pastries, coffee, and juice."

"I had breakfast, but I could use a cup of coffee."

Shane jumps up from nowhere, startling us. "I'll get it for you!" His smile is large and eager. "You take it black? Cream? Sugar?"

I work hard not to recoil. Shane is a nice enough guy. He's just always so…near.

"Black, thank you," Grandmama says.

He turns to the rest of us. "Mom?"

I grimace. Did Shane just call *my* mother Mom?

She frowns. "No, thank you, Shane."

"Anything for you, Magnolia?" Shane asks.

I point to my plate and cup. "I'm covered. Thanks."

As Shane hurries to fetch the coffee, Grandmama bumps her shoulder against mine. "I think that young man is sweet on you."

I force a smile. Grandmama doesn't always try to play matchmaker, but when she does, you have to be firm.

"You mean Shane? He's in college. So probably five years younger than me."

"That's not so bad," Grandmama says. "I sure don't understand why young ladies these days don't want to settle down."

My thoughts immediately swivel to my sister. She's settling down, in a way. I wonder what Grandmama is going to think of that. "We have our careers to think of."

"Well, in my day," Grandmama begins, but I'm saved when Shane returns with the coffee. She smiles up at him. "Thank you, young man. You should sit with us."

Seriously?

Shane eagerly drops into the chair beside me.

Mom looks around. "Where's Havannah? I thought she was coming."

"She is," I say quickly. Havannah was puking her guts when I left this morning. I told her I would cover for her. "She's probably in the back somewhere. She'll be here before it starts."

If she's not, I'm hoping everyone will be caught up in the show and won't notice.

Mercifully, the theme music begins. Everyone quiets. Eileen stands in front of her set. "Welcome to today's edition of *Mornings with Eileen*. Today we have an amazing lineup of interesting people to start your day."

She mentions an actor first, which makes sense as his movie is coming out this weekend. Then the image of me sitting next to Anthony fills the screen. Everyone in the party room cheers.

Dad reaches over and squeezes my shoulder. "You look beautiful, sweetheart."

Quite a few people shift their gazes between the screen and me as if to compare how I look on television to my current state. Grandmama says what everyone is probably thinking. "Oh my, Magnolia! Why don't you wear makeup all the time?"

I plaster on a smile. I am acutely aware of how different I appear on the show. To be honest, I *have* left my hair down today. It makes the difference a little less, and there's no sense sticking it in a ponytail until I start working.

Havannah wasn't able to go with me to L.A., of course, but Eileen's staff used the footage from Milton's show to recreate the look.

Eileen starts every episode with a featured charity. In our room, staffers whisper amongst themselves. I suspect my altered appearance is still the subject.

During the commercial, Mom stands up to look around. "Magnolia, can you text your sister? She should be here."

"Sure thing, Mom!" I jerk my phone out.

Mom's asking about you.

Havannah writes back quickly. *I'm in the back parking lot. Hopefully just puked my last puke. Eating a cracker.*

I look up. "She's here. She's in the back." All true.

Mom nods and sits down. The show returns with the actor's interview. I grip my coffee cup with both hands, trying to calm my nerves. I know the show won't go completely as we recorded it. They will cut it to fit their time allotment. Our answers could be shortened, and some questions might be skipped.

I wonder what Anthony and his crew are doing this morning, if they are having a watch party, too.

As the actor's segment ends, Mom pushes back her chair as though she might go look for Havannah. Thankfully, Eileen says, "Next up, two young deli entrepreneurs address the charges by a prominent cooking show host when we come back to *Mornings with Eileen.*"

"The commercials aren't very long, Mom," I say. "You don't want to miss it."

Mom frowns but she doesn't get up.

Dad rubs his hands together. "This is going to be amazing." His eyes shine with happiness. I can only hope I live up to whatever he's hoping for.

Havannah slips into the back of the room and stands against the wall.

"Oh, there she is," Mom says. "Havannah, over here!"

"Too crowded," Havannah calls. "Back here is fine!" She does look green around the gills. I'm sure she wants to stay near the door in case she needs to race to the bathroom.

The music returns, and the studio audience claps. That must be added after the fact, because we sat there for ages as they rearranged the lights. The screen shows all three of us, and a great cheer goes up in our room.

Then the focus is on Eileen. "A few days ago, popular talk show host Milton Creed of *America's Spiciest Chef* levied accusations at two Colorado delicatessen owners, claiming they had set out to humiliate him by doctoring pickles on his show."

The camera shifts, and Eileen adjusts effortlessly. "This brought up a lot of questions. Why would two business owners, with everything to lose, pull a prank on such a prominent show? What did they stand to gain? After reading the statements made by Milton Creed and his staff, I decided to get to the bottom of this mystery. I present to you the deli owners themselves, Anthony Pickle and Magnolia Boudreaux."

The view switches to the two of us on the sofa. The angle makes us appear to be sitting closer together than we were in real life.

"Don't they look cozy?" Shane says.

No one responds. I don't even look his way.

This is nothing like the shaky footage that went out from the cell phone. This is high definition on a big screen. I quickly scan my dress, my hair, my face. My feet look awkward. I shouldn't have worn sparkly shoes.

Anthony looks perfect in charcoal pants and a sports jacket. He's calm, cool, and collected, handsome and friendly. They're going to love him. My palms start to sweat.

The first questions are exactly as we recorded them. Both of us reiterate that we didn't do anything nefarious to the pickles. Anthony makes the point that it's ridiculous that we would attempt this, since Milton wouldn't air anything that embarrassed him. There was no point in trying.

But then we get to the argument where I accuse Anthony of stealing our new location.

Dad glances over at me. Heat rises to my face. I appear way more hostile than I thought. I'm practically in Anthony's face due to how the angle shrinks the distance between us.

At least I still have my speech about our family business. It's heartfelt and I know it will take the edge off this confrontation. It'll be a great triumph and the staff will be so pleased with my performance.

But the speech doesn't start. The footage cuts to a close-up of Eileen!

I sit forward as she says words I don't recognize. She must have recorded them later. "The rivalry between Anthony and Magnolia has taken a turn. There's no wonder why Milton Creed believes them guilty of trying to use his show to ruin each other." She pauses, letting that ominous conclusion sink in. "Stay tuned for our next guest, singer Emilio Cruz."

It cuts to commercial.

What? It's over?

It can't be!

Eileen just said we hated each other! That our rivalry would ruin us!

That can't be it!

But Shane lifts the remote and clicks off the television. Silence blankets the room.

I open my mouth, but I don't know what to say.

My mother speaks first. "Magnolia?"

"They edited it a lot," I spit out. "They made us look terrible!"

"Anthony sure sat close to you," Shane says.

I resist the urge to tell him to shut up. But there's no need to say anything else, because everyone starts shuffling around, picking up plates and heading for the door.

Dad squeezes my wrist. "It's okay, Magnolia. These talk shows are only after the ratings."

Mom shreds a paper napkin into bits. "I bet Eileen's in cahoots with that terrible Milton Creed."

Grandmama hasn't said a thing. The staff clears the pastries and drinks and moves to the kitchen. Then the four of us are the only ones in the room. Even Havannah has made herself scarce. Hopefully, I haven't made her puke more.

"Where do we go from here?" Mom asks. "Will people stop coming to our restaurant?"

Dad shakes his head. "Our customers are loyal. The whole thing will die out in a day."

Grandmama taps her coffee cup on the table. "We got a lot of publicity today," she says. "Who's in charge of our social media presence?"

My eyebrows hit my hairline. I didn't know Grandmama knew what "social media presence" meant.

"I am," Mom says.

"You'll want to stay on it today. There's going to be talk. We'll want to answer it with a steady hand. Who's manning the phones? People will be calling."

"I can do that," Dad says. "I'll handle any fallout."

"I think I'd like to do it today," Grandmama says.

"I'll take over your office. Route all calls to me. If there's more than one at a time, you can take the overflow."

"All right, Mom," Dad says.

It's been a long time since I've seen Grandmama take charge of the deli that she and my grandfather founded. I realize what this means.

The new generation has threatened what she built.

She's going to have to do something to protect it.

It's all my fault.

11

ANTHONY

I don't get a chance to watch Eileen's show until after the workday.

We had several emergencies at the deli, and I had to field quite a few phone calls from reporters and other talk show hosts wanting us to appear. I forwarded the messages to Charity.

When I finally get settled at home that night, I unwrap the sub sandwich Marie packed for me and locate the recording of the show.

And damn. They emphasized the animosity between me and Magnolia. I run it back and listen again. Eileen's practically saying we're guilty of Milton's accusations.

This is bad. I scroll through the web hits on my name. Most seem primarily amused that Magnolia went off on me. A few accuse me of being heartless for taking away her opportunities.

I rub my eyes. I'm tired. I want to sleep.

But a text message pops up from my dad. *You were great. That Boudreaux girl has made a mess of things.*

I pause, unsure what to say. But then I type. *She was upset. She's taking a beating online.*

Is she? I switch my search to Magnolia's name to see what is being said about her.

My eyes nearly bug out of my head. The negative mentions tagged with my name are small compared to what's being said directly to her.

Back off, you jealous bitch.

Goes to show women shouldn't be running restaurants.

Someone needs to knock some sense into that 'ho.

Everybody knows she did it.

A few of them shouldn't be mentioned. They're terrible. They're words people should never think in their heads, much less type into a comment box.

A protective urge flares hot. I've got to do something to help her.

I send her a text. *Just now watching the segment and reading the comments. I'm sorry people are so terrible.*

And I wait.

Nothing.

Maybe she's busy.

I send a message to Charity. *Just saw everything. Talk?*

Within thirty seconds, my phone rings.

"I've already put together a tentative plan," Charity says.

"Good evening to you, too."

"Sorry, but the situation has been on my mind all day."

"Did you see some of those threats?"

Charity sighs. "I did. I don't like this situation for either of you. Right now, the sentiment is overwhelmingly against her. But what will happen next is you will see women rise to defend her, and it is going to turn against you."

"But I didn't do anything."

"You were called out by a woman who feels she has been wronged. We probably have twenty-four hours to get control of this before it starts to backfire."

This is not what I want to hear. "I was hoping to work directly with her so we could fight this together."

"That is absolutely the best scenario. Have you contacted her?"

"I sent her a text, but she doesn't tend to respond to me."

"You want me to reach out?"

"She didn't seem to like the idea of you. She calls you 'Spin Doctor.' No offense."

"Nope. I get it. But that doesn't mean you shouldn't team up."

"Should we do another show?"

"Not without a coordinated plan. She's obviously got some feelings, and she doesn't have enough control to avoid saying them on television."

"What do we do?"

"I've taken control of all the official Pickle deli accounts. My assistant and I will be doing the responses. Let us do our job."

Now that *is* what I want to hear. "How long do these things normally take to play out?"

"If no one else fuels the fire, it should die down within three to four days. We'll handle your side. But if

Milton or Magnolia decides to provide new content, it could flare back up."

"I wish everybody had someone like you."

"Oh, trust me, Milton does. What he's doing is calculated and planned. He's using you for publicity, and it's paying off. The segments that he's been airing have an incredibly high market share compared to the ones before all this happened. Everyone wants to see what he's up to."

"What will his next move be?"

She hesitates, then says. "He's ruthless. And ambitious. It's a difficult combination to predict."

"Great."

"Get some sleep. You sound exhausted. Call me if you hear from Magnolia."

"Will do."

I drop the phone on the sofa. We have to do something. But all I can do is wait.

I must've fallen asleep, because I wake to a buzzing near my ear. It's my phone.

I squint at the screen. Five a.m. I have about three hours until I need to get to the deli.

The buzz is a text from Charity.

Sorry for the early hour. We've been monitoring your media accounts all night. I need approval to take control of several more websites because your reviews are starting to tank.

Our reviews?

I head over to some of the prominent sites. And I see it.

One star. Boulder Pickle serves its sandwiches with a side of misogyny.

One star. The only thing worth ordering here is Anthony's pickle, chopped into pieces.

Ouch.

One star. Just what we need, a mansplainer telling a woman how to run her business.

And so many more.

We've racked up fifty one-star reviews on this site alone, all since I fell asleep.

This isn't good.

I text Charity.

Sending you some logins. Can we do anything about this?

She responds right away.

I'm deactivating your business profiles until this blows over. It's the best choice for the moment.

Well this sucks.

I'm about to shower when I decide to check the reviews for Magnolia and the Tasty Pepper.

Same story as mine, but on steroids.

One star. Who does this bitch think she is?

One star. The real reason this bullshit deli hasn't expanded is because everything there sucks. I wouldn't swallow anything there any more than that chick would…on a date.

And more of that ilk.

I have to get through to her.

I send her another text. I hope it doesn't wake her up, but it can't wait. *I know you don't want to talk to me. But I have a strategy. Let's work together so we can beat this thing.*

This time I get an answer. It's not much. But it's something.

Okay.

We decide to meet before the workday gets heavy. I imagine that Magnolia is a lot like me, overseeing the morning preparations. Since her family sent her to do the cooking show originally, she's probably their top chef.

I chat strategy with Charity on the drive to the hole-in-the-wall coffee shop Magnolia suggested. Charity says she'll send me a list of ideas to review to get this resolved the fastest.

When I arrive, Magnolia's already sitting in the back corner nursing a coffee. Her hair is up today, swinging in a long ponytail. She hasn't taken off her puffy white coat, but I can see that today she's wearing leggings and cute boots with sheepskin inside.

I place a quick order and slide into the chair opposite her. "How are you holding up?"

She lifts her coffee cup and swirls it in circles. "I would like a time machine so that I can go back and never call Milton Creed."

I grunt my agreement. "Was the segment your idea from the start?"

"Dad and I came up with it. I'd been trying to think of ways to get more business to warrant a second branch. I thought beating you at your own TikTok game would get our deli some credibility with a younger age bracket."

She stares past me, lost in thought. Those long

eyelashes about kill me. She isn't made up like the show, but her eyes are a vivid blue and her lips are soft pink.

It's hard to focus.

The barista calls my name, and I pick up my latte, glad for a breather to get my thoughts straight. When I return, she seems to have pulled herself together.

"So, what's your expert's big plan?" she asks.

Talking business is way easier than fighting the urge to sit closer. "Charity took my business profiles down to stop the flood of one-star reviews. She can do that for you as well, if you want to try to work together on this."

Magnolia idly rubs her thumb along the edge of her cup. "And what would we do together?"

A thousand answers flash through my mind, mostly involving extremely compromising positions. I squeeze my coffee cup so hard the plastic lid pops off. The liquid that leaks out the sides thankfully misses my fingers.

Her gaze flicks to my face. God. She probably has me all figured out.

I carefully press the lid back on and wipe up the spill with a napkin. "Maybe a joint promotion? That way people know we don't hate each other."

"I guess." She doesn't seem very enthusiastic.

"Charity had some suggestions. Let me pull them up." I open the document Charity sent and scan the options. My jaw drops.

"What?" Magnolia asks. "What's the big solution?"

I turn the screen face down on the table. There's no way I'm going to suggest it.

She squints an eye at me. "Out with it."

I shake my head. "We can brainstorm ideas for ourselves."

"But you said she was such a hotshot!" She snatches up my phone. It hasn't powered off the screen, so the list is right there.

Oh, boy.

Her mouth drops open. "Is she serious?"

"Just because she suggests it doesn't mean we have to."

She slides the phone across the table. "She wants me to apologize to you on national TV!"

"Like I said—"

"Not in a million years."

I hold up my hands. "I'm not asking you to."

"Charity can stick it up her butt."

"You've made your point."

But Magnolia won't let it go. "I can't back down now. I've got an army of women in business behind me."

"I saw that."

"The jerks are out in force, but so is the support."

"It's a double-edged sword, for sure."

She squishes her nose in a way that makes my chest tighten. "I saw what they wanted to do to your pickle."

My neck flashes hot. "The Internet doesn't play nice."

My phone buzzes, but I don't turn it over to see who it is.

Magnolia looks down at it. "You think that's your superstar? Asking if you got me to agree to apologize?"

I shrug. "Could be anything."

But then it buzzes again. And again.

Then Magnolia's starts going.

"That is never a good sign," she says.

"Agreed. On the count of three?"

She takes a deep breath. "One. Two. Three."

We both pick up our phones.

"Oh, God," Magnolia says.

I quickly see what she means. An entirely new set of statements have come from Milton Creed's camp. These have footage.

"I totally forgot those things we said on his show," Magnolia says. "Before the leaked footage."

"Me too."

Both of our phones auto-play similar clips, a fraction of a second apart, like an eerie echo of our checkered pasts.

In the video, Magnolia's face is in close-up, full-res, nothing like the shaky footage. Her expression is saucy. "I stole one of the jars of Anthony's pickles from your very own fridge."

Milton's hands smack on the counter. "You tampered with the set?"

Magnolia shows zero remorse. In fact, she looks proud. "I did."

I jam my thumb on the screen to stop the video. "It's nothing they didn't already know. You already said you altered one of the jars."

"But it's right there on video. Did you see my face? I look guilty as hell!"

"It's out of context!"

"It's going to sink me," Magnolia says. "I practically say I did it." Magnolia holds her head in her hands.

"Magnolia," I say, but she stops me.

"Milton is going to keep going and going. He's got beautiful footage he can use any way he wants. He can cut and splice. He'll never stop."

"We can fight him!"

She looks up, her eyes wet. "At what cost to my family?"

I don't know how to answer.

"I'm going to confess." She points at my phone. "And apologize. Just like she said to do. Let's get the biggest show they've got. Ask Charity which one is the best. And let's get on it." Her eyes lift from the phone to meet mine.

I'm struck again by how perfect she is. How exquisite. My gut tightens as our gazes remain locked.

I see everything clearly. She's trying to do right by her family's business, same as me. She's made some mistakes, as public as can be.

But I can't let her do this. "I don't want you to take the fall. You didn't doctor those pickles."

"I can't prove I didn't. And we can't wait any longer. The rivalry angle was all me. I did this. I started it. I made it worse on Eileen's show. I have to end it."

"It's not what I want. Can't I confess instead?"

She spins her phone around, paused on the frame of her looking smug, like she'd pulled the biggest prank in the culinary universe. "I'm the one they caught. So please, let's get this over with."

All I can manage to say is, "Okay."

12

MAGNOLIA

Charity chooses the afternoon talk show *On Spec*. It has a roundtable format, so we will have three people interviewing me along with Anthony. They have been promised a big reveal.

She also books us on the same flight this time.

I grip the armrests as the airplane takes off. We're headed to New York, so the flight is longer.

When we're safely aloft, I let out a long breath and release my grip.

"Don't fly much?" Anthony asks.

He's been over-the-top friendly since he picked me up at the Tasty Pepper. He constantly chats me up in the car, in the security line, while we wait to take off.

And here he goes again.

"Often enough," I say. "Dad and I go to the big trade shows."

"I do those sometimes."

The conversation peters out, and I try to relax. I

should save my anxiety-ridden angst for my big, televised confession.

Anthony seems to accept that I'm not going to be very talkative and leans his head back.

The quiet is blissful for all of three minutes. Then he's at it again. "Did you review the statements Charity sent?" He's asked me this three times already.

"I did."

"Crazy that this show will be live."

I wonder if he's nervous too, and that's why he's so chatty. The roundtable format means that they like to keep everything spontaneous. We will do a run-through of where to sit and what to expect. But we've only been given two questions to prepare. All the rest will be off-the-cuff.

Including my confession and apology. Which I have to work in somewhere.

And most of all, *not lose my temper*.

The next morning, the green room is full of people waiting for their turn with *On Spec*. I hide in the corner nursing a cup of tea and watch everyone. I'm way too introverted to mix and mingle. But it's fascinating to people-watch.

An actress holds court near the door, carefully perched on the arm of a leather sofa. Her dark skin is luminous, her expression eager and friendly. Laughter frequently erupts from her side of the room.

I can't imagine what it is like to be comfortable with your fame. Or at least to be able to fake it so well.

Anthony seems to be in his element, speaking to a man who must be clergy as he's wearing a flat white collar. He's young and reasonably handsome. I wonder what he'll be doing on the show, but whatever it is, it will be nothing compared to what I'm about to do.

Confess to a prank that I didn't commit.

A young man dressed all in black steps in and calls for the actress. She pops off the edge of the sofa with a big smile for the room. "Good luck, everyone!"

Her eyes rest on Anthony for a split second, and a tendril of jealousy stirs in my belly.

What is that?

Anthony gives her a sheepish nod. Then for some reason, his gaze shifts to me. Like he's concerned I might have seen it.

I turn back to the hospitality table to warm up my tea.

I begged off from dinner last night, although he asked. I needed to keep my head clear and to go to bed early. It definitely wasn't the time for me to manage awkward exchanges with the person about to witness my downfall.

Besides, Charity warned us not to be seen together more than necessary. She has arranged for a private escort through rear entrances at both the airport and the hotel where we're staying.

During the conference call after we reached New York, she emphasized the necessity of controlling the message from here on out. Once this blows over, she'll restore our social media accounts, request the worst of the reviews to be removed, and all will be as it was.

That's all I've wanted for two weeks.

I plan to return to my corner of the room, but a voice calls from the door. "Anthony Pickle and Magnolia Boudreaux." It sounds like a drill sergeant.

I set my cup on a tray and follow Anthony to the door. Our handler is a stern older woman who looks like a villain from a spy thriller.

Her arrow-straight eyebrows form a V on her forehead as she turns to us. "Pick up the pace."

Anthony glances at me, his eyes wide, an expression you might make if you and a classmate were headed to the principal after shooting spit wads.

We follow her down the maze of corridors. "What did we ever do to get Cruella?" he whispers.

The woman's head turns sharply as if she has heard him. "Remember this is a live broadcast with a studio audience."

"Yes, ma'am." Anthony gives her a salute. As we continue through the bowels of the studio building, Anthony starts humming the tune to "Cruella de Vil."

He's trying to keep me calm. I'm not sure it's possible.

When Cruella leads us to the sound stage, we wait a moment in the wings beyond the set. Hushed crew wanders around us, tiptoeing in the red glow.

The bright jazzy theme song of the show blares through the speakers, signaling the commercial.

Cruella turns to us. "Come along. Make sure you behave. There is an audience."

"She's only said that three times," Andrew whispers.

When we walk out into the lights, the audience erupts in a mix of cheers and boos.

I didn't expect this.

I glance at Anthony, fear shooting through my gut.

"You okay?" he asks.

I'm not. Not at all. My voice feels stolen.

The three hosts swivel in their chairs as we approach.

"Welcome, welcome!" Jenae, a statuesque Jamaican woman with a beautiful accent, stands to greet us. "So glad you're here."

"We're glad to be here," Anthony says.

Cruella takes off in another direction as a man from the stage crew leads us to our seats and checks our mic packs. "Say a few words," he says.

"Hello," I say anxiously. Another round of boos.

Jenae lifts her arms and motions for everyone to settle down.

"Good afternoon," Anthony says. Cheers erupt.

Of course they do. These people have taken their sides.

Angie, a friendly redhead who is considered the kindest of the three hosts, leans forward to pat my hand. "Don't you worry a bit. Nobody goes crazy during *On Spec*."

I give her a quick nod, but I don't feel any better.

Lauren, the third host, makes Cruella look like a Disney princess. Her blond hair is sculpted with hairspray, which sets off her fire engine red pantsuit. She swivels in her chair and stares me down. "I've got some questions for you, honey."

Angie shoots her co-host a look that says, "*Save it,*" and I feel like I'm going to throw up.

A stocky man with a headset walks across the stage. "Thirty seconds."

The crowd goes quiet.

"You've got this," Anthony says.

The thing is, I don't *got this.* I'm terrified. Our memorized statements have flown from my head.

All I can think about is getting booed or yelled at. They can't rush the stage in an angry mob, can they?

The sudden blare of the intro music startles me, and I jump in my seat.

"Steady," Angie whispers. She's immediately to my right, and beyond her are the other two hosts. Anthony is on my left.

Several cameras glide into place and turn to aim at us.

"Welcome back," Angie says. "We have with us two people who have been making quite a stir in the culinary world. Anthony Pickle and Magnolia Boudreaux own competing restaurants in the mountain city of Boulder, Colorado. But when they were invited for a segment on *America's Spiciest Chef,* something went terribly wrong."

Angie turns to us. "Anthony, what can you tell us about that day?"

This is one of our prepared questions. Anthony will not accuse me. He'll stick to the story until I make my confession. At least that's the plan.

Anthony's grin is charming and warm. I sense the audience sighing.

"Well, Angie, I made a perfectly amazing pickle, and Magnolia had a brilliant adjustment to my recipe. But when Milton Creed tasted mine, it was inedible."

"Inedible how?" Janae asks.

"It burned his mouth," Anthony says.

Lauren makes a shocked sound. "So, who did it? You say it wasn't you. She says it wasn't *her.*" She points to me and pauses as a long *boo* slithers through the audience.

A trickle of sweat slips down my back. This is a tough crowd. I should've known.

"It's been a great mystery," Anthony says smoothly. "Magnolia and I talked about it in the parking lot after Milton threw us out."

Anthony's going off-script. I feel light-headed. What is he doing?

Jenae sits up very tall. "Milton threw you out?"

Anthony nods. "Into the cold. Without our coats or cell phones or keys. Unceremoniously tossed us out like he had something to hide."

The crowd makes an *ooh* sound.

He's baiting Milton. This was not part of the plan.

Angie turns to me. "Magnolia, what was going through your head when you're standing out in the cold after a huge talk show host has thrown you off the set?"

I'm supposed to be confessing that I wrecked the pickles and apologizing. But Anthony's taken us off course.

"I — I"

I sound guilty, is what I sound like.

Anthony chimes in. "Magnolia wisely pointed out that staff members on the set were saying that Milton was not popular with his crew."

What is he doing? This will make it worse! But I don't contradict him. I can't. My throat feels frozen.

All three hosts seem to be on board with the story, their faces brightening at the idea of the mystery unraveling on their show.

Anthony continues. "When the rogue cell phone footage released, that cinched it for us."

Lauren is all ears. "Why?"

"Because if you are going to risk your job to humiliate your boss, you will absolutely make sure someone is there to record what you did."

Angie turns to her cohosts. "They have a point."

"I don't buy it," Lauren says, her siren red nails tapping the table in front of her. "You believe someone managed to poison the pickles, record it, and get away with the whole thing?"

"I do," he says.

Lauren shakes her head so hard that her dangly earrings swing. "Then I have some oceanfront property in Colorado to sell you."

The audience laughs. My anger burns hot that they're baiting Anthony. I'm no longer frozen, and my words come out in a rush. "Do you get off by making guests look horrible?"

Lauren snaps, "If the shoe fits, honey."

Anthony cuts in. "We had nothing to do with this."

"Maybe *you* had nothing to do with it," Lauren shoots back. "We're not sure about *her*."

The audience lets out a long *boooo*.

This is my chance. Lauren has thrown the gauntlet. I stand up. "The thing is—"

Anthony stands up, too. I have no idea what he's doing. We had a plan! He's ruining everything!

My frustration boils over as I face him "This was a trap all along, wasn't it?"

"No!" Anthony says. "It's not!"

"Right. That's why you flew me here. Why you put me in the same hotel. You had to win. You and your four-year-old deli with unoriginal sandwiches and stupid pickles that are more gimmick than food."

Lauren lets out a whoop. "Oh no she didn't!"

The audience roars.

Angie holds out her hands. "Let them talk."

Anthony's face has gone red. "I can't believe after all this you still don't trust me!"

My anger bursts so hot that I practically see stars. "How can I trust someone who would poach a long-standing deli's territory!"

"There's plenty of room in Boulder for both of us!"

He's so close that every breath of his words brushes my cheeks.

"Not if everybody hates us!" My voice cracks.

"I don't hate you!"

"Then what are you doing?"

His eyes shine as they look into mine. "Trust me."

I want to ask him why, when suddenly, his lips are on mine, warm and gentle. His hands move to my waist.

We're kissing.

Kissing on national television!

Live!

I vaguely register one of the hosts saying, "Well, this is unexpected."

The intensity of the moment makes everything go quiet. I'm floating in the ocean, and Anthony is a life preserver. I cling to him like I'm drowning. Maybe I am.

But it's quiet here in his arms. His mouth is careful, seeking, and easy. He's like home.

But soon, sounds start to penetrate, then the blazing lights. The audience is roaring with cheers and applause.

We pull apart.

I stare into his eyes. They are the darkest blue, like smoke. Neither one of us speaks. I'm not sure we could be heard over the noise even if we did.

The blare of the music sounds. It's a commercial. The hosts stand.

"Well, that's going to get some press," Janae says.

"Told you we should bring them on," Lauren adds.

I'm afraid to turn around, to look at them, look at anyone. I let go of Anthony's arm and smooth my dress nervously.

Cruella returns. "Come along," she says.

And just like that, as if nothing's happened, we're ushered off the set.

13

ANTHONY

The most important thing to know about a live show is that—it's live.

Monitors broadcasting the show hang in the corners of each hall so guests and crew can keep tabs on the progress of the live feed.

Before we make it to the sound room, two crew members rush up to us.

"I told you we should ship them!" one says with a squeal.

"Congratulations you crazy kids!" the other cries.

Guests from the green room pass by, clapping me on the back and winking.

Once we're free of mics and have collected our things, Cruella practically knocks people out of the way to get us out the back door. Apparently, she doubles as security.

I'm liking her better all the time.

The town car Charity arranged for us waits in the private lot.

We jump into the back of the car, and I give the address of the hotel.

Magnolia stares out the window, fingers pressed to her lips as if I hit her, rather than kissed her. I wonder, all too late, if she has a boyfriend I don't know about and I just made things terribly, terribly worse.

Finally, she asks, "What was that?"

I want to tell her that it was the result of all my pent-up feelings. The way I felt about her since she shocked me by walking on the set of Milton's show.

But I have to get the new problem out of the way.

"Did I cause trouble for you with a boyfriend?"

She seems taken aback by the idea. "No. I don't have one."

Thank God.

It all comes out in a rush. "So, we were sitting there. And people kept booing. And I started thinking—why should you take the fall for this?"

Magnolia interrupts. "Because I was the one in the footage, you numbskull. It had to be me."

I ramble on. "I decided that instead of you having to confess and take the fall, for us to be united."

"United?"

"Yes. I thought, Milton's trying to ruin both of us by having everyone take sides. You versus me. What if there were no sides to take? It's like Charity said. A united front."

"Go on."

Her tone isn't very encouraging, so I stick to the concept and leave out any feelings.

"Now all the speculation will be on our relationship

and when it began. People will completely be on our side."

Magnolia's hands fold tightly together. I wonder if she's imagining choking the life out of me for what I did. "And now that you've started this, I assume we have to keep up the ruse?"

My heart thunders down my chest. She hates this. I should have known. I was foolish. But I have to keep going. "We will have to see how it plays out. Maybe not."

Magnolia doesn't reply, simply staring out the window.

I resist the urge to reach over and touch her. "I thought you'd be glad. You didn't have to confess to something you didn't do. Or take that heat."

"What about our family?" she asks. "My dad will wonder why I'm suddenly hooking up with the deli owner across town."

"We can tell our families it's not real." I have to swallow my disappointment. I thought there had been something in that kiss. It felt perfect at the time.

But I was dead wrong. "As long as we don't antagonize each other online or in public, no one's going to know we're not actually seeing each other."

She lets out a long sigh. "All right. It makes sense." She opens her purse. "Don't forget we had to turn our phones all the way off."

"Oh, that's right." I jerk mine out of my coat pocket.

When we power on, both our phones start buzzing with notifications. Everyone saw it live, all right. I have messages from Dad, both my brothers, Grammy Alma, and my cousins. I steal a glance at Magnolia. She's tapping away as well.

I say the same thing over and over again.

Brilliant tactic, right?

I think we've solved it.

This should blow over now.

When I finally look up, I realize we've barely moved three blocks. I lean forward to tap on the glass between the front and back seats. The driver rolls it down.

"What's going on?" I ask.

"It's rush hour," he says. "Midtown's a beast. Are you in rush to get somewhere? I could try some side streets."

"No. Just the hotel. Thanks."

He rolls the window back up.

I glance over at Magnolia. She's absorbed in her phone.

I fire off a call to Charity. She answers after one ring with, "Bloody brilliant, Anthony! Have you seen what's happening online?"

"We're still in the car."

"The Internet is rooting for you two. I've had my people push out the hashtag #ShipBoudrickle with clips from the live broadcast."

"Boudrickle?"

"Yes! Boudreaux. Pickle. Isn't it cute?"

So, I have a "ship" name.

Charity goes on in a rush. "My writer is preparing a *Buzzfeed* article titled 'Ten Times Anthony and Magnolia Accidentally Revealed Their Secret Love on

Television' with associated stills from your appearances."

"You found stills that work?"

She sounds breathless. Clearly this scenario is her jam. "Tons. This is the easiest fake news I've ever had to sell."

"Really?" I want to ask her to send them to me, but Magnolia's in the car. Later. "You're worth every penny."

"You bet I am. So, what are the plans for tonight?"

"Should there be something?" I glance over at Magnolia. Her fingers have stilled on the phone. In fact, the screen is dark. She's been listening for a while.

"I would suggest a romantic dinner. I can make the reservations. I'll tip off some photographers. We could milk it. A short stroll. Buy some flowers for her at a street vendor."

Whoa. "Let me put Magnolia on, so she can have a say in this."

Magnolia's eyes catch mine, one eyebrow lifted.

I lower the phone and switch to speaker. "Okay, Charity, we're all here."

"Magnolia, you were magnificent," Charity answers. "Wait. Magnolia. Magnificent. Let me note that play on words."

Magnolia shakes her head, but her serious expression loses some of its strain.

Charity returns. "Magnolia, this is a very time-sensitive opportunity. If you two can pull off enough of a romance to push out any negativity Milton has been spreading, he'll be toast. If he tries to put a wedge between you again, *he* will be the one getting boos from the audience."

I haven't taken my eyes off Magnolia, but she stares down at the phone. "You think it will work?"

"Of course it will work! I'm only angry that I didn't think of it! Shipping the two of you is the simplest and cleanest solution to this publicity challenge!"

"But Milton can still say we doctored the pickles."

"So what if you did! He'll be the villain, and you are the romantic leads in this story."

"What do we have to do?" Magnolia asks.

"A short walk. A romantic dinner. A few meaningful glances if you can pull it off. I won't ask for another kiss. But if you can—another kiss!"

The car goes silent.

"Are you two in?"

Magnolia's eyes meet mine.

"Up to you," I say. "But I'm game."

Still, she hesitates.

But Charity is a master seller. "Here's the thing. Magnolia, you're after a younger market and opening a second deli, right? You need capital, right? Seed money?"

"Yes," Magnolia says.

"I say let's go full-tilt romance. You two create something you can package and sell online. A love pickle, maybe."

Magnolia sounds like she's choking. "A love…pickle?"

"You two can argue specifics. My team can have an online shop ready to roll in a few hours. You just need to create the magic. We can even farm this out. Chocolates. Whatever. It's all about the label. I feel like we could raise six figures in the next two months. For each of you. Then you're well on your way to opening that new branch, right? The relationship can die off and you'll be yesterday's news, but with a lasting legacy."

My mind is already buzzing. "Dad was already working on a pickle line for distribution," I say.

"Perfect," she says. "We can lead that line with the love pickle, or whatever you decide. I'd recommend packaging that ghost pickle too. It's a hit already."

I glance at Magnolia. "It could work."

Charity can't seem to stop. "In the meantime, Anthony, you be your brilliant self and come up with a shared menu for both your delis. A Boudrickle sandwich. Do it up big. Give it to all the delis. You'll have them lined up to get it before the ink is dry on the sign."

"That's something we could discuss over dinner," Magnolia says. The fire is starting to light in her eyes. "We could create new combos from ingredients we already have. Maybe a dessert for upselling."

"I love the way you're thinking, Magnolia. Strike while the iron is hot!" Charity is practically preaching from the pulpit. "Ride the wave!"

Now we're both laughing. Laughing because we're through this ordeal. The future feels wide open. Not just for me and Boulder Pickle. But for Magnolia. We're going to get her that second branch.

"Don't get sticker shock from my bill!" Charity says with a laugh. "I'll text directions to your dinner tonight. Magnolia, dress romantically. Something that will *whoosh* if Anthony spins you in a circle. Anthony, spin her. Buy her flowers. I'm going to call a few tasteful photographers who won't stalk you, but stay discreetly away. Let's do this thing."

She clicks off the line. We stare at the dark phone for a moment, then I manage to say, "What do you think?"

The car inches forward, and Magnolia leans back against the leather seat. "I need a couple of hours to process all this."

"I think it's going to be fun. We can pretend we're in a sweeping romantic movie and ham it up."

Magnolia gives me side-eye. "Are you a Hallmark movie fan?"

I press my hand to my chest. "I might own a 'This is my Hallmark movie watching sweater.' I may or may not have bought it for myself."

Magnolia's laugh is loud and genuine. It's music to my ears. "Well, I'm delighted to hear it. We can both be the heroes of our story."

"You can be the small-town girl trying to save her family deli," I say.

"And you can be the promising young chef who aims to help her succeed," she says.

We grin at each other, and for the first time since I met Magnolia, I feel hope that we will work things out.

14

MAGNOLIA

Soon I will have to go downstairs to find a romantic dress. I have no idea what makes one fit well, and certainly not one that will "whoosh" like Charity requested.

The only dresses I've worn past the age of ten were those I've borrowed from Havannah.

I call my sister in a tizzy and explain the situation. She already knows my big kiss was fake. She was the first person I texted in the car.

"You have to help me!"

"Where are they sending you to look?" she asks.

"The boutique in the hotel. But I doubt I can afford anything in it. This is a high-end hotel."

"Take pictures and send them to me."

"How am I going to look like a smitten girlfriend?"

She pauses. "Are you sure that kiss was fake? Because it looked damn real from where I was sitting."

"I didn't even know it was coming. I'm probably more shocked than anything."

"I'll agree with you on that. But it keeps going well past the shock point."

"Did it?" I haven't sought out any clips from the show. I'm scared to look. "But Havannah, focus, I need a dress! I'll go down to the boutique. If it's obviously too much, I'll walk a few blocks. Surely there's something nearby."

"Is your makeup still good?"

I rush to the bathroom mirror. "I'm solid. The show was only an hour ago." It feels like a year since then, though. Life is rushing at me.

"You should go. You've only got two hours until this date. That's not a lot of time to shop."

"I'll ring you if I need help. Don't leave your phone!"

Havannah laughs. "I'll glue it to my hand."

I hang up and scramble for my bag. I keep our checking account lean, but I do have a credit card. If our future is everything Charity says, it might make sense to invest in a pretty dress.

Thank goodness I have nice shoes on. I guess the dress will have to match them. Splurging on a new pair doesn't seem smart.

When I arrive at the downstairs boutique, my anxiety rises. It's gorgeous, all gold columns and heavy draperies. The racks are spread apart, with what appears to be exactly one size of each item. It carries a wide range of apparel from dresses to jeans to tailored jackets.

A young pink-haired salesperson approaches eagerly.

I'm wearing the same outfit from the show, which might've been a mistake. I could be recognized.

But if this woman knows who I am, she doesn't let on. "My name is Esmée. I will be your personal shopper. What are you looking for, *ma chérie?*"

I want to browse and see if the prices are way out of my league, but Esmée's clearly going to be stuck by my side, so I say, "I need a dress that will swing in a circle."

At that request, she spins to the rear counter and waves at an older woman with a vintage beehive. "Sonata! It is her!"

What does that mean? While the other woman approaches, I finger a silk blouse on a rack close by. No price tag. My face flames. Nothing here has a tag on it. That means the people who normally buy clothes here don't care what things cost.

I'm totally out of my element.

Sonata arrives and reaches out her hands to grasp mine. "Magnolia, you made it."

"You know who I am?"

"Charity called and said you'd be coming. I have already found three beautiful dresses for you to try." She releases my fingers with a quick squeeze.

Sonata leads me to the back of the store, where two elegant dressing rooms lined with gold silk wait for customers. It's like the bedroom of a princess. My chest goes tight. I know for sure I can't afford anything here.

"This one is yours," she says, pushing open the door.

Inside are three dresses the likes of which I would never have considered for myself before.

All are knee-length with miles of fabric on the skirt. The first is all white, with a scoop neck and long sheer sleeves. The second is the wintry floral in cool blue and silver. It's sleeveless but is paired with a silvery blue wrap.

The third is poppy red with a scalloped neck and hem. The sleeves fall to the elbow, then flare out.

They're beautiful. I might as well try them on. It's not often you get treated like a star. I step inside to choose one.

I glance at my black shoes. They won't go with the white dress or the silvery blue.

Red it is. I switch out from my skirt and top and into the dress. It fits like a dream. The waist is fastened with a sash that requires tying in a bow. I do the best I can and step into my shoes. When I open the door, both ladies are standing outside.

"It is very lovely," Sonata says. "Come see."

She leads me to a carpeted platform surrounded with mirrors, something you might see in a bridal store. I step up.

Esmée hurries away as I turn in the mirror.

"Let me get that bow," Sonata says. She swiftly reties the sash.

My cheeks grow warm as I examine myself in the dress. The red makes my hair shine like gold. I turn in a circle and the skirt flares as promised.

Esmée returns with three shoe boxes. "I pulled three styles for you. Size seven, *oui?*"

"That's right."

As she sets them in a line at my feet, I hesitate. There's no way I can afford all this.

"How much is the dress?" I ask.

Sonata waves my question away. "It is already covered. Have no fear."

What does that mean? I can only assume Charity will take the money from whatever we earn with the online store. Or charge it to Anthony. We can make it square later.

I assess the shoes. One pair is stilettos so high that my ankles cry for help just looking at them.

The second have a more modest heel, red with a closed toe.

The third are ballet flats like I wore to the second show, patent leather with a small gold bow.

I should probably go for the flats, but I might be able to manage the modest ones.

I kick off my shoes and slide my foot into the heels, feeling very much like Cinderella.

"They're a touch tight across the instep," I say.

Esmée nods. "We can have them stretched if they're the ones you want. We will run them over to the dry-cleaning service. They have someone who can do it on the spot."

"Did you want to try on the other dresses?" Sonata asks.

"I'm tight on time," I say. "And we have to stretch the shoes."

Sonata nods, straightening the flowy sleeve. "All three are lovely, but I think this is the best choice. You have a good instinct."

I don't, I only chose it because of the shoes, but I give her a small smile.

"Why don't you leave it on," she says. "Then you won't have to worry about the bow. Your date is in an hour, right?"

"What time is it?"

"Six-thirty."

I suck in a breath. It's all happening so fast. "Yes."

"I'll run the shoes over," Esmée says. She waits for me to step out of them, then rushes out the door.

"What about accessories?" Sonata asks. "Perhaps a necklace?"

"I'm not sure."

The woman bends down conspiratorially. "If I were you, I would make the most of this opportunity."

Except this is probably going to come out of whatever profits I make.

Sonata gestures to a glass case on the side wall. "Just let me show you. If nothing looks good, all is well."

It can't hurt. My bare feet pad on the floor as we head over to the counter lined with jewelry.

"I think you are more of a modest girl, not one for statement pieces, correct?"

I nod.

Sonata lifts a gold chain with a perfect teardrop ruby. It twinkles in the light like a hypnotist's charm.

It's beautiful.

"This will complement that neckline perfectly," Sonata says. She walks behind me and fastens the necklace. I bend to an oval mirror on the counter. She's right. It is the perfect thing.

"And these earrings," the woman says. Small rubies drip in a cascade. She holds one to my ear.

They are so lovely that my stomach quivers. I touch the sparkling waterfall of gems.

"I've never seen anything so beautiful," I say.

"I must agree," Sonata says.

"I'm assuming these are real gems?"

"But of course."

My heart falls. "I couldn't."

Sonata spreads the glittering earrings on her palm. "I was specifically told that any jewelry you chose would be a gift from the gentleman."

I snap my gaze to hers. "Really?"

She smiles. "Really."

Now I'm even more concerned about accepting. What are we doing here? And why would Anthony buy me jewelry?

I bite my lip. "How much is the necklace?"

Surprisingly, the sum isn't much more than I would have paid for a plane ticket and hotel if the show hadn't covered those. "I'll take it. But not the earrings. And I would like to pay for the necklace myself."

"Whatever you like," she says.

By the time we finish the transaction, Esmée has run back with my red shoes.

"Try them now."

I slide my feet inside and sigh. "That's perfect." I wish I'd known I could do this. There were so many beautiful shoes in my life I could have bought.

Esmée claps her hands. "I cannot wait to see the pictures. Everyone is breathless to catch you together again."

"Really?"

Esmée leans in. "You are, as they say, a viral hit." She holds up her phone. "I saw the whole thing while I waited for the shoes. So *romantique*."

Sonata closes up the fabric bag holding my old outfit and shoes. "Should I have this sent up to your room?"

I take it from her. "I can manage it. Thank you so much for your help."

I cross the lobby with my bag.

Now it's time for the date.

15

ANTHONY

I have to take a deep breath before I knock on Magnolia's hotel room door to start our pretend date. A thousand competing worries buzz through my head.

The fact that I actually *like* Magnolia is the biggest and most pressing. I know it will do well for appearances that I feel so strongly about her.

But I practically dragged her to New York to do this, and she only agreed to any of it because of the benefits for her business. So I most certainly need to proceed with caution.

She calls out, "Coming!" The ensuing flutter of footsteps makes me smile.

The door flies open, and I immediately have to take a step back. Magnolia is stunning. She shines like a jewel, her red dress fitted at the waist, leading to a neckline that draws my gaze like a beacon in the night.

Nestled in the cleavage that has me already breaking out in a cold sweat is a glittering pendant. If all went correctly downstairs, it is my first gift to her, even if she doesn't know it.

Her choice feels like an omen. My mother's favorite gem was a ruby. And although she didn't live long enough to see any of her sons find their brides, both my brothers have reported small signs that suggested her approval.

I wonder if I will look back on this day and know that the ruby necklace was mine.

"Have I rendered you speechless?" Magnolia's mouth is pressed into a bewitching smirk.

"Completely," I say. "I don't think I've ever seen anyone look so beautiful."

She rolls her eyes. "Flattery will get you nowhere. But watch this." She backs away from the door and turns in a quick circle. The flowing skirt lifts in a perfect swirl of red, showing off a long expanse of slender legs. My mouth goes dry.

Magnolia holds still, letting the dress fall. "I've been practicing so I know exactly how fast I can spin without showing off my knickers."

"Knickers?"

She laughs. "My sister and I love the *Great British Bake Off.* Sometimes we forget certain words aren't actually American." She leans forward. "Besides, I feel like *panties* is too much for us, don't you think?"

At the word *panties,* my mind goes completely blank. I can only stare at her like a big dumb rock. She waves her hand up in my face "Anthony? Are you in there? Is red your kryptonite?"

No, but *she* is. I try to shake myself free of the wild

thoughts racing through my head. *Concentrate, Anthony.*

"Maybe." I draw in a steadying breath. "Charity found us a clever Thai place to go to. Sound good?"

"Sure!" Magnolia turns to snatch up a short black coat. "Is it freezing out?"

"Pretty cold, but for the few blocks we're walking, I think we'll be fine."

"I guess you keeping me warm will make the photographers happy!"

I can only nod lamely as she slides her arm through mine. For a moment, everything good in the world settles around my shoulders.

We head toward the main elevator instead of the secret one in the back. Tonight is the absolute opposite of everything we've done before. We want to be public, witnessed, talked about. Magnolia seems completely on board. Charity's optimism must have infected her, because I've never seen her so happy and easygoing.

I press the elevator button. "Imagine the Tasty Pepper Two, serving the finest pickle relish in the Rocky Mountains."

That gets a big smile out of her. The doors slide open, and we step into the elevator.

Magnolia's face is mischievous. "I love that you are known for the pickles, and I will be famous for the very same item, only chopped into tiny bits."

I can't help burst out laughing "You have to use that line on one of our future shows. It's epic."

She seems pleased by the compliment, and by the time we cross the lobby and exit the hotel, she's glowing. Good. I want her to feel like we belong.

Even if this is only a big fake to the world, the product of what will happen between us is very real. Her dreams for her deli coming true. And for me, an end to this stressful part of my life.

"So, when can we expect photographers?" she asks.

"Anytime. Charity thought we shouldn't know exactly when they'll appear because she doesn't want us to overact. We're to look as natural as possible."

"Makes sense. We must convince everyone we're a happy new couple."

I draw her closer. As we pass shop windows, I glance over to see how we look. Magnolia is perfect in her black coat and golden hair. I'm awkwardly hunched over, so I quickly straighten my posture and plaster on a smile.

"Are you checking out your reflection?" Magnolia asks.

"Busted."

"How do we look?"

I squeeze her arm. "Absolutely perfect."

Our gazes clash, and for a moment I think she understands that I mean it, no fakery. But then she bursts out in a peal of laughter. "You're so funny!"

Wait. What? "You don't think we look good together?"

Her voice drops to a whisper. "I see a camera across the street."

"Oh."

She bumps me with her hip. "Laugh, so we look like happy lovers."

My mind stumbles, this time on *lovers*. But I pull

together enough to crack a jocular, "Should I break out in song?"

"Don't you dare!"

"Don't I dare? What wouldn't I dare?"

I grasp her hand and initiate a move I haven't tried since high school. It's risky. We could go viral in the wrong way if this fails.

But I spin her out and away from me. Her dress swirls, and she gasps.

I circle her back toward me, not stopping until our bodies are flush against each other. "Want to do it again in case they didn't get the shot?"

"I'm glad I didn't eat anything, or I'd be puking down the front of my coat."

I touch the tip of her nose. "You're so romantic."

Now she's really laughing as I twirl her out again, this time creating a big finish that draws her to my side.

When we walk again, our bodies touching, my heart beats painfully. If only this were real.

After another block, we pause at a flower vendor approved by Charity. I choose a cluster of red roses that match her dress and pay the elderly gentleman in a vivid green apron.

"I'm the luckiest girl in the world!" Magnolia exclaims, her eyes wide. She pauses. "Too much?"

I can't help but grin. "Maybe a little."

She draws the flowers to her face. "These do smell amazing."

"I'm glad you like them."

"I guess this is when I should kiss you," she says.

My heart hammers at the thought of having her in

my arms again. "Only if you want to."

"Maybe we should save it."

Disappointment washes over me. "Of course."

We reach the restaurant, and I open the door for her.

Despite not knowing for sure if the cameras are following us, she pauses in the open door, her eyes gazing up at me, her face close to mine. It's an almost-kiss for the camera. I can barely stand it.

"How's that?" she asks.

"Perfect." It takes all the control I can muster not to press my mouth to hers.

We head inside. I assume no one will follow us into the restaurant, but when we arrive, the host seems to know we were coming. "We have a table by the window," he says.

Of course he does. Charity is thorough.

When we're seated, Magnolia examines the menu as if it's a textbook.

"Do you make a lot of Thai?" I ask. We've never had much opportunity to talk about our culinary pursuits.

"Not really," she says. I wait for her to expand on that, but she doesn't.

"I took an entire course on Far East cuisines in culinary school."

She continues to study her menu. "Nice."

I follow her lead and keep reading. I choose the spiciest item on the menu, just for fun. "What are you going to try?"

"Pad Thai."

"You're going for tangy instead of spicy today."

She nods and sets down the menu.

The waiter arrives with a bottle of white wine. "Compliments of Charity," he says.

When he's poured two glasses and taken our order, I figure it's time to talk shop while we can.

"What did you think of Charity's ideas? Relish? Pickles? Maybe something completely different?"

Magnolia's face grows serious, then she seems to remember herself and plasters on a smile. "I can't forget where we are," she says. "I like the idea of the shared menu. I think anything that could draw extra foot traffic into our delis in the short-term will have the quickest impact."

"Agreed. Just know we are limited on how many people we can draw in Boulder. When we open our products up to shipping anywhere, we will make the most of this opportunity."

She nods. "I agree with that, but we have to remember that there will be a delay between when we will be up and running and taking orders. We don't even have our products figured out. Then there's the matter of manufacturing and upfront costs."

"Don't worry about those," I say.

She hesitates. "Like I wasn't supposed to worry about the jewelry?"

I glance at the ruby. "I love what you chose."

"You should know I paid for this myself. As much as I appreciated the gesture, it didn't seem appropriate to accept such intimate gifts."

I glance around, but the diners all seem oblivious.

"Sorry," she says. "I should be more careful about what I say, but I wanted to put that out there."

"Point taken," I say, disappointed again. "We'll keep it strictly professional."

"Other than when we're making out for cameras?"

I assume she's trying to make me laugh, but I'm feeling crushed. Sometimes this hope in my heart is too much to bear. "Except for then."

"I enjoy talking shop," she says. "Let's plan our imminent total world domination." Her smile seems genuine.

That's good at least. She no longer seems to hate me.

If nothing else, I'll have yet another friend-zone to add to my collection. I'm not the Casanova that my brothers are. Women flock to them. They think of me as a friend. This is my lot.

We hash out tons of ideas for dishes to add to our menus, and some preliminary concepts for things that can be shipped. We take notes on the back of napkins, and I carefully fold them and tuck them in my pocket.

Occasionally I take her hand and bring it to my lips, holding it there in case someone might be taking a photo. We find ease in moving in and out of normal business talk and romance-for-show.

Our food arrives. Even the steam from the extremely potent spices makes my eyes water. "This is gonna burn," I say. "Since you were already working on a recipe to adjust my ghost pepper pickle, though, you must be able to take spice with the best of them."

Magnolia's eyes stay downcast as she busily stirs

together her noodles and tofu. "Sure," she says.

I lift a slice of beef bathed in fiery red curry. "This will wake the dead."

"I bet." Magnolia stuffs a bit of tofu in her mouth.

I take my first bite, savoring the fire. "Hurts so good."

Magnolia doesn't comment on that, carefully twirling noodles with chopsticks.

"You have to try it. It's amazing." I capture a bite and hold it out. "Besides, it'll make a great picture."

"Did you say it was red curry?"

I lower the chopsticks. "Yes. That's the main spice in Pad Prik."

"Sorry. I'm allergic."

I set the bite down. "Red curry allergy. That's good to know."

"If you want to share a bite for the camera, I can give you some of this," she says.

I nod. "Sure."

She spins a bit of noodles and holds them out to me. We take it slow, enabling a photographer to get the shot, if anyone's even out there.

"What is your family business culture like?" she asks. "Mine swear that if we don't spend every moment in the restaurant, we're somehow going to cause it to close forever."

"I hear you on that. In fact, a year and a half ago, my dad staged a competition to see which of his three sons could turn the biggest profit. He decided to retire, and he wanted one of us to take over the chain."

"Really? Who won?"

"I did."

"Are you the oldest?"

"The youngest. Jason's the oldest, down in Austin. He got married last summer. And Max is the middle brother. He's in L.A."

"I'm so jealous how you've managed to expand."

I point my chopsticks at her. "You're going to get there. That's what this is all about."

She seems pleased, tucking back into her meal. Even though there won't be any real romance here, I realize that makes things easier. I don't have to worry about making a move or blowing it. Everything is for show.

When we walk out the door, Magnolia pulls me close. "I see a photographer over there."

I glance across the street. A long lens is trained on us.

"We should probably do that kiss," she said. "That's probably what he's waiting for."

I lead us closer to the light below the awning, nerves firing up again.

This kiss won't be like the one on the show. That was spontaneous. Full of emotion. It fit.

This one is manufactured. I take the flowers from her, so they don't get smashed between us.

"Here goes," I say.

"Ready when you are." She closes her eyes and lifts her chin.

I look at her a moment. Her long eyelashes rest on her perfect cheeks. Her lips are no longer shiny with gloss. She seems more natural, like when I saw her at the coffee shop. I like it.

I rub my thumb across her cheek. She relaxes her stance, resting against me. That's better.

I lean in. When our lips meet, they are cool at first, chilled by the frosty weather. She exhales, her breath feathering against my skin. I claim her mouth slowly, bit by bit. I gently bite her lower lip and she smiles.

Her body sinks into mine, her hands moving to the back of my head.

I don't intend to deepen the kiss, as the lighter one probably will look better for the picture. But it happens anyway. Her lips part. My tongue traces hers. She tastes slightly sweet, like the Pad Thai she ate. I realize that I've been eating something she's allergic to and back away in an instant.

Her eyes fly open.

"Are you okay?" I ask. "There might be some trace of the curry. How sensitive are you?"

She sinks down, and I realize she's been standing on her tiptoes. "It's fine. I'm fine." Her eyes are wide, her lips pinked up.

I let out a long breath. "Okay, good. I won't make that mistake again. If I know we're going to be staging a kiss, I'll be careful what I eat." I take her hand and lead her back toward our hotel.

That was close.

We walk back in silence. She holds her flowers close to her chest, as if to have a reason not to hold my hand.

I went too far on the kiss. And I had put her at risk.

This is my fault.

It seems I can't even fake date correctly.

16

MAGNOLIA

I'll admit, the first time I walk in the back door of the Tasty Pepper after returning from New York, I sneak into my office on tiptoe like a teenager after curfew. Pictures of my kiss with Anthony on a New York boulevard are *everywhere*.

I don't want to talk to anyone about it, least of all my dad. I'm barely allowing myself to think about it in my own head.

Readers, I could use advice. I'm in a hot mess. You all know I'm a spice wimp, and I LIED to Anthony about being allergic to red curry to avoid him finding out.

But worst of all, I liked the kiss.

Liked it, liked it, liked it.

What is that all about?

And of course, he had to shut it off when he remembered the curry.

I guess that's what you call poetic justice.

What will happen next? Your guess is as good as mine.

I turn on my computer, wincing at the startup beep. Dad surely heard it next door.

I'm not sure why I'm delaying the inevitable. The only reason I haven't been pestered to death by my parents since the live show is that they don't like to text, especially when it's important. I badgered Havannah into explaining about the fake kisses and why we did it.

I thought I had gotten off scot-free and could focus on work when I roll back in my chair and smash into the metal filing cabinet.

It tilts and smacks the wall I share with my dad's office.

I freeze, hoping the noise won't send him over immediately.

But the telltale sound of his chair rolling back on the hardwood floor next door tells me he's coming. Sure enough, Dad's gray head appears in the doorway.

"There you are! Your mother and I thought you would stop by for dinner with your sister last night."

"My flight was late," I lie. "I should've let you guys know that. I'm sorry."

In truth, I'd been home when Havannah left for the dinner. After all the covering I've been doing for her, so no one knows about her morning sickness, she knew good and well not to mention I was back in town.

"You never know about those airlines," he says. "Back in my day, it was a big deal if they were more than ten minutes off schedule. People would get fired."

I glance at the clock. The deli's about to open and I know Havannah isn't here. She was heaving up dry toast when I left.

"You need me on the floor? Havannah's going to be late."

He lifts a hand. "No, no. Your mom has it handled. To be honest, I think she prefers greeting customers over running social media. I think we've got those two roles reversed."

I seize on this new topic of conversation. "I think it's a great idea to switch them. When Havannah came back from college, we should have put her on social media. She's amazing at it. She can do that from home in the mornings and not even come in."

She better thank me for this.

"I'll see what your mom thinks about it. Ever since that TikTok thing happened, she's realized she might be slacking. It took her years to get up to speed on Facebook. New apps pop up like mushrooms."

"They do."

I'm hoping our talk is over, but I don't get that lucky.

He absently taps on the door frame. "I guess you're gonna tell your old man about what happened on that show?"

"Havannah didn't mention it?"

"She did. But apparently there was also a date?"

"Oh. That."

"Yes. That. It was quite the talk among the staff yesterday."

"Well, to be honest, Anthony Pickle's family hired a social media coordinator."

Dad nods. "And."

"She thought it would be beneficial for us to have a

united front, so we planned the whole thing. It's all fake."

Dad's face screws up in confusion. "What is?"

"The kiss. The date. They hired a photographer to capture it all. We're trying to make sure that Milton Creed can't do any more damage to us."

Dad claps his hands together, a sound so startling in the quiet that I jump an inch off my seat.

"How about that. And here we were so worried about you. Thought that boy might be providing unwanted attention to our little girl."

I hadn't expected this reaction. "No. Nothing like that. I'm fine."

"This is good news. It seems like all the publicity has been really positive."

I decide to go ahead and tell him some of our ideas, since he's so jovial about it. "We're thinking of creating some joint items on our menu. You know, to take the opportunity to upsell."

"Sure, sure. That sounds fine. Run them by Dan and Sakura to get them on the line."

Well, that was easy. "I'll do that!"

I swivel my chair to face my computer, but Dad doesn't leave. I cautiously turn back to face him.

His face is the picture of concern. "Magnolia, you'd tell me if you were in a bind, wouldn't you?"

"Of course," I say. "Just don't spread it too widely that the relationship is fake. We don't want any leaks ruining the plan. This whole thing has been weirdly popular."

"You might be grown, but I'm still your dad."

"I know."

Thank goodness I don't have to lie.

Except for maybe what I felt both times Anthony Pickle kissed me.

Nope. I'm perfectly content lying to myself about that.

When Dad's gone, I review all the ideas that Anthony has already typed from our napkin notes. He's suggested a combination menu with a soup, sandwich, and dessert. In addition, the Tasty Pepper will come up with a recipe for Love Relish, and his deli will serve an original pickle called The Kiss.

These sound really clever.

I wonder what our relish should be. I pull up the supply lists for our orders. I can't cook my way through a box of mac and cheese, but I can analyze our shipments and see what sells.

Our menu hasn't changed since before I was born. But it looks like years ago, we would place a large order for cranberries this time of year. The practice ended around the time Grandmama stepped back from the deli for retirement. Interesting.

I spin and turn to the safe that holds the family recipes for our menu.

I sort through various breads, potato salad, sauerkraut, and a few other classics. Then I come across a whole sheaf of relishes. There's one with cranberries. "Boudreaux Thanksgiving Relish," it reads.

Perfect.

Suddenly I remember a few jars in the back of the supply pantry marked like this. They'd be old but could give me an idea of what the relish looked like, and if it seemed suitable for long-term shelf-stability and shipping.

The kitchen is all hustle as I pass through. The lunch hour has already begun.

I squeeze past staff members chopping and replenishing trays for the sandwich line and head into the supply closet.

I'm not familiar with the order of things in here, but I know those jars are in the back. I walk deep into the pantry and begin shuffling boxes around. They're not here anymore. Rats.

I sense someone has followed me in. I turn.

It's Shane.

"Hey. Can I help you find something?" he asks.

"Just looking around."

"Nothing in particular?"

I can't let him in on what I'm thinking. He's totally adopted my rivalry with Anthony. I step forward as if I'm going to push past him, but he doesn't move.

My face is level with the chest of his red apron, signaling that he's the manager of the line.

"Did you need something from me?" I ask.

He's tall, and his blond curls add to his youthful appearance. There's nothing wrong with him, really. He's too young and aggressive for me.

"I saw the show," he says finally.

Oh.

He shoves his hands in his apron pockets. "What was that all about?"

"Nothing."

"It didn't look like nothing. Do I need to go crack his jaw?"

I try to picture Shane's long, lanky body trying to impact Anthony's quiet strength. "It's nothing to worry about."

"So, are you dating this guy? Because he's the enemy, remember. He's the one who poached on our territory."

"It will be okay."

"Are you sure? I'm looking out for you. I don't like to think he's playing you."

"He's not. It's fine."

"It didn't look fine. Listen, I can talk to reporters. Get this man off your back."

Whoa. That would be the worst. "No! Don't do that. It was a publicity stunt."

"A what?"

"It wasn't real. Just a way to get Milton Creed off our backs."

His whole body relaxes. "That's a relief."

"It's a ploy. And a big secret. You can't tell anyone, okay? Milton might come after us again."

His face breaks into a grin. "I like knowing your secrets." He smacks his chest over his heart. "You can trust me with anything."

"Thanks. I need to go."

He steps aside.

When I return to the kitchen, my head buzzing from the encounter, our head chef Dan is by the freezer.

I head over. I could use Dan's expertise. "Hey," I say.

"Did you ever make Grandmama's Thanksgiving relish?"

His gray-whiskered face breaks into a smile. "Sure did. You know, we should bring that back this year."

"I agree! Could we order the cranberries and make a batch to test?"

"Will do, Miss Magnolia! Good to see some old traditions coming back!"

"We might be doing a new soup and sandwich combo as well. I'm running the ideas by Dad."

"Sounds soup-er!" Dan lets out a loud guffaw.

He's a card, that's for sure. But he's worked for my father since before I was born. "Thanks, Dan."

I'm feeling better as I head back to my office. I have a time-tested recipe for Anthony, and I don't have to admit I can't cook.

Finally, something is going right.

17

ANTHONY

The first spontaneous text from Magnolia puts a smile on my face.

I have samples of Love Relish for you to try!

She sounds happy. I quickly text her back. *I'm testing the new sandwich and soup this afternoon. Want to pop over?*

I sense her hesitation in the three dots that remain flashing for an inordinately long time. Sometimes I forget that she hates me and my territory-poaching deli.

I quickly text her again. *We can meet on neutral ground if you think that's better.*

She finally replies. *No, it's fine. Just weird to think of going into your kitchen.*

I'm happy to have you here.

Okay.

My staff has been ribbing me about the televised kiss ever since I returned from New York. Charity kept my dad informed of our plan, so thankfully I never had to clarify to him that everything was fake. He told Jason and Max.

Even so, I saved all the images that surfaced from our date. There are great ones from when I gave her the flowers. There's the almost-kiss in front of the restaurant door. But my favorite? A whole series from the actual kiss after dinner.

They're convincing. Sometimes I look at them and wonder how it could have been fake at all. It didn't feel that way at the time.

I've sworn off red curry forever.

Milton's crew hasn't commented publicly on our TV kiss or date. Hopefully, he's decided to back off.

I purposely suggest a time in the afternoon when the deli is minimally staffed. When Marie leads Magnolia through the door from the dining room, I'm surprised at how seeing her here affects me. It's like the room got brighter just because she walked into it.

Her blond hair is pulled back today, and she wears jeans and a sweater. I like seeing laid-back Magnolia.

She sets her puffy coat on a stool and passes me a small glass jar. "This is the Love Relish. It's a sweet relish with gherkins, pickled onions, and cranberry."

I lift the jar to the light. It's pink and red with hints of green. Perfect for a Love and Pickles line, which Charity has suggested.

"Was this your creation?" I unscrew the lid.

"It's an old classic I've revived."

"Lots of talent at the Tasty Pepper, and you're right in the middle of it." I rummage around for a spoon and dip it into the relish. It's tangy and sweet. "I love it."

"It has an apple cider vinegar base that should be

shelf stable. I think we could put this one in the online store."

"Perfect. I haven't started working on the new pickle yet. But Charity has a team mocking up the branding." I hesitate. "Unless you have someone you want her to coordinate with."

Magnolia shakes her head. "No. Our branding has been the same since I was born."

"Same here."

I love that these long family traditions are something we have in common. I lead her to a large pot on the stove. "So, the soup I've devised is sweet-potato based. It's savory, with a hint of heat on the backend."

When she looks into the pot with trepidation, I add, "No red curry. It's chili powder."

I dip a ladle into the soup and fill a bowl. "While that cools off, we can try the sandwich."

I carry the soup to the center workspace. "The cranberry relish tells me we've been on the same brainwave. Because the sandwich is turkey with a sweet mustard cranberry compote."

"I guess we're all feeling the approach of Thanksgiving. Any spice to it?"

"Not at all. Only in the soup."

I grab a slice of our signature white bread. The compote glides across the surface, and I add two layers of turkey, a slice of Swiss, and thinly sliced bread and butter pickles. A second slice of bread tops the sandwich.

"I hope you came hungry." I slice the sandwich into two triangles and pass one to her.

"I can eat." She accepts the sandwich and takes a bite from the corner. Her eyebrows shoot up. "Delicious."

I stir the soup to cool it down. "I think the sweet potato in the soup complements the sandwich. It has a Thanksgiving feel without being traditional."

I fill a spoon with a chunky bite of soup. "I can't wait to hear what you think."

Feeding her here is different from the chopsticks in the restaurant. There's no one taking pictures. No proof of what we're doing. The kitchen is empty, Kennedy is manning the line, and Marie's busy collecting supplies from the walk-in fridge.

For these few seconds, we're alone.

Her gaze meets mine as her mouth closes over the spoon. She takes the bite and lets out a long *mmmmm*. I set the spoon on the counter.

"That's good," she says, then claps her hand to her mouth. "Oh, there's the heat!"

"Is it too much?" I can't imagine it would be for someone like her.

She shakes her head. "No, it's just a surprise. Even though you told me." Her laugh is shaky and nervous as she looks around.

I race to the sink and fill a clean cup with water. "Here. If it's still too hot, I can get you some cheese or milk."

She tries to look casual as she accepts the water, but then gulps it like the soup set fire to her mouth.

Huh. Something tells me Magnolia isn't as big on spice as she's let people believe. It doesn't matter to me, but it's interesting. She talked differently on Milton Creed's show.

But then, she was trying to make a splash.

I take the soup bowl to the sink, so she doesn't feel obligated to eat any more. "Do you think it's too spicy?"

Magnolia runs her hand across her mouth. She's trying to downplay her distress. "No. It's fine. But it should have a warning. A little flame by it or something."

I sit on a stool across from her at the prep table. "Do you want to sell the kiss pickle? We were going to have our own exclusive item, but we can share."

She lifts her relish jar and turns it in circles on the table. "I don't know. It's all happening so fast."

"Charity says we have to seize the momentum."

"How do we do that?"

"Stay visible. She wants to know if you would like to do another show. She's got six lined up."

"Six?"

"Sure. The talk show offers are getting smaller, but the cooking shows are starting to heat up."

"So we'd cook?"

"Sure, just like on Milton's show. Hopefully with less drama."

"And she thinks it would help sell all this?" She gestures to the sandwich and the jar.

"It's our best shot at maximizing this opportunity."

She bites her lip. Maybe this is hard for her, consorting with the enemy.

I have to step up. "For what it's worth, I don't like

that my deli has caused your family distress. I want to make it right."

She doesn't respond to that, and my belly churns at exactly how much she hates having to work with me to improve her situation. I fiddle with my half of the sandwich, lining up the edges more exactly. "Maybe the kiss and the date were a bad idea."

She doesn't comment on that. "Will the shows cover travel and all that?"

"Yes," I say. "Maybe not first class—"

"Will you not book me on fancy things? It makes me feel like I owe you."

I remember the jewelry mistake. "I won't pay for extras. I'll get Charity to negotiate them with the shows."

She slides off the stool. "Okay. See if she can book them in a row, so I can be in one place a little longer. It's nice to see a bit of a city when I'm there. I can't afford travel otherwise."

"Will do." She's on board. I can breathe again.

She pushes the jar toward me. "You keep this. I hope the kiss pickle is worth the wait!"

"It will be."

As Magnolia picks up her coat and leaves the kitchen, I can't take my eyes off her.

Even if it's all fake on her end, I can't wait for us to travel together.

18

MAGNOLIA

Once Anthony and I launch the new joint menu, everything starts to happen fast. Charity books us for five appearances in Los Angeles.

My wardrobe for the upcoming shows is carefully crafted, along with Anthony's complementary outfits. Everything is based on cranberry and cream, with some grays and blues mixed in. Charity has worked magic with several designers who let me borrow items to give them exposure on the shows.

I have a fleet of dresses, pants and jeans, skirts and tops. The show outfits are well planned for being wired for sound. Two of the dresses swirl like the one I bought in New York, so we can occasionally re-create the moment.

Before leaving for L.A., we go on a local Boulder morning show to reveal the new menu items. We bring the new Boudrickle sandwich and the soup, titled "Hot and Sweet."

We don't mention the new relish, love pickle, or

dessert, because Charity has promised exclusive reveals to three hosts in Los Angeles.

The Boulder show is easy. Anthony and I serve the soup and sandwich to the hosts, who fawn over it. We hold hands and smile at each other, blissfully telling the audience that despite the initial hardship, we are grateful that Milton Creed brought us together.

We'll be in L.A. for a full week. As I requested, Charity has booked us for three shows, one every other day.

In between, we have appearances at a local restaurant and a gourmet food store. Two of the shows plus the food store are cooking demonstrations. Dad carefully plans what I will prepare, and I practice each step. We make sure there are no feats of culinary skill that would reveal I haven't had any training. Or that I can't cook much at all.

I figure if I can fake an entire relationship, surely, I can muddle through a recipe. Havannah helps me practice giggles to make my mistakes cute and prompts me on how to flirt my way into convincing Anthony to help if I get in a bind.

It's a lot.

Charity makes sure we get first-class tickets, since she's able to pool the resources of the appearances, and our entire hotel stay plus expenses are covered. It's a big win.

As long as I don't blow it.

Anthony and I aren't recognizable out of context, so we're able to maneuver through the airport and hotel lobbies with minimum fuss. Charity has warned us that our relative obscurity might change by the end of this publicity run.

"Our goal is to get you everywhere," she tells us during a phone call once we settle into an office space that links our two hotel suites in L.A. "Remember, it's critical you look happy and in love when you're out in public. Milton Creed will look for an opportunity to expose you if he gets even a whiff of insincerity."

"Thanks, Charity," Anthony says.

"Have fun. Give me a debriefing after each show. Ta-ta!"

I let out a sigh and sink down in the armchair. Now we can chill for a bit. "We're free today, right?" I ask.

Anthony kicks out his legs and rests his head on the back of the leather seat. "Absolutely. The first show isn't until tomorrow afternoon. We don't have to deal with the stylists until noon."

I stand up. "I've got two L.A. bucket list items I didn't get to do last time."

"What are those?"

"A stroll on the Hollywood Walk of Fame and a tour of the Queen Mary."

"Those are great stops," he says. "You want company?"

I hesitate. I don't want to go alone, but he'll have to pretend to be my boyfriend even in our off-hours. "Sure, if you're game for the charade."

"Totally game." His expression is eager.

I head for my door. "I'll change into the most casual thing they have allowed me to wear."

"Me too. I think I got my jeans approved."

I have to laugh. "This is the craziest situation, right?"

"It is." He looks like he wants to say something else, but then opens his door. "See you in half an hour?"

"Definitely."

I step into my room and close the door. It's weird, but I find I dislike Anthony a little less every day. He's risen to the occasion on these menus. I think we have something incredibly powerful happening for our delis.

I switch into a pair of cream-colored jeans and a cranberry sweater. The weather here is nothing like Boulder, mid 70s and perfect for walking.

My wardrobe includes a pair of cute cream sneakers with dark pink trim, so I slide them on, marveling at the memory foam inside. This only took five minutes, so I take a moment to text my sister. *Made it to L.A. Anthony is charming. He plays the role well.*

She writes back. *I'm telling you, it's not a role to him.*

I shake my head. Havannah is ever the romantic. *I don't see it.*

Open your eyes!

There's no good response to that, so I send a quick note to Dad. *Made it to L.A. Hotel is nice.*

He writes back.

Good. We had a line waiting for us to open today.

Really?

It's the show you did yesterday. Everybody wants to eat the new sandwich and soup combo.

Yay!

You two have fun. Try not to fight.

Dad imagines Anthony is like Sherman Pickle,

Anthony's father. There is no love lost between my dad and Sherman. They once got into a booming argument at a restaurant convention.

It's probably a good thing we're not actually dating. That would be one awkward family dinner.

I pack my phone and a few essentials in the tiny messenger-style purse that matches my shoes. I peek in the mirror. Havannah prepped my look for the day before we got on the flight in case we were seen. I need to refresh my lipstick.

I have to get used to a full face of makeup. A stylist will arrive every day in L.A. to put me together. I'm trying to learn how to do it myself, so that I don't have to go through these grueling appointments forever.

Maybe by the end of the week, I'll have it down well enough to only need one for the shows.

I recolor my lips and pop a kiss at my reflection. In some ways, I've reversed roles with my sister. She's the one at home most of the time, doing the deli social media from our sofa. She rarely gets out of her sweats, her hair in a messy ponytail.

And here I am, with designer clothes and a stylist.

This is the craziest life.

"I'm doing this for you, little baby on the way," I whisper. I wonder if I'm going to get a niece or a nephew. A thrill zips through me. Havannah's appointment with the doctor is next week. Then we will start project find-the-baby-daddy.

A door in the office space opens and closes. Anthony must be ready. I grab a tissue to blot my lips. But then I picture placing a big colored kiss on his cheek. It would be fun if there are cameras around. So I leave it and stick the lipstick into the tiny purse for a refresher should the moment arise.

Without cameras, I know he won't kiss me today.

But maybe, if we're lucky, paparazzi will find us.

I pause at the door, my hand on the knob.

Whoa, everybody. Did you catch that?

What's happening to me?

Am I looking for an excuse to kiss Anthony Pickle?

When we arrive at the Hollywood Walk of Fame, security guards oversee the process of a crew taking down a canopy for guests.

"What happened here?" I ask.

Anthony cranes his neck. "Looks like somebody got their star today."

"Good thing we missed it. It was probably a madhouse."

A woman in a giant straw hat passes by. "Mmm hmm. Totally crazy." She pauses to take a picture of the star at her feet.

We push through the crowd milling around. The sidewalk is partially taken up by a stage covered in red velvet. I notice an inordinate number of people holding fancy cameras. "I guess photographers are still hanging around," I tell Anthony.

A man with a neck weighed down with equipment overhears me. "They're saying Jennifer Aniston is in the juice joint." He tilts his head at the pressed juice store across the street.

"Really?"

His dark eyes fix on me as he slowly lifts one of the cameras. "Hey, aren't you those two who got in the fight on *Mornings with Eileen*?"

I turn to Anthony. He grimaces.

"Let's go!" I say and push Anthony up the street.

But they're on to us. We slip through the crowd for several blocks, but as soon as we're free of the bulk of the bystanders, we're easy pickings. When the first flash goes off, more photographers arrive. Some have long lenses, others get close.

"Look here, Magnolia!" they call. "Over here."

They are definitely not chill like the ones Charity hired in New York.

I lean close to Anthony. "What do we do?"

He shrugs. "I guess we give the people what they want."

He drags me close and bends me over his arm. "No red curry this time," he whispers. Then his lips are on mine. A cheer goes up. Flashes pop.

I'm self-conscious at first, the position, the people, being outdoors. I think about my purse dangling and my sweater riding up my belly.

But Anthony's lips soften, and the world goes still. He holds me steady and close, his body over mine, arms bracing my back. His breath is warm. He smells of woodsy cologne and toothpaste.

His neck is hot under my hand, the muscles corded as they hold me in place. His tongue greets mine, and I fall into him a little more. I'm cocooned by him, held tight.

Maybe I don't want this to end.

But my body begins to lift, and Anthony sets me upright. Whistles and cheers start to penetrate the perfect silence. I look up at him, then laugh. His lips are as cranberry as mine. I never blotted my lipstick.

I use my thumb to erase the color. His cheeks pink up. He's adorable.

"Cute," I say.

He points at himself as if to say *who me?* And grins. Flashes pop pop pop.

I point down. We're standing on Fred Astaire's star. He takes my hand and twirls me in circles around it. I wish I was wearing a swirly skirt, but my cream-colored jeans have to do.

When he pulls me close, I say, "Charity is going to love this."

He grins. "I know. We're her prodigal clients."

"How are we going to escape?"

He spins me again, then we continue walking. "I don't know."

The cameras continue to follow us.

We spot someone exiting a taxi a block ahead. Our gazes meet.

"Yes?" he asks.

"Totally."

We make a run for it.

Right as the woman is about to close the door, Anthony grabs it and we duck inside.

"Step on it!" he says.

The taxi driver, a forty-something woman with a helmet of black hair, turns to prop her elbow on the seat and stare us down. "This ain't a movie set, mister."

"Can you take us to the Queen Mary," I ask.

"That's forty minutes, you know," she says.

"That's all right," I say.

She gives a nod and heads down the street. The photographers have started to fade into the tourists. Show's over.

"That was fun," I say to Anthony.

He snakes his hand over and squeezes mine. "It was."

My heart hammers.

He's holding my hand and nobody's even looking.

19

ANTHONY

I don't know what came over me, taking Magnolia's hand. I think I ought to pull away, but Magnolia's looking at me with something I can only describe as contentment.

What's happening here?

We drive along Hollywood Boulevard, the sidewalks filled with tourists. Magnolia takes it all in, bending down to get a look at the shops and people. I hope she saw enough of the stars to make her happy.

I clear my throat. "So, how many times have you been to L.A.?"

"Just when we were here for *Mornings with Eileen*." The car turns away from the interesting sights and she settles back in her seat.

"So why the Queen Mary?"

"My parents stayed there on their honeymoon and had a swoony meal at Sir Winston's on board. We heard about it a million times growing up."

"Really?" My mind is already buzzing with how I can make a dinner there happen.

We enter the freeway and the skyscrapers of downtown Los Angeles begin to appear. Magnolia lets go of my hand and turns back to the window. "That's a lot of tall buildings."

"You really get a sense of it from the freeway."

"Sure isn't downtown Boulder."

While she gazes out, I quickly tap a message to Charity and Max.

How can I get into Sir Winston's on the Queen Mary in the next hour?

Charity responds quickly. *Looks available. Want me to make reservations?*

But Max pops on. *I got your back, bro. Check your inbox.*

By the time we leave the cab, the reservation confirmation has chimed from my inbox. While Magnolia stands on the sidewalk admiring the giant ship, I pull up the email.

"Want dinner?" I ask.

"Can we go in the ship first? I think you can walk up and do a tour."

"Absolutely," I say. "And we have a reservation for Sir Winston's."

Her face lights up. "Really?"

I extend my arm. "Let's take a look around. Then we'll see what the chefs here can do."

Magnolia squeals as we walk into the entry pavilion.

When we cross the bridge into the ship, Magnolia is enchanted, exclaiming at the lamps, the wood, the floors. Replicas of the ship and several others line a long hallway. We cross to a promenade full of shops.

"Don't you love how it smells!" she says. "It's like ocean water and history!"

I have to laugh. Our hands brush, and she takes mine. It's not a bad idea. We could be seen here.

She stands beneath the big bell that reads *Queen Mary*. "Let's go on the sun deck!"

We head outside and walk along the wood planks. The breeze picks up, adding curl to her hair. She's completely happy, almost giddy. Just watching her awe makes me smile.

"We can go on the bridge!" she says. She cranes her head sideways to look at the words painted onto the steering mechanism. "Slack away! Let go! Hold on! Heave in!" She laughs. "What silly options!"

We pass curtained windows with diners inside a fancy room. "Is that where we're eating?" she asks.

"I think so."

"I can't wait to picture a young version of Mom and Dad in there. We'll have to take pictures!"

"Anything the lady desires."

"Is it time?"

"We have about five minutes."

We lean on the rail a while, letting the sea air wash over us. Then Magnolia takes my arm. "Take me to dinner!"

We're seated in wide leather chairs near a window with an ocean view. A server instantly brings us glasses of water and a basket of bread.

"I'm starving," she says, gulping water and choosing a soft warm roll.

"I hear the Beef Wellington is the famous offering here," I say.

"My dad got that. He never misses a good slab of meat wrapped in pastry."

"And your mom?"

"She ordered the stuffed salmon." Magnolia sits back, taking the room in "Did you know you could do dining with the spirits on Friday nights?"

"Is that what you wanted?"

"No! I have enough skeletons in my closet without worrying about ghosts."

"I can't imagine you have a single thing to hide."

She sips her water and shrugs. "Maybe they're not terribly sordid by modern standards." Her eyes meet mine. "I haven't killed a man. Yet."

I laugh so loudly I startle a few guests at other tables.

She tosses her napkin at me. "Hush up! I can't take you anywhere!"

I catch it and toss it back. "I'm probably better stuck back in the kitchen."

She spreads the linen across her lap. "Do you eat at a lot of fancy places to learn new tricks?"

"Not as much as I'd like, but I've been to every place in Boulder."

"Do you eat at La Fontaine D'or?"

I hesitate. I hate that place. "I've been there."

She leans forward. "Isn't it awful?"

Thank God. "Yes! I was worried you loved it."

"No way. Dad calls it *Twenty Ways to Ruin a Steak*."

I clap my hand over my mouth to avoid startling our neighbors again. Usually this isn't a problem for me. But with Magnolia, it's different. I laugh too loudly, too much.

The waiter arrives with menus. "Can I interest you in a bottle of wine?"

"Do you have a nice Pinot Noir for the Beef Wellington?" I ask.

"I have several." He lists them off.

I turn to Magnolia. "Are you going to do the Beef Wellington or the salmon, or should we try both?"

"Both, for sure," she says.

I order a Pinot Noir for the beef and a Chardonnay for the salmon, as well as order the food, since we already know what we want. When the man is gone, I say, "We can try both wines, too. I think the germs have already been shared. On camera, no less."

She smiles down at her bread. "That they have."

I want to ask her what's happening. What's real. What's fake. But instead, I stare out the window at the blue water where it meets the darkening sky.

The view is spectacular. Lights have begun to twinkle along the coast.

Magnolia surveys the room. "I'm trying to picture my parents here, right after their wedding. They would have been younger than I am."

"I guess they're very happy?"

"I think so. They have squabbles. But they've been married for thirty years." She takes a sip of her water. "What about yours?"

Thinking about Mom always robs me of my voice

for a moment. I pick up my water glass and sip until I feel in control again.

"They were the happiest people I know. Our deli legacy didn't come from nothing. It was built from how much they loved each other and wanted to create something lasting for their family."

Her eyes search mine. "Why does this make you sad?"

I realize that she doesn't know. It's funny, most women I date Google me immediately. The whole story is there.

"My mother died twelve years ago. I was fifteen and didn't think I would ever be happy again after I lost her."

Magnolia sucks in a breath. Her hand slips across the table to clasp mine. "I'm so sorry. I didn't know."

Her fingers are cool from the water glass. I squeeze them. "I'm glad your parents are happy."

"You said your brother is married. Does his wife support his deli?"

The vice on my chest loosens. "Absolutely. Nova was the acting manager at Jason's deli when he met her. It's quite a story. He pretended to be a new hire because he was trying to investigate some missing money."

"So, she didn't know he was her boss?"

"Nope. It all came crashing down when she found out."

"I bet. But they're married now?"

"Totally happy. It worked out."

The waiter arrives with the glasses of wine, placing the red in front of me and the white in front of her.

"Your pick for the first try," he says. "Then we'll swap spit."

Her smile is bright and reaches her eyes. "I'll go with white first."

She takes a tentative sip and nods. "It's good. So, what about your other brother?"

"Max and Camryn are different. She works with athletes on the bodybuilding circuit. That's how she met Max."

"He does bodybuilding in addition to running the deli?"

"Yep. But my brothers only have one deli. I have two."

"Do you spend much time at the one in New York?"

"A fair amount. But Dad helps out. I've been staying close to home since this whole Milton Creed thing started."

She frowns. "Should we have done shows in New York then? I took you away from both your delis for a whole week."

"No, no. It's fine. Everything is running smoothly. And all this publicity helps grow the business. I'm sure you've heard sales are up at both our delis. Charity forwarded me some mentions on Twitter about lines out the door. My manager is adding shifts."

She nods. "Dad told me. It's great, right?"

"We've only just begun. We still get to introduce the joint dessert. We'll announce my pickle and your relish. Lots of reasons for them to come back. And then of course the online store."

"By the end of this week, it will all be in place." She lifts her wine glass to her lips and closes her eyes.

It's grown fully dark outside, and the candlelight flickers across her face. Our table is softly illuminated by an overhead light. The big leather chairs feel like something you would relax in at home.

I like this. Being with her. Seeing our joint venture succeed.

Her voice is husky as she says, "Just a week ago, I thought everything was going to fall apart." She opens her eyes. "But you fixed it."

"All I did was kiss you."

"Biggest stroke of brilliance I've known in my lifetime."

I want to tell her it was so easy. That she is infinitely kissable.

But the waiter arrives with two salads.

I sigh. Dinners are great, but I'm ready for time alone with Magnolia.

20

MAGNOLIA

I wake up at the crack of dawn. The first night in a new hotel always gets to me.

But I'm willing to admit something to all of you.

It's also about Anthony Pickle.

Last night's sightseeing and dinner were amazing. In fact, for a hot minute I thought something might happen when we returned to the hotel.

But Anthony was a gentleman. We entered through the office between our two suites, and he wished me good night and headed to his own room.

I have to admit, it confuses me. Is this real or not? I keep thinking I sense genuine emotions from him, but then I'm not sure.

I feel like a sixteen-year-old girl.

But I want to do something for him. A gesture like the dinner at Sir Winston's he arranged.

I do some early morning Googling on the pickle theme. Yodeling pickles. Silly. Pickle candy? Gross. Pickle…bouquets?

Then I see it. The perfect thing.

It's unusual. A little bit naughty.

I grab an Uber to the small boutique plant nursery.

I walk the aisle, and when I spot what I'm looking for, I start laughing so hard that other shoppers look my way.

It's a cactus. Officially, it's *Trichocereus bridgesii*.

But there's only one way to describe it.

A penis cactus.

Spread out in front of me in small decorative pots, are row after row of tall girthy cucumber-like cactus plants in various stages of appearing to be a green penis.

An elderly woman shopkeeper in a red apron sidles close to me. "These are very popular. Getting one for someone special?"

"You could say that." I bite my lip to control my giggles.

She tilts her head as she gazes at my face. "You look familiar."

I figure she gets a lot of celebrities here, given the exclusivity of the store and its proximity to the big studios.

"I'm Magnolia Boudreaux. I'm going to be on *Daytime with Anastasia* in a few hours and I'm thinking of giving my fellow guest one of these on the show."

Her eyes light up. Of course they do. I'm about to give her shop major promo.

She glances at the display of green penises. "We should pick the best one."

We sort through the plants. "What about this one?"

she asks. She holds up a particularly accurate specimen, uncircumcised.

"That's a good one," I say.

She walks around the table. "Unless you want something huge."

She holds up a monster. Tall and fat but with the right tip to make sure the connection is made. Circumcised this time. The pot is cream-colored with a broad green stripe. "Perfect," I say. "How much is it?"

"I'm happy to provide it to you since it will be on air," she says. "Would you like us to deliver it to the studio to keep the surprise?"

"Can you do that?"

"Do you have a publicist working with the show?"

Clearly, she's experienced with this. "I do."

"Call them and have them notify their contact that a delivery driver will be arriving with the cactus. They'll have it ready for you in the green room or possibly somewhere on the set. Your handler will let you know."

I feel tingly with excitement. "This is going to be fun."

She carries the cactus behind the register. "You bet it will. I'll have my driver get on this right away. Don't forget to call the publicist. They'll list our store in the credits."

I pull my phone out of my purse. "Doing it right now."

My steps are light as I walk down the sidewalk. I request a ride back to the hotel, then place the call to Charity, who says she'll handle it straight away.

I've pulled many fun pranks in my life, particularly

on my sister. But never for such a big audience. I think I know Anthony well enough that he will find it hilarious.

I can't wait.

Anthony and I ride over to the studio together. This one is part of a big commercial lot. By the time we are through the gates and onto the property, I'm starting to feel like an actual celebrity.

I spot a woman in a gold gown. "Is that Gal Gadot?" I ask, my breath catching.

Anthony leans over me to peer out. "I'd say that's probably her stunt double."

More people wander the long drive between buildings, and I watch with strained attention, wondering who I'll see.

The car slides to a stop by a beige building that looks like all the others.

"I guess this is us," Anthony says.

The driver walks around the car to let us out. We've barely stood up when the back door of the building opens and a beefy Hispanic man with a headset waves us forward. "Anthony. Magnolia. So good to see you."

We follow him into the bowels of the building. "I'm Marco. I'll be with you all afternoon through rehearsal and recording. Anthony, I'm going to drop you in the green room. Magnolia, we need to get you approved by makeup and hair. But you look fantastic."

I'm glad they're separating us, so I can ask him to check on the location of my penis cactus.

When I'm settled in a chair in front of a large lighted mirror, Franco sidles up close. "Your item has arrived. It has been approved by the show. And I have to say, it's hilarious. Anastasia's going to bring it out about two-thirds of the way into the segment, right after the dessert tasting. It will not be rehearsed."

I nod. "Thanks, Franco."

"I'm going to meet up with your boy."

My boy. I forget that everyone thinks we're together.

But aren't we?

The makeup artist tweaks the highlights on my cheekbones and adds extra shadow to my eyelids. "Give me your phone so I can snap your look," she says.

I pass it over.

"It looks like the stylist is good but not experienced with show lighting. Show her this before your next appearance."

I nod. Within minutes, Franco is back and leading me to the green room. "You lovebirds can hang out here until your rehearsal," he says. "Don't do anything I wouldn't do. Admittedly, that's not much."

Then he's gone.

Anthony waits in a chair, scrolling through his phone. "They're really hyping us on here. I've seen two ads with our faces."

I sit in a chair close by. "That's good. I'm glad we get to announce the dessert."

"I brought four. Hopefully, nobody has tampered with them." He flashes a wry grin.

I bump his arm with my elbow. "Are you feeding me?"

"You know it. We've had lots of practice."

Our gazes lock for a moment. I remember last night, passing bits of Beef Wellington and salmon back and forth.

"Feeding each other is becoming a habit," I say.

"I like it."

I glance around, but no one else is in the room. He isn't having to act right now. And yet he's saying all the things I would want to hear.

Is it real? Or is he prepping me for being smitten on camera?

It's hard to know.

The door opens with a roar of raucous laughter, and five young men in ripped jeans and leather vests tumble into the room.

They don't seem to be totally sober.

"Hey, hey, hey!" one of them says. "We're here for our munchies."

I glance over at Anthony with a smile. He pinches his thumb and finger together and holds them close to his lips, pretending to suck in.

Another of the guys sees me and lowers his sunglasses. "There's a bitchin' broad in here."

Anthony puts his arm around me.

"I get it." His sunglasses go back up. "You licked it. It's yours."

Franco calls for us. We hold hands in the hall, and crew members pass us with a smile. We are rushed through the rehearsal with Anastasia, who is dressed in sweatpants, the stylist working on her hair.

"I'm behind schedule this morning," she says. "You

two are pros. Be genuine. Sit close. Are you going to kiss her? Because everybody's hoping that you kiss her."

Anthony smiles in my direction. "I never miss an opportunity to kiss Magnolia."

The talk show goes perfectly. Anastasia is sweet and graceful. Every few questions she asks, "Do you have another kiss for the audience?"

I'm assuming she wants several, so they can use the best one or two on the show. I don't mind.

We walk to a tall table and show off the new dessert. Anastasia pronounces it divine, two soft sugar cookies with a thick raspberry filling. Each cookie is piped with a heart on top.

Anthony feeds me a bite of cookie and gives me another kiss. We're standing this time, so it's less awkward than sitting together on the straight-backed sofa.

We both taste of sugar and fruit. My lipstick has been sealed so that it doesn't smear.

We linger on this one, our hands clasped tightly between us. I keep my eyes closed, and my chin uplifted. For a moment I wonder what will happen when the talk shows stop. Will I see him again? Will this simply end? Will we say we broke up?

My chest tightens, and my grip on his hand squeezes.

He pulls away. "Are you all right, my love?"

He's never said that before. *My love.*

I nod. "I love doing the shows with you."

The audience lets out a long *awwwww*.

"All right, lovebirds. Before I get a sugar rush, let's see what we have over here."

A man walks out with a tall narrow box that must contain my gift for Anthony.

He looks at me. "What is this?"

"I picked something up for you this morning at a shop called Old Juanita's. Since your *pickle* brought us together, I thought it would be perfect."

The audience roars at the joke.

Anthony takes the lid off the top of the box. It's well-designed, because the sides fall flat as soon as the top is removed.

The penis cactus is revealed in all its glory.

Anthony almost chokes. "Is this what I think it is?"

I open my eyes wide and innocent, like when we'd double entendre'd on Milton's show. "It's a pickle, Anthony. Just like your ghost pepper one. It's how we met."

Anastasia doubles over with laughter. "Magnolia, I think that's more than a pickle."

I turn it around by the bowl. "Whatever do you mean?" I wrap my fingers around the base where there are no cactus spines. "It's so much like you, Anthony."

The laughter in the room lasts so long that Anastasia calls for a cut so everyone can compose themselves. "Good stuff," she says. "Keep it coming."

When the cameras are rolling again, she says, "I had no idea that these even existed."

"It's called *Trichocereus bridgesii.*" I've been practicing the pronunciation since I bought it that morning.

"That's a mouthful," Anthony says, sending the entire room into outrageous laughter again.

"I have to get a picture with Anthony and Magnolia and their *pickle* plant." Anastasia uses her fingers to make air quotes.

She pulls out her phone and makes a big show of taking a selfie with us and the cactus.

"And that's our lovebirds," she says. "For those of you lucky enough to be in driving range of Boulder, Colorado, go try out their new dessert at either of the delis. And if not, I hear there's a new online venture coming where you can pick up some of the wonderful things they are going to create together."

"Absolutely, Anastasia," Anthony says smoothly. "The online store is already up and running."

The audience claps, and we head off the side stage. The crew gathers the rolling table with the dessert and Anthony's penis plant.

He squeezes me close to him as we walk down the hall. "Finally, one that goes exactly as planned."

I agree. Everything is perfect.

21

ANTHONY

I pace my hotel room the night of Anastasia's show. It's been a long day.

But I want to see Magnolia.

I pace more.

We had so many kisses today. It should be strange in front of so many people. Especially since we're not actually a couple.

But it's not.

I pick up the room service menu, intending to order something. But then set it down again.

Maybe we can order together.

No.

I should leave her alone.

I pace again.

I decide to put the cactus in the room between our suites. Maybe if I'm loud enough, she'll hear me. If she's interested, she might come out. And then I can casually say, "You want to order some food together?"

I pick up the plant, but before I reach the door, my confidence runs for the hills.

Is she sick of me? What if she's in there thinking *Why can't I go a single day without having to deal with Anthony Pickle?*

But I'm not asking anything. I'm just moving to the middle room.

I draw a deep breath and turn the knob.

I pull it closed hard enough that it could be heard, but not so loud that it would wake her if she was already sleeping.

I wander the office space, trying to decide where exactly to place this crazy plant. There's a telephone table between the two chairs near the window where we sat earlier.

A counter on the side wall serves as a place for setting out snacks and water for meetings.

In another corner, a heavy round table is surrounded by six rolling chairs.

If we do have dinner together, that's where we'll go, so I place the cactus smack in the center.

I hold still, listening. Magnolia doesn't come out.

Is she even in there? I guess she could've left and gone to dinner on her own.

My gut plummets at the thought.

I return to the table and pick up the plant, this time setting it down more firmly. It gives a resounding thud.

I pause.

Still nothing.

I plunk into an armchair, tapping my thumb on my

knee. Maybe I should let this go. Return to my room and order dinner.

But I don't want to.

I pick up the hotel phone receiver, then drop it down again.

And listen. Still nothing.

Shoot.

I'm going to have to be bold.

I walk over to her door and lift my hand to knock.

But right as I'm about to make contact, the door flies open.

She's changed into a loose pink sweatshirt that reads *Get Juiced* across the front and Army green sweatpants.

"Oh!" she says.

"Hey." I drop my hand.

"I thought I heard you out here." She sees the penis cactus and heads right for it. "You brought Penny out here. I love it."

"Penny?"

She shifts the bowl holding the plant. "That's what I named it."

"Penny is a weird name for a cactus that is proba-bly…male."

She shakes her head with a laugh. "Think it through, Anthony." She watches me, turning her hand in circles as if she's waving the answer at me.

"But Penny is generally a shortened form of Penel—" and then I get it. It's short for *penis*.

"Clever."

She claps her hands. "I knew you'd think so." She gestures to my outfit. "You're still all fancy."

"And you are no longer wearing Charity-sanctioned outfits."

She plucks at the pink sweatshirt. "I was tired of wearing fancy clothes. Normally you only see me dressed like that at weddings and funerals."

Interesting. She's always been so put together when I've seen her. "I feel overdressed."

"You need to go put on something more casual."

This is going better than I thought. "Done. Should we order some room service? Charity would kill us if we got caught out in public in anything less than the designer wardrobe."

Magnolia giggles. "Oh, the scandal. Young lovers spotted at a lowbrow burger shack wearing Target sweatpants."

"I don't risk the wrath of Charity."

"I hear you. Room service it is. Is there a menu out here?"

"In the drawer." I head over to the small table and pull one out. "Why don't you look it over while I change?"

She accepts it with a grunt. "It's heavier than a Cheesecake Factory menu. It'll take an hour to decide what I want."

"We have all night."

She glances up from the menu to raise an eyebrow at me.

What does that mean? *Don't press your luck?* Or *come hither?*

I wish I were as smooth as my brothers. They'd know exactly what to do.

I head back to my room and dig through my bags to find something to match her. Jeans. No. Workout shorts. No. Do I even have the right thing?

I find something unexpected. I hadn't gone through everything, mostly dumping the contents of the boxes that arrived from Charity directly into the suitcases.

Plaid pajamas in navy and cranberry. What did Charity think I would do with these? A photo shoot in sleepwear?

Regardless, they're the same casual level as Magnolia's sweatpants.

I pull them on. I think of all the scenes in movies where the woman goes and prepares herself for the man, putting on a négligée and brushing her teeth.

Should I brush my teeth?

It might be weird right before we eat. Toothpaste and wine? Not a thing.

What else did they do?

Shave things. That's come up in movies.

I head to the mirror to check out my face. My look is always scruffy. When I get rid of all my facial hair, I look ten years old. So, nope.

What about my balls? Should I shave my balls?

I have no idea.

I'd text my brothers, but they'd probably take a screenshot and put it on Twitter.

Will Magnolia even be *seeing* my balls?

Does she have opinions about manscaping?

I shouldn't be thinking about this.

It's just dinner.

Besides, I can't confuse our real relationship as business partners with the public relationship, which is well, a lot more.

Especially after the penis cactus.

Penny didn't shave *his* balls. He's downright thorny.

I settle on a quick rinse with mouthwash and a light application of cologne.

And I'm ready.

When I make it back to the meeting room, Magnolia is deep into the menu. "Did you know they have four types of grilled cheese?" She glances up. "Hey! You got fancy sleepwear, too."

I sit in the chair next to her. "You got some?"

"You bet I did. And I won't be caught dead in it."

Now she has my interest. "What is it?"

She runs her finger down the menu page. "Wouldn't you like to know?"

Yes. Yes, I would.

I'm guessing she's not going to tell me, so my imagination runs wild. Baby doll pajamas. Négligées. Peephole bras. Crotchless panties.

Whoa. Gotta get myself in check.

Magnolia snaps the menu shut. "It's going to sound like a ten-year-old got hold of the menu. But I want tater tots, butter pasta, and chocolate cake."

I take the menu from her. "That's quite a combination."

"Everything was tempting me." She tilts her head, her ponytail swinging.

I could tell her exactly what is tempting me.

But instead, I flip quickly through the menu. "I'll get this ordered."

She walks around the room while I talk to the kitchen. I watch her every move as she runs her hand along the side table and spins one of the chairs. She picks up the cactus, and when her finger taps the tip of the shaft, I start to wish I had worn something more structured. I shift the menu onto my lap.

I focus on describing all the menu items to the woman on the line, adding a bottle of champagne for the success of our show. I squeeze my eyes shut so Magnolia can't distract me. By the time I hang up, I have my crotch under control.

She drops into the leather armchair next to me. "I've been thinking about something."

I can come up with a hundred things I'd like her to say. Naked showers. Hot sex. More showers. My pants stir again, so I leave the menu where it is. "Oh?"

"We haven't figured out who tampered with the pickles and released the video." She gestures to the room. "At this point, we ought to thank them. They've made all this happen."

She's right. "I'm assuming it was someone on Milton's team, and he's kicking up this big fuss to make sure none of it makes him look bad."

"He's been awfully quiet lately. Nothing since that montage making me look guilty."

"I'm not sure how we would find any leads."

Magnolia draws her knees up to her chest. "If he got rid of employees as often as that one woman suggested, there might be somebody who's been fired since our show. They might talk."

"Maybe we could ask around. Or Charity could."

She stands up to pace the room, animated now. "That would be the ultimate high point of our story. Mystery solved by Anthony Pickle and Magnolia Boudreaux."

"You mean BoudRickle."

She bursts out laughing. "I forgot about our 'ship' name."

"I never thought I'd have a hashtag of my couple name with someone."

She pauses by the round table. "I never thought I'd give a Pickle brother the time of day."

My body is chill again, so I shove the menu in the drawer and head her way. "Are we good about the past? My coming into Boulder with a new deli without even reaching out?" I stop only a foot away from her.

Her gaze meets mine. "We're good. I'm glad my terrible plan worked out to bring us together rather than apart."

I decide it's time to take a risk. "Are we? Together?"

"All of them think so." She lifts her hand to gesture at the door, but en route, smacks me in the nose. "Oh no! I'm sorry!" She presses her hand to my face. "I got you good!"

"It's fine." It doesn't hurt, but she's really close. I can smell a floral hand lotion and a fruity shampoo.

"Are you sure?" Her face is full of concern as she examines my nose.

I lift my hand to her cheek and brush away a line of worry. "I'm sure."

Now we're super close. Her breath feathers across my lips.

It's like all those times I've kissed her.

But this time, we're alone. I'm not expected to do anything. There are no cameras. No live studio audience. But Magnolia might be expecting me to try.

I lean in, but not all the way. She can bridge the distance if she wants to. I'll know in her hesitation.

She closes the gap.

Her mouth is warm and opens to me immediately. Her body presses into mine, her hands at my neck. Every outline of her curves feels carved into me, breasts, belly, hips. Adrenaline shoots through my body, landing in my groin.

I draw her tightly against me, and she should be able to feel that I'm not faking this part. She sucks in a breath, then we're in again, mouths slanting against each other, hands touching every accessible part.

The longing I've felt for her for weeks explodes into need. I've been waiting for any sign from her that this is more than pretend. That what started as a ruse has become real.

My fingers slip beneath the bottom of her shirt, connecting with the warm skin of her back, her ribs. I slide up and realize there is no barrier to her soft breast, no bra. Just her, a taut nipple budding beneath my touch.

She sucks in a breath, and fire licks through me. We've made it here at last. She's mine. I've wanted her to be mine for so long.

We bump against the table and I sit her on it. Her legs wrap around my hips, and I grind against her, my free hand clasping her neck, the other kneading the plump breast.

I want to feast on her, so I move, lips shifting to her jaw, her neck. I push the sweatshirt up and bend down to tease the tight nipple with my tongue.

Her head falls back. Our bodies rock against each other. Everything I've envisioned is happening. Magnolia is in my arms, my hands, my mouth.

I jerk the sweatshirt over her head, tossing it to the floor. I pause a moment to take her in, the alabaster skin, pale pink nipples. Her long blond ponytail falls down her naked back. She's perfect. Absolutely perfect.

I lean down, feasting on every newly exposed part of her. Neck, collarbone, both pert breasts. I'm on fire, desperate to know every inch of her delectable body.

She unbuttons the front of my pajama top, her hands learning the breadth of my chest and sliding down my abs. Her breathing is heavy.

For a moment, our gazes meet again, and I pull her face to mine. This kiss is frenzied, hot, and we hold nothing back. A groan escapes my mouth as she pulls me close, our naked chests making their first contact.

I move both hands to the waistband of her sweatpants to make absolutely clear where I want this to go. How much I want her. How I've waited. I start to slide them down.

Then comes the knock on the door. "Room service."

Shit.

Shit. Shit. Shit.

I hold her another second. "I guess we have to get that."

She nods. "We ordered it."

"We can't be assholes and ignore them?"

She slides off the table and reaches for her sweatshirt. "We're not asshole types."

I step away and button my shirt while she pulls on her top.

As the busboy rolls in the linen-covered table with its silver dishes, I watch her. She retreats to the leather chair to fix her ponytail, not making eye contact with me or the delivery boy.

When he's gone, she scurries to the silver domes and lifts them until she finds all of hers. She takes them to the table like nothing crazy just happened between us. "I'm starved."

I'm not sure what to say, so I chime in with, "Me too."

But I'm pretty sure we're not talking about the same thing.

Dinner goes on like it might have before the frenzied kissing.

When we're done, she slips back to her room with a quiet, "Goodnight, Anthony."

And just like that, the moment is gone.

22

MAGNOLIA

R eaders, that was close. So, so, so close.
         I almost lost my head there.

I need to focus, right? We need good publicity. We need me to get us out of this mess.

Not get into a bigger mess!

But the next morning, as the makeup artist prepares me for the demonstration at the gourmet food store, I can't stop thinking about last night.

Was I going to have an affair with Anthony Pickle after all?

I definitely feel like I might.

You already know this, don't you?

Anthony has always struck me as a cinnamon roll kind of guy, tender from the early loss of his mother.

But last night, he was all heat.

I've never felt like this before.

I've done the deed a few times. But I thought the reason I never had a long-standing relationship was because I was unwilling to have sex right away.

So I did.

Even doing the whole number was nothing like that encounter I had with Anthony.

That was fire.

But I can't afford fire. We need a business relationship. We need to be able to travel. Something like what happened last night could blow up in our faces. Or burn too hot and extinguish, leaving us in an awkward place if we still have to pretend to be lovers in public.

I can't do it.

I turn in the mirror to double check the gold A-line dress and cranberry apron that Charity provided me for this kitchen demonstration.

I run the recipe over in my mind. It's simple. Roasted acorn squash covered in spices.

Today I have to prove I am a chef. I have no training, so I'll stick with stories about how I grew up next to the stove while my parents planned recipes. Deflect on questions about culinary school or my qualifications.

I can do this.

I hear Anthony's door open and close in the room between us. I check my hair and lipstick one more time. This event won't be televised, so there probably won't be any need to kiss. I'm relieved. I have this terrible feeling that our next kiss will lead to much, much more. I'm glad there will be a little distance between them.

I grab my cell phone and my purse and head into the meeting room.

Anthony waits in his leather chair. His navy pants and cream shirt set off the cranberry apron folded in his lap. "All set?" he asks.

I have to set a professional tone. "Yes. It will be fun. Cooking. Smiling. Selling food."

"Good. Let's go."

When we drive up to the two-story smoked glass store, I'm in awe. Even from the street, you can see that the bottom floor is filled with beautifully presented displays of gleaming pans, bakeware, and well-appointed linens.

"This is something," Anthony says.

We head inside. The owner Joe Franken greets us. "Anthony, Magnolia. I'm so glad you could make it today. Our test kitchen is upstairs."

We follow him up the glass staircase. Everything gleams.

The top floor houses their collection of cookbooks, plus a test kitchen that rivals Milton Creed's. A significant chunk of the space is taken up by rows of chairs for audience members.

"We're expecting a full house," Joe says. "Mostly press. But we have also invited some VIP customers."

Anthony seems to remember that we're supposed to be a couple and puts his arm around my waist.

Joe and his crew beam at us. "Young love," he says. "I will let you get acquainted with the set."

The demonstration starts smoothly with a staff member explaining we will be giving fresh takes on Thanksgiving dinner sides. Anthony announces he will make a potato-leek au gratin with crumbly blue cheese.

I watch while Anthony describes how to prepare the leeks to avoid the grit between the fine layers. I had no idea they had that.

He chops the potatoes swiftly and with great skill, tossing the knives like he did on Milton's show. No one ever got to see that amazing footage, and I'm glad he gets to do it here.

Beyond that, his ingredients are already prepared, and he quickly layers his dish and slides it into the oven.

Then it's my turn.

I face the audience. "My great-grandmother made roasted acorn squash at Thanksgiving when my mother was a girl." I lift two expertly cut sections of squash, done by the crew before we arrived. "You want to leave them in big chunks, like this."

The next part will be easy, tossing on the spices from the pre-measured cups.

But a voice comes from the crowd. "I understand that cutting acorn squash is quite difficult."

My heart beats faster. "You must have confidence and a good sharp knife." I lift the small bowl of ground pepper.

Another voice, "I've tried cutting big squash, too. We would love to see your technique."

Panic starts to set in. "Do we have time for that?" I turn to Joe, who stands off to one side.

He grins. "You guys do whatever you need to do."

I force a smile. "Of course."

I lift an uncut acorn squash from the bowl. It's green with patches of orange and gold.

"We're lucky acorn squash is in season this time of year," I say, wincing at the shake in my voice. I reach over to the knife block and select the largest handle. I'm fairly sure that's the one Dad used when he taught me the steps. He warned me not to even try to cut it, but let the prep crew do it.

But here I am.

"We'll be cutting it into four pieces." I step sideways to the cutting board. Anthony watches from the end of the counter. Sweat trickles down my neck.

Please don't be tough, I pray as I set the squash on the board. *Please don't be super hard to cut.*

I hold the acorn squash carefully. It's round and difficult to keep in place. I press the knife down.

It digs in about a quarter of an inch, then stalls completely.

I push down harder. It sinks a little farther, but now the knife won't go any direction, not down, not up.

My face flames. I wiggle it, shifting my hand. I feel a prick on my finger and panic flares. I can't bleed on the dish!

The room has gone silent. I smile unconvincingly. A few cell phones are raised, recording me. Cameras snap.

"I wanted to show how tricky this is," I say, but I can hear the fear in my voice. This is bad. So bad. My finger feels wet. Am I bleeding? I quickly swipe it on my apron, so glad it is cranberry and will hide the stain.

Anthony swoops in. "That is a brilliant tactic, Magnolia," he says. He takes the knife from me and lifts the acorn. "Now we have a hammer."

He moves the knife up and down, demonstrating that the acorn squash is well attached. "This is no way to start a Thanksgiving tradition unless you have a beef with your uncle." The room erupts in laughter.

He taps the acorn squash on the cutting board and

wiggles the knife in some subtle way I can't fathom until it comes free.

"I'd love to show my favorite technique, with Magnolia's permission."

I want to kiss him for real. "Be my guest."

"When Magnolia said you have to cut with confidence, she meant it. Notice that when she hesitated, the knife got caught in the squash."

He turns the acorn squash in his hand and places the tip of his knife on the cutting board. "You have to imagine that you're murdering someone." He grins. "I'll take nominations." This gets a renewed roar of laughter from the crowd.

He brings the knife blade down hard and fast. The acorn squash falls into two perfect halves.

"So it's not so much about the technique, as the speed. Just be sure no fingers get in the way."

His smile is charming as he holds up the two pieces of squash, and the audience claps.

He fixed my problem. Again.

Despite Anthony's prowess in turning my embarrassment into a lesson, I'm a wreck by the time we get back to the hotel. My thoughts are spiraling.

I should've known they would ask me to perform a task I couldn't do. And I still have all these cooking shows to go. If anyone figures out the fraud, they'll ask me to do all sorts of culinary feats I'm not trained for. I'll get roasted more than a Thanksgiving turkey.

I fling myself onto the bed. I barely spoke to Anthony in the car on the ride back. I didn't know what to say. What person who claims to be a chef doesn't know how to slice a freaking squash?

I lie there, wondering if I can die of embarrassment, when I hear a gentle knock on the interior door, the one that faces the meeting room between our suites.

It has to be Anthony.

I lift my head. "What?"

"I ordered hot tea and chocolate cake. Thought it might help."

Why does he have to be so sweet?

"I think I need something stronger," I say.

"Will tequila do it?"

I sit up. "That might be too far."

"How about a nice bottle of red wine? An Australian cabernet will go well with chocolate cake."

Anthony always knows the perfect pairings for everything. I drink whatever's on sale at the supermarket.

But he's trying to make me feel better, not worse. "Okay."

After about twenty minutes, he knocks again.

"The food's here. Should I bring it in?"

"It's open."

A shaft of light falls over the bed as Anthony cautiously opens the door.

"It's dark in here."

"I didn't bother to turn on the lights."

He rolls in the cart. "I went a little crazy. There's cake as promised. And pie. Tater tots, in case you needed real sustenance."

I sit up. "You're too much, Anthony Pickle."

He sets the cart close enough to the bed that I can use it as a dining table. "I've been told that." He lifts the smallest silver lid. "Tater tots first?"

"Wine first."

He nods. "I'll pour your glass."

I sit on the edge of the bed, tucking my bare feet beneath the hem of my dress.

Anthony opens the bottle and pours a glass through an aerator. "Glad I brought my own," he said. "It wouldn't do to drink it straight from the bottle without letting it breathe."

He's rambling. He's nervous. Because of me? Or what happened at the food store?

I take the glass. "All right. How bad was it?"

"How bad was what?" He pours a second glass for himself.

"You know what."

"You mean catching a knife in the heart of a squash?"

"Yes, that."

He leans against the wall, swirling the red wine glass. Like me, he's in his fancy outfit, minus the apron, but he's rolled up his sleeves. My gaze is drawn to his strong, bare forearms, but I force it away.

"I should probably do most of the cutting should it come up," he says carefully. "Not everyone is good with knives."

Time to confess. "I never went to culinary school."

"But you did go to school. You mentioned that in an interview."

I nod.

"I guess you wanted to study the business part?"

I nod again and take a sip. The wine is heaven.

"That's important. Since Jason got some liberal arts degree, and God only knows what Max studied, it turns out we have to hire out help on financial planning. Nova's getting her MBA. That will help as we keep expanding."

"You seem to know everything."

"I ask a lot of questions."

I chug another gulp of wine.

"Time for tater tots?" he asks.

I nod. He passes me the plate.

I set down the wine and start inhaling tater tots like they are the last marshmallows at the campfire.

"So what would you consider your strengths in the kitchen?" he asks. "That way as we go into these cooking segments, I know where I might need to shore up the presentation."

I have trouble swallowing my bite. I don't know how to tell him that I have no strengths. That pouring cereal without spilling it might be the shining star of my culinary skill set.

I switch out my tater tots for the wine again. I should get it over with. "I can't cook."

His head tilts. "Like, not at all?"

I hold the wine glass to my forehead and nod.

"Okay. That might explain a thing or two."

"Sorry," I say quickly. "I didn't want to be the one to do Milton's show. We had to draw straws because my sister didn't want to do it and I got picked." My words are a rush. "I practice dishes ahead, but I can't always predict what I might be asked to do. Like cutting acorn squash."

"In hindsight, we should have picked something simpler."

"They wanted something fancy. My family isn't fancy. They are deli owners. We make sandwiches."

"I get it. I think we salvaged it. I really think we did."

I set down my wine. "Really?"

"We were Abbott and Costello, riffing off each other."

He circles the food trolley to sit beside me on the bed. "Besides, it was just a food demonstration. There was no big press junket. Nobody's going to think anything of it."

"But I have to cook again tomorrow," I say. "And this one's on live television."

He brushes my hair behind my shoulder. "I'm glad you told me, Magnolia. We're in this together. Now that I know, I can predict what you might struggle with and make sure I handle it. I'll make it look like I'm being a good boyfriend."

"You are a good boyfriend."

Something flickers behind his gaze, and I know he's thinking of last night.

"Should we talk about it?" I ask.

"I don't know." He lets go of my hair. "I'm not sure what's happening here."

"I didn't either for a long time," I say. "I thought you

were doing this out of a sense of obligation. To fix the problem."

His smoky eyes fix on me. "I was and I am. But last night, it felt like more than that."

"It is." I squeeze my fists. This is hard. "I don't have a ton of experience with men. I mean, I have some. But not a lot. It's scary. And this tour is so important. I'm afraid."

"I am too," he says, astonishing me. "Because I have been falling for you ever since New York, and it's been killing me to think that this was all an act for you. You clearly did not like me one bit before New York."

Butterflies flitter through my belly. "You were the enemy."

"I know. And I wanted to fix it. Then you were about to confess on that show, and I couldn't stand it. So I kissed you, and suddenly I realized it was just an excuse to do what I'd wanted to do all along."

I can't stop looking at his face. Anthony wouldn't lie. He's not that kind of guy. He's the sweet kind. The sort of guy you look for and think you'll never find.

He lifts my hand. "You cut yourself on the squash, didn't you?"

I feel drunk even though I've only had a few drinks of wine. "I did. I'm a mess."

"This one?" He lifts a finger to his mouth and kisses the tip.

"It's fine."

"Is it?" His attention moves to the finger. "Yes, you'll live."

My belly flutters. We've come so far. "It was a tiny nick."

Our eyes meet. "Should I leave?" he asks.

I shake my head *no*.

He holds onto my hand, letting my fingertips trace down his chin until it rests on the rapid thump of his heart.

He was so ardent last night. I know he wants me.

I'm ready to explore. I lift my hand to run through his light brown hair. His eyes close, reveling in my touch.

I move down to his shirt. "Is it okay if I unbutton these?"

He nods, not opening his eyes.

It's been quite a while since I last dated someone, and even longer since I slept with anyone. The memories are distant and forgettable.

I reach the bottom button and push his shirt open. His chest is smooth and warm. I remind myself of all muscles, hills, and clefts I felt last night. His abs are subtly defined.

I push the shirt off his shoulders. My hands glide along his arms, then back into his hair. I want to memorize him.

He reaches behind me for the zipper of my dress. It slides down my back, cool air hitting my skin. His mouth finds my neck, then moves along my body as the dress falls to my waist.

The cream-colored bra is trimmed in lace, and his warm breath flutters along the edges as he kisses his way into the cleft between my breasts.

He reaches for the back of the bra, and some of my

tension dissolves with the release of the band. He drags it away and tosses it to the floor.

"So beautiful," he murmurs as his mouth feasts greedily, taking a nipple into his mouth.

My hands run along his back. I let him play, drowning in his perfect attention after the stress of the day.

He slides me onto my back. "Can I look at all of you now?"

I nod as he presses me down on the pillows, my hair spilling everywhere.

He eases the dress over my hips, and I'm left only with a pair of cream lace panties.

"I'm going to kiss every inch." He starts with my mouth, delving deeply. He tastes of wine, his tongue sliding along mine. I shiver, already feeling lost. Every worry, every thought, every care falls away except for him.

He moves down my neck, between my breasts. Then his breath tickles my ribs and belly. He nibbles along the lace of my panties, then his fingers slide inside the edge and ease them down.

My body hums with anticipation, one arm thrown over my forehead.

When the panties have gone, he murmurs, "So lovely."

He kisses the inside of my knee and begins moving up my thigh.

"I could never have pictured how beautiful you are in all the times I've thought of it."

So he has been thinking about this.

His stubble brushes my inner thigh, and I suck in a breath.

"I can't wait to taste you," he whispers. "Is that all right?"

I grip the pillow with both hands, the fire licking through my body like nothing before. "Yes."

He places a kiss at the apex of my thighs and slides his tongue lower.

He makes his way slowly, and a moan escapes my lips.

Anthony is a man who takes his time. I begin to throb, aching for more.

He pauses to say, "You're delicious. This is what we need to bottle."

I choke out a laugh. "Whatever would we call it?"

"Magnolia's petal…" He hesitates.

"Sauce?" I suggest.

He laughs, pressing his face into my belly. "Now that's a title. What have I done without you?"

I tangle my fingers in his hair. "I think the question is what are you going to do next?"

As if I've given him a dare, he drops his face and sucks lightly on my clit.

My hips lurch forward with the sudden explosion of pleasure. "Oh!"

Heat spreads through my center as he licks, his tongue warm and wet, then he does it again, with more suction.

"Oh my God!"

"You like that?" His voice is husky.

"Yesss."

He licks again, and this time when his lips fasten on my clit, I slide over the edge, my body shuddering with orgasm. I'm released, pleasure spiraling through me, my breathing labored. "Oh my God, God, God." My arms fall to the bed.

"Not a bad start," he says. He kisses his way back up to my breasts, his mouth closing over a nipple to mimic the sucking he did below. "Mmm. Who needs food when I have Magnolia Boudreaux?"

I reach between our bodies to unfasten his belt. The leather slides from the belt loops with a sensuous hiss. I pluck open the button and zipper and push the designer pants down.

He kicks off his shoes. In seconds, the pants, and the boxers beneath them, are crumpled at the end of the bed.

I drop my gaze. He's long and hard. A thrill zips through me.

I slide my hand down. Everything is smooth. Did he shave his balls?

My eyes meet his. "Manscaping?"

He grins. "Maybe I planned ahead."

A giggle escapes. "Anthony Pickle, you're terrible."

He touches my chin. "Before we do this, you should know my last name is actually Packwood."

I sit up. "What?"

"Dad wanted us all to use Pickle as a last name to support the franchise."

"But Packwood, it's—" I can't even say it.

"I know. It's basically the same thing."

I glance down at him. "Well, you're definitely packing wood."

He rolls over on top of me. "Magnolia, you have one filthy mouth."

I can't stop laughing. "Only when I say your name."

His breath is warm on my ear. "I'm hoping you're about to say it a whole hell of a lot."

He reaches down and slides his fingers inside me. His thumb circles my clit.

The same ache I felt when he first began floods me a second time. I clutch his shoulders.

"I want inside you," he says. "What do we need to do to make that happen?"

Unlike my sister, I'm on the pill. But I flash to her situation and wonder if we Boudreaux are somehow super fertile. "Do you have condoms?"

"I do."

He rustles around in his pants pockets, then returns.

I relax again. I'm protected. Twice over.

He leans over me and parts my thighs with his knee.

For a moment, our eyes lock again. "I knew I was meant to be with you," he says.

He slides inside. I am so wet and ready that he glides in as if he was made for me.

Maybe he is.

He moves carefully, propping himself up on his arms to watch my face. He's attentive, and at the same time intense. I can feel the pleasure ripple through him as I spread my hands across the muscles of his back.

I don't want to close my eyes. I love seeing him. But

he reaches between us, circling my clit again, and need of him overtakes me.

"Anthony, yes."

"Yes," he breathes in return. I realize I've said his name, just as he asked.

His strokes increase in speed and intensity. He lowers his head to capture my nipple with his mouth.

His thumb on my clit works in quick circles while he slides in and out of my body.

The tension I felt earlier when he licked me is nothing compared to the burgeoning need in my body now. Bright flashes of pleasure start to spark from where we are joined.

His mouth moves from one breast to the other, and my back arches up to meet him.

I clutch his shoulders, moving with him, finding our rhythm.

"Anthony, Anthony, Anthony." It's happening again. "Faster. Harder."

Anthony is more than happy to oblige.

We rock together, the bed shifting quietly beneath us. I feel hot and swollen around him as he moves over me again and again.

"Magnolia," he says, and that first beautiful expression of my name sends me up the spiral even farther.

There's a distinct sensation that we're floating, that we're no longer even on the bed. We clasp each other.

I kiss his cheek. "Make me come again," I whisper.

His motions slow down, become more deliberate. His hand moves in tandem with his strokes. Our bodies sync, blending together like the perfect ingredients of a favorite dish.

The tension gathers, clenching where he works my body.

But suddenly, it flashes like a hand grenade. I cry out, shocked at the intensity, and say his name, God's name, every word I know.

"Magnolia, Magnolia." His thrusts become fierce. I'm already coming, my body pulsing when I feel him begin to shudder as well.

We hold onto each other, waiting out the storm. The beauty of it settles around us, and we rest, clinging to each other on the bed.

His hand twists into my hair. "Magnolia," is all he can say.

I nod against his neck. "I know."

"I never will leave here," he says.

"Me neither."

So we don't, curling tightly together. We sleep until the buzzer reminds us that it is a new day, and we have a cooking show to do.

And our fake relationship might not be nearly so false.

Readers, you were right.

23

ANTHONY

Mama Nita's cooking show the next day goes perfectly.

During rehearsal, Magnolia and I go over every step to ensure she knows how to handle the ingredients.

But it wouldn't have mattered. Mama Nita is a warm grandmotherly chef specializing in interior Mexican cuisine. She treats everyone on her set like family.

It's a long show, though, and the recording takes most of the day.

We have our driver grab a deep-dish pizza as we sit close in the backseat to head back to the hotel.

"Three down, two to go," Magnolia says.

"That means we're over halfway."

I rub my thumb up and down her arm. Today was good. I woke up with Magnolia in my arms, and I look forward to ending the day the same way.

After we return to the hotel and devour the pizza, Magnolia says she has something to show me.

I kick off my shoes and lie back on the bed in her room. We seem to have unofficially chosen it as our resting place.

I glance around. Her suitcases are organized, propped open on racks. She's neat and orderly, but I could have guessed that.

Her shoe boxes are stacked on the dresser. I have a similar set straight from Charity. I remember that we're supposed to call her to say how the show went. It can wait.

Magnolia peeks her face through the cracked door. "Are you ready for this?"

"Do I get a hint?"

"Well, you remember that first night when you showed me your plaid pajamas?"

I do. "You said you had something you would never wear."

"I changed my mind."

Now I'm interested. I sit up on the edge of the bed. "Well, let's have it."

When Magnolia steps out, I'm momentarily struck dumb.

She wears a satin cream silk robe that barely tops her thighs.

Her feet are encased in satin kitten heels, leaving her legs long and exposed.

"This really is a gift from Charity," I tell her.

Magnolia glances down. "Isn't it?"

"You think she suspected we would end up together?"

Magnolia takes a couple of steps closer to the bed,

her hand on the belt. "Based on this, I'm thinking she did."

In a flash, she unties the belt and lets the robe fall to the floor.

If I were a fourteen-year-old boy, I would have completely shot my load.

The cranberry négligée Magnolia wears is completely sheer. It falls across her body in a sheen of shimmery gauze.

Her pink nipples taunt me, caressed by the fabric.

The panties could barely be called anything at all, two tiny strings tied in bows on her hips, ending in the narrowest V.

She follows my gaze. "I had to do some lady-scaping to wear this sucker."

I'm practically salivating. I simultaneously want her to never take it off, and to take it off right now.

"I'm going to fuck you so hard," I say.

She touches her cheek with her finger, her eyes lifted to the ceiling. "Why, Mr. Pickle, such language from a gentleman."

I reach out for her with a growl and drag her close to me. I want to memorize her. Then I want to touch every inch of her, and lick.

But she whirls away from me.

"Not so fast." She walks over to the enormous plate glass window on the wall. It's covered with blackout curtains.

She whisks them open in one quick move.

Outside, the Hollywood Hills sparkle with lights. It's titillating, seeing her, so naked against an outdoor scene.

But we're on the top floor. No one should be able to see in.

"I want you right here," she says.

I have underestimated Magnolia Boudreaux. Quiet and unassuming.

Not tonight.

She looks me up and down. "You should be naked."

I have never pulled my clothes off as fast as I did right then.

When I've got the condom on, I stride over to her, pulling her body roughly against mine. "Sometimes I think I know you, and then you surprise the hell out of me."

"Do I?" Her sparkling eyes search mine. "I wouldn't want to be predictable."

I flash back to that very first time we met, on the set of Milton's show. This fire in her was there then. I see it now.

"Miss Magnolia, prepare to get fucked."

I press her against the window, trapping her hands beneath mine. Those pert breasts lift as she sucks in a breath.

I blow hot air across her skin, easily passing through the thin wisp of fabric that hides nothing.

I take a nipple in my mouth, teasing it into a tight bud.

So she wants something different. I'm game.

I move my hand to grasp both her wrists, and jerk the tie holding back the curtains.

I wrap it around her joined hands and pull them high.

"I like this," I say. "I really like this."

Her gaze lifts to mine. "Me too."

The glass is cool on my forearm as I hold her hands above her head. Beyond the window, lights twinkle, and down below, cars cruise along the street.

But up here, it's just us. I grasp her thigh with my hand and part her legs.

My mouth claims hers as my fingers easily shift aside the flimsy fabric of the panties and slide inside her.

She's slick and wet. This night is getting her, the window, the outfit.

I lift her thigh and wrap it around my body.

"You ever scream?" I ask her.

She shakes her head. "No."

I enter her in one swift thrust.

She sucks in a sharp breath. "God."

I press her into the chilly window, thrusting upward, hard and firm.

She gasps, again and again. "God. Anthony."

She liked it gentle and easy last night.

But I can see she likes this, too. Hard and fast and relentless. I lower my head to gently bite her nipple.

"Oh my God!"

I release her hands and grasp her other thigh, wrapping both legs around me. I hold her with both hands, my body pushing into hers without mercy. My thighs work, muscles clenching. Her face is tight with concentration.

She can't stop calling out. "God. God. Anthony."

I grind against her with every thrust, activating her clit.

The tone of her voice goes up with each connection until it reaches a keening cry.

Her legs began to tremble. I thrust in again, this time keeping the connection, grinding and pressing, gyrating in a circle against her wet, slick body pressed against the window.

She screams.

Her body shudders. I pump all the way through the pulsing. Only when she begins to settle in my arms do I unleash in her.

By the time it's all spent, we're both shaking. I shift her in my arms to carry her to the bed. I lay her down and untie her wrists.

Her eyes are closed, her face the picture of bliss haloed by her golden hair.

The fabric floats along her body, and I take a moment to gently run my hands along every curve, across her breasts, rising and falling gently with her breath. Then her ribs, belly button, and down across her hips. I tug on the strings of the tiny panties and they fall away.

"Maybe something to bring you down?" I ask. "A gentle nightcap."

"Mmmm hmmm."

I lean low near her belly, sliding her thighs apart.

She moans gently as my tongue finds those tender overworked parts.

I tease her carefully, bringing her up slowly. When I think she's back in that space, I gently suckle at her clit.

Her body trembles, and she cries out. "Oh my God."

Her body pulses gently until this orgasm also subsides.

She turns onto her side with a long, slow sigh. I slip in behind her, pulling the covers over us. By the time I properly spoon behind her, she is already asleep.

And I'm pretty sure I'm falling hard.

24

MAGNOLIA

The rest of our trip is like a dream. More shows, Anthony by my side.

More sex. So. Much. Sex.

We explore every side of ourselves. Tender. Hot. On fire. There seems no limit to how differently we can do the same act.

I've never known anything like this.

But all good trips must come to an end.

And now we're back in Boulder with no idea how to approach the not-fake fake relationship with our families.

I'm hoping to broach the subject with Havannah, but with her upcoming sonogram and baby daddy search, she's terribly distracted.

The morning of the doctor's appointment, we have to straight-up lie to our parents about why neither of us can be at the deli.

I take the fall, saying I'm having a girl problem and need Havannah with me at the doctor's office.

Depending on how you interpret it, maybe it's not such a big fib after all. Because we definitely have a girl problem. My sister needs a conception date.

I sit outside the room while Dr. Briggs does the pelvic exam. I love my sister, but there's only so far up her biz I need to see.

But when the nurse rolls in the sonogram machine, I follow.

"Everything looks good so far," Havannah says when I stand near her head. "Since I'm nine weeks, we should be able to make out the baby's body."

Nine weeks. That seems like forever. I lean down to whisper, "Did you make any headway on the...you know?"

"Possibly. The sonogram will tell us almost certainly."

The nurse passes the doctor something that looks like a curling iron. Is that what's going inside my sister?

I grip her hand. Havannah watches the black screen.

"Here we go," the doctor says.

I stick to the screen too, not interested in seeing the long wand disappear or thinking about where it's going.

The white dots on the black screen shift and move. I can't make out anything.

There's a black hole in the center, and then, a round edge of white. Is that the baby?

Then I see it. The baby's silhouette, a belly and a head. "There's the wee one," the doctor says. He holds the wand with one hand and types with the other. "We'll take a shot of that for home."

"Do we have a conception date?" Havannah asks.

"Once we do the measurements, it will pop up some dates," he says. A tiny print scrolls out of the machine. "Here's the head. The body. And look, there's the heartbeat." He turns a dial and a *whomp, whomp, whomp* sound fills the room.

Tears squeeze out of my sister's eyes, and I instantly start crying, too. "There he is," she says. "He's real."

Numbers begin to fill in the right-hand side. "Looks like the LMP is September 16," the doctor says. "That would be when you bled last. The baby's due date is June 22."

Havannah squeezes my hand. "A June bug!"

I peer at the numbers. "So, conception is...?"

The doctor shifts the wand and the view changes. "Right at the end of September. Maybe the 30th, give or take a day. Does that sound right?"

"It does. Thank you," Havannah says.

We watch as he takes more measurements, then withdraws the wand. "Everything looks good. On your way out, you'll set up several appointments. Feel free to call any time you have worries. Angie will give you lots of things to read. What to eat. What to expect. Congratulations." He shakes her hand, then mine. "See you soon, Havannah."

When they've left, Havannah sits up. "I'm going to get dressed, then we'll look through my texts. September 30 was mid-week, and there was only one guy I didn't bang on a weekend."

"So, you think you've narrowed it to one?"

"I think so." Her mouth is set in a tight, serious line as she pads to the corner for her clothes. "We'll want a paternity test, but I feel sure it's going to be the first of the three-boy run I had. The others were too late."

When we get in my car with Havannah's books and pamphlets, she starts searching her phone. "So, Mark was October 3 and Jessie was October 9. That's too late."

"Who was September 30?"

"It was September 29. And all I have is his username."

I brake too hard at a red light, shifting us forward in the seat. "What?"

"He was the one who paid cash. We got tacos and then did the deed in his car."

"You conceived your baby in a car?"

"Yeah, the dark might explain the condom incident. Maybe he didn't even put it on right."

"Havannah!"

"Water under the bridge."

A horn honks and I realize the light has turned green again. "Well, is he still on Blendr? Can you score another hookup and find him that way?"

"Already on it."

She's quiet for a moment, so I focus on driving. No sense getting us killed before we can even find the baby daddy.

"We should probably go to the deli," I say. "We've missed a good chunk of the day already."

"Fine," she says. "I'm going to have to tell Mom and Dad eventually." She waves the sonogram. "They're going to be grandparents."

"You're going to do that today? At the deli?"

"No. I should figure out this father thing first. It will be easier if I at least appear to be in a relationship." She bumps my arm with her elbow. "Hey, maybe I can take a few lessons from you about faking it. You and Pickle Boy have convinced the world."

Yikes. Right. I need to tell Havannah about my change of status with Anthony. I haven't had a chance yet.

"Shit." Havannah's voice is laced with fear.

"What is it?"

"He hasn't been active on Blendr in over a month."

"What does that mean?"

"Blendr is location-sensitive. So he might not be in Boulder anymore."

"Did he live here?"

"We didn't get to that!"

"But he had a car here. So he didn't fly in for a trip."

She pokes at her phone. "True. It was his car for sure. Full of his clothes and random stuff. Definitely not a rental."

"Did you two talk at all?"

"I wasn't in it for the conversation, Mags." She huffs out a breath.

"Are there any clues on his profile?"

She reads the text. "I'm a cool bro looking for a real ho for a good time. I will treat you right."

"God, Havannah. Standards?"

She turns the phone to me. "What about these standards?"

When we hit the next red light, I take a look. The

man peering out has a huge laugh, shaggy blond hair, and could pass for Kurt Cobain in a heartbeat.

"Whoa. The baby is going to be one good lookin' kid."

"I know, right!" She turns the phone back. "See?"

"I get it." We're only a few blocks from the deli. "What's your next move?"

"His username is CheetahGuitar. That's got to mean something."

"Do you know his first name? You had to say something during the act!"

She thinks for a second. "Jesse."

I relax a little. "The guitar's a clue. Did Jesse say he was in a band?"

"There were guitar picks all over his back seat."

I picture Havannah banging a Cobain look-alike in a messy back seat and have to shake the image away. "So, start looking for a Jesse in a band related to Cheetah."

We pull into the deli lot and Havannah tucks her phone away. "Mags, I'm going to go in and say hi, then head home to do social media alone." She gestures to the pile of baby paperwork. "My mind is not going to be on pastrami."

"I'll get Dad to drive me home," I say.

We head inside. Havannah is true to her word, and after a quick stop by Dad's office and a short exchange with Mom, she's off.

"Keep me posted," I say. "I want to know."

She nods. "I will."

I head to the kitchen to see how the new menu items have been faring. We added the new dessert the same day as the announcement. We *must* improve profits to help Havannah.

Stupid Jesse and his craptastic condom.

Sakura oversees two crew members at the metal prep table. They have an entire line of freshly baked sugar cookies set out.

"How's it coming?" I ask.

Her face brightens, and she tucks a bit of shiny black hair under her cap. "The cookies are flying out the door! We have people coming in just to buy some."

"Good!" I'm anxious to head to the back and review the daily receipts since we introduced the new menu. "Keep 'em coming!"

"Will you be doing more shows?" she asks. "I'll want to know when to taper off the supply order."

My mind flashes to more cities, more wild nights with Anthony. "Certainly. It's going very well."

Sakura's gaze rests on my face. "You are glowing, Magnolia. I think the publicity agrees with you."

My cheeks warm. "Thank you. I'll make some projections based on sales so we can decide on the orders."

She nods and turns back to the assembly.

I've barely sat in my chair and powered on my computer when someone knocks. I've left my office door open.

I expect it will be Dad, but when I swivel in my chair, I'm surprised to see Shane.

"Oh—hey," I say. "Did you need something?"

Shane's grin is sheepish. "Just checking in. You doing okay after a week with the enemy?"

I try not to stiffen. He's only following up on our pantry discussion. "It went well. Seems like it's helping business. And that's the whole point!" I spin back to my computer in hopes that this will send the signal that I'm working.

But he steps inside the door. "So, I wanted to ask you about something."

I sigh. He's not going to go away. I turn back around. "What is it?"

He shuffles his shoe on the hardwood floor. "So there's that new Avengers movie. Would you like to see it?"

Oh, God. He's asking me out.

He's an employee I'll be seeing every day, so I try to avoid a direct rejection. "Is there a group of staffers going?"

His cheeks redden. "No. I meant just you and me."

"Oh."

He takes another step closer, and I resist the urge to roll backwards to escape him.

"I think we both know what's been happening between us," he says.

"I don't think I do." I try to keep the shakiness from my voice. He's harmless. We're at my work and my dad is on the other side of the wall.

"Grandmama seemed to think we were a good fit."

I can't stop myself from saying, "Don't call her that."

He frowns. "I thought we were all like family here."

"Then we definitely shouldn't be going on a date." I

give him a weak smile. "It would be like dating your sister."

"I don't think of you like a sister." He leans down, and my panic rises when I realize he intends to kiss me.

I push hard with my feet and sail across the room in the rolling chair.

He opens his eyes and realizes I've avoided him. His eyes darken.

"Are you sweet on Anthony Pickle now?"

"No!" I sure as hell wouldn't tell Shane first. Anthony and I haven't decided how to approach our families with the news. They still think it's all fake.

"Are you sure? There was a lot of kissing on those shows."

"Those are scripted! Practiced! It's what we have to do to sell sandwiches!"

Shane relaxes. "Good. I wouldn't want to think you were falling for him."

I press my hand to my heart and draw in a deep breath, so I won't overreact. "No, of course not."

"Then I still have a chance." He shoves his hand in his pockets and heads for the door.

I want to nip this immediately. "No, Shane, you don't," I say. "I'm too old for you. You work for my dad. It's not going to work."

He doesn't turn around, staring into the hall. "You sure about that?"

"I am."

Shane walks the rest of the way out of my office. I jump to my door, closing and locking it. I had no idea his crush on me was so intense. I should have set some boundaries sooner.

It's a full five minutes at my desk before I'm calm enough to pull up sales figures. Things are looking good. We're almost doubling our gross sales, and the cookies are leading the rise in revenue. I wonder if they can be packaged for the online shop.

Things are good.

A text comes through from my sister.

Found him.

I respond immediately. *Really! Who is he?*

H: Part of some crappy band that plays the hole-in-the-wall bar circuit.

Me: Still, that's fun. Where is he now?

H: Hold on, I found something else.

There's a big delay. What did she find?

Me: Havannah? Are you okay?

After what feels like an eternity, she finally responds.

No.

She sends a link, and when I pull it up, my stomach revolts. I can barely contain my shock and disgust. I'm sure she's probably throwing up.

I immediately gather my things. I have to go home to her. I'll take Dad's car. Call an Uber. Whatever I have to do.

As I click off my phone, the headline of the story sears my brain.

Local band member Jesse Smith arrested for beating wife after she accuses him of dating app cheating spree.

25

ANTHONY

Magnolia calls in tears. She won't say exactly what's wrong, only that her sister is devastated, and everything is falling apart.

I try to comfort her, but she doesn't stay on long. She thought her sister had fallen asleep but realized she wasn't. She had to go.

I sit with my sales figures at home, but I worry about Magnolia and her family. At least money is less of an issue. The burst of sales has kept the staff busy, and it's been an incredible boost to both of our bottom lines.

Magnolia finally texts me an hour later.

She's sleeping again. Can't talk but I wanted to say goodnight.

You sure you're okay?

I am. Not sure about her. I'll tell you about it soon. Just not yet.

Okay. Good night.

I lift my arms and stretch in the desk chair. I should go to bed. I don't know how much I can see Magnolia now that we're back. We're supposed to leave next week for the New York leg of publicity. But if Magnolia is having a family crisis, maybe we should cancel.

I head to bed thinking of her. Maybe someday soon I can bring her here, sneak her inside for at least a while, if not the night. I hold on to those thoughts, since I'm not sure when she'll be part of my reality again.

By Wednesday, our trip is a go. Magnolia says her sister is better and has a lineup of girlfriends to hang out with her while we're gone. She's still not ready to explain.

This trip butts against Thanksgiving. Our original flights had Magnolia flying back on Wednesday to be with her family while I stay north to celebrate with mine.

But I hope we can take the opportunity to tell my family about us, then come back to Boulder to announce it to hers.

She listens to my plan as we settle into our seats on the flight out. "Can Charity change my flight?"

"Charity can make planes stop mid-air."

She smiles. "The only trouble is that if I skip my family Thanksgiving, they'll want to know why."

"Your sister knows, right?"

Magnolia shakes her head. "Not yet. She's going through some stuff, and I'm not bringing up my crazy life."

"How about this. I'll talk to Grammy Alma about an early dinner. You see if you can push yours until evening. We can make both."

"It's a three-and-a-half-hour flight, plus security and all that."

I hold up a finger. "If Grammy serves at noon Eastern, that's 9 a.m. Boulder time. We'll gain all those hours back on the flight."

Understanding registers on her face. "Right. So, we fly out at, say four o'clock in New York, then get back hours and touch down at four-thirty in Boulder, we can easily make a six o'clock dinner here."

"See?"

"I'm in."

I lean over to plant a kiss on her mouth. "This is going to be the best holiday of my life."

Even without Mom, I think, but the sadness at another holiday without her is softened by the idea of having Magnolia there.

We only have one official talk show in New York, but a news crew will be filming us at the Manhattan Pickle for a segment as well. When we arrive at my deli, Dad and Grammy Alma are already there, guiding the stage-hands who are shifting tables and shining up the line.

Dad is dressed up today in a blazer. He stands at least a foot taller than Grammy in her floral dress and gray curls.

"Anthony! There you are!" Grammy draws me into a hug. I breathe in the familiar scent of her, rose powder and bread dough. It's the best smell in the world.

Dad pounds me on the back. "You going to introduce me to Magnolia?"

She extends a hand. "We met once before. At the Albuquerque restaurant convention six years ago."

He peers at her. "You've grown up a mite since then."

"And you've opened a deli in my town." Her gaze bores straight into his.

"I hear yours is doing well, and you might open a second."

"We might." Magnolia stands tall. She isn't the least bit intimidated by Dad. Good for her.

I glance at Grammy, who gives me a wink. She likes Magnolia already. I can tell.

Dad holds out an arm. "Shall I show you around? No trade secrets between deli owners."

My chest squeezes when Magnolia slides her arm through his. This is working out even better than I had hoped.

The segment is easy compared to our usual filming gigs. Magnolia and I serve customers side by side, making our new sandwich and ladling soup. We each take a bite of the same cookie, like Lady and the Tramp. It's all silly and fun.

When we've returned the deli to its normal state, Dad suggests we all go to dinner. Magnolia is game, and in the car on the way I whisper to her, "Should we tell them?"

But nothing gets past Grammy Alma. Her hearing is so fine that she can pick out a line of gossip about her family in Grand Central Station. She turns around in the front seat. "Tell us what?"

Dad catches my gaze in the rearview mirror. "Is something wrong?"

"There's been a new development," I say, and Magnolia starts to giggle. "What?" I ask her.

"You're calling it a *development*?"

Grammy wags her finger at us. "If you're here to admit that you're actually a couple, I could have told you that three weeks ago."

"Three weeks ago?" I glance at Magnolia. "That was before Los Angeles."

Grammy turns back around, all smug. "Then I knew before you."

Dad pulls up to a red light and turns back to us. "So, are you confirming or denying that you two are the real deal?"

Before I can answer, Charity texts in all caps. WE HAVE A PROBLEM. PLEASE CALL.

Charity never uses caps.

I show the text to Magnolia. She nods.

"Hold on to that thought, Dad."

I put the phone on speaker and dial.

Charity answers instantly. "First, how did the filming go at the deli?"

"Smashing," Dad says.

"Hello, Mr. Pickle," she says. "You're all together."

"Grammy too," I say.

"How delightful. Unfortunately, we have a situation. Is Magnolia with you?"

"I'm here," she chimes in.

"Does this sound familiar to you?" Charity asks. "It's a recording."

A scratchy sound comes over the phone. Then, a male voice, hollow, like he's in a small room.

"Are you sweet on Anthony Pickle now?"

Then Magnolia. *"No!"*

Then the male. *"Are you sure? There was a lot of kissing on those shows."*

Magnolia sounds agitated as she says, *"Those are scripted! Practiced! It's what we have to do to sell sandwiches!"*

"Good. I wouldn't want to think you were falling for him."

"No, of course not."

Magnolia's face is ashen as she listens.

Charity speaks. "Is that a recording of you? Or is it fake?"

Magnolia's voice shakes as she asks, "How did you get that?"

Charity says, "So it's real. That's fine. I just have to spin it."

"How are you going to spin that?" I ask. "It blows the lid on the whole thing!"

Magnolia meets my gaze with wet eyes. "I'm sorry. He had me in a bad place. I wanted him to go away."

I squeeze her hand. "Did he upset you?"

"He hoped we could be a couple."

"I get it." I squeeze her fingers on the seat. "We'll get through this."

The car goes quiet.

Grammy Alma breaks the silence. "So, I have an idea."

"We're all ears," Charity says.

"A proposal," Grammy says. "If they get engaged, no one will believe the lie."

"But it's another lie," Magnolia says.

"People believe what they want to believe," Charity says. "And they love this love story."

Dad pulls the car into a loading zone. "We were about to go to dinner. Should we go ring shopping instead?" His eyes meet mine. "Or should we go somewhere else?"

I know what he's asking. I hesitate. I shake my head no. "A jeweler is fine," I say.

"You have a place?" Charity asks.

"Of course I have a place." Dad glances at us. "Is this an acceptable solution?"

"What do you think, Magnolia?" I ask.

She meets my gaze. "Well, I got us in this mess in the first place. And the second place. Now a third. I think I have to agree with whatever you all decide to do to get us out."

"Ring shopping it is," Dad says, pulling the car back into the flow of traffic. "Charity, should we have a crew?"

"No. Let's make it a surprise for viewers on the show tomorrow. Anthony can tip off the host."

Grammy claps. "Diamonds are a grammy's best friend."

We laugh, although when I look over at Magnolia, she's staring out the window. We never truly confirmed with my family that we were together, and I sense that right now is not the time.

Instead, we're apparently getting engaged.

26

MAGNOLIA

I sit in front of the mirror in the dressing room of the *Kitchen Time with Dawn* set, practicing my surprised look. "Oh, Anthony! Yes! I will marry you."

Gross. I look like a low-budget jewelry commercial.

I try again. "Yes, Anthony. I would be honored to marry you."

Yeeech.

The shave-and-a-haircut knock on the door can only be Anthony.

"Come in!"

He opens the door a crack and peeps through. "Are you indecent?"

"I might like to be."

He steps inside. We've broken the cranberry color palette finally, and he wears a navy shirt and khakis. "Fancy digs on this show, right? Dressing rooms?"

"It is." The nook is small but private. Dawn has been doing cooking shows for a decade and has been able to customize her studio.

"I've been practicing my big speech," he says. "Want to hear it?"

"Should I? Every time I go over my acceptance, I sound like a soap opera diva."

"Maybe we should keep it spontaneous." He leans down to kiss my head. "I like the headband."

I turn to the mirror. I'm wearing a sapphire dress with a gold stripe along the neckline and sleeve hems. It seems too much for a cooking show, but Charity was adamant. "It's a proposal. It will be shared relentlessly."

To give me a touch of royal feel, who knows why, she sent a stylist with a metal headband decorated with gold flowers. My hair is curled for the first time in an appearance, long loose ringlets cascading over my shoulders. "I'm a Cinderella wannabe."

"You look like a princess, for sure."

I lean back against his belly. "Why the hell did Shane record me?"

"Spurned men can be just as vindictive as women scorned."

"Dad fired him. He texted me this morning."

"Good."

"He could do more damage."

Anthony squeezes my shoulders. "We're going to make this right. And then, maybe, retire from public scrutiny."

"I hear that."

"You've practiced answers in case Dawn asks about the recording?"

"I don't think she will. It's not her style. But I have

my answer ready. It was me, but from weeks ago, before we fell in love. I have no idea why he released it now."

"Good."

A young woman steps up to the doorway. "Ready?"

I stand. Here we go again.

We meet Dawn, a mid-sixties woman with a pouf of gray hair and merry blue eyes. "So glad to have the cooking love birds on my show!" She grasps my hand warmly. "You ready for Christmas cookies with a kick?"

Anthony says, "I've got my Cayenne shaker ready! You've never made Christmas cookies like this!"

Spicy cookies. I would never have thought our pickle rivalry would lead to this. The show will air next week, after Thanksgiving, as everyone gears up for the holidays.

The cameras move into position. There's no audience for this show. Final cookies have already been made. In fact, every stage is prepared ahead of time. We're mostly ornamental, chatting with Dawn and prepping a batch that is destined for the trash.

We mix the dough and roll them out. Anthony dusts my nose with flour and kisses it. I act the part like I always have, but inside my stomach quakes.

The pear-shaped diamond Anthony paid for last night cost two years of rent for me. I had such a wonderful time with him in L.A., but the experience of buying the ring with his family was a struggle. As much as I'd dreamed of a day like this, it is hollow to do it for a fake proposal. It's like having your first kiss be someone who only did it after losing a bet.

We cut out a dozen cookies before the first break. As planned, Anthony takes Dawn aside and tells her his surprise —he is going to propose to me on her show and I have no idea.

Dawn lights up, glancing over at me, her hands on her cheeks.

The set crew cleans up our mess and brings out trays of unbaked cookies artfully arranged on the cooking sheets. Baked cookies already wait for us inside the oven.

"You want me to clean your apron?" a young woman asks. I glance down. I have a line of flour from where I pressed against the counter.

"I've got it. Thanks." I brush the flour off. My ringlets keep falling over my shoulder. It feels wrong. If I were cooking for real, I'd want to pull my hair back. And who bakes cookies in a dress?

Everything about me is fake. From the makeup to the hair to the clothes to the big moment about to unfold. I want to run.

But this is bigger than me. I want that second branch. For me. For Dad. And for Havannah. I've almost made it to the end. With the holidays approaching, we can take a step back. Sales are up at our delis and preorders are excellent for our online store.

We've already succeeded.

We just have to fix this one stupid problem Shane caused.

Anthony returns, all smiles. "Ready to decorate?"

I nod. Two crew members arrange pre-filled squeeze bags of royal icing. I practiced my technique, ensuring I could reasonably pipe "M" and "A" inside a heart. If I screw up, they'll cut to the final, already prepared by Dawn's staff.

That's right. I'm also a fake chef.

The cameras move into position. Dawn shifts next to us. "Show us that beautiful pan of cookies," she says.

We lift the sheet to the cameras, then pause so Anthony and I can share a sweet couple look. We're the ideal, happiness and joy, cooking together.

Fake, fake, fake.

We move down to the frosting counter and the cameras reset.

I pipe my heart. Anthony expertly decorates an elaborate Christmas tree with tiny candles on each bough.

Dawn passes a cookie to me. "Try one, Magnolia. I added a special ingredient to yours to rival Anthony's Cayenne."

I accept the red stocking with trepidation. At least if I choke on the spice, they can cut it out of the show. I take a bite.

Heat sears my taste buds, but I manage to keep the shock off my face. "Wow! It's hot! It's not Cayenne?"

"No, it's red curry!" Dawn beams. "Isn't that clever?"

Anthony lunges for the cookie and knocks it from my hand. "Spit it out!"

I freeze, then remember he thinks I'm allergic. More fraud. "It's okay, Anthony," I say.

"But it's curry!"

I give him a weak smile. "I'm fine with curry."

He opens his mouth, understanding dawning. "I see."

Right. I can apparently lie about anything.

We record that segment of the show again, this time with me taking only the tiniest nibble. Dawn shows off more completed cookies, and I'm guessing it's time for the proposal.

Anthony leads me to a part of the set not hidden with a counter, a table and chairs set for Christmas. A plate of perfect cookies waits for us there.

Anthony lifts a candy cane. "It's fun to add a little fire to the red frosting to make a spicy surprise on your cookie platter."

Dawn turns to the camera. "Fire cookies. How is that for a Christmas with kick! Thank you for watching this episode of *Kitchen Time with Dawn*."

Anthony taps her on the shoulder. "I have one more thing," he says.

"Oh really?" She feigns surprise.

Anthony takes my hand and leads me to the other side of the table, where a lace napkin covers a plate.

"What's this?" I ask.

He shifts me so that we're in the optimum position for the camera and lifts the plate.

He gets down on one knee and holds the plate up to me.

I'm confused. Did he put the ring on the plate?

I lift the lace napkin. Beneath is a huge Christmas tree cookie. It reads *Magnolia, will you marry me?*

My hands fly to my face. "Anthony!" He pulls a box from his apron pocket.

Dawn takes the plate and sets it strategically behind us on the table.

Anthony opens the box to reveal the ring. "Will you make me the happiest chef in the world?"

He did a smart job of bringing out my surprised face with the cookie. He's good.

Despite the farce, knowing it's all for show, my eyes mist up. Anthony's expression is so earnest. It feels real. How could that face tell a lie?

I can only nod at first, then squeak out a tiny, "Yes."

He slides the ring onto my finger and stands, pulling me to him. His thumb caresses my cheek as our eyes lock. A single tear slides down my cheek. If only this were real.

He moves close and whispers, "I love you," in my ear, but it's on the camera side, so it's only a tactic.

His lips meet mine and it's a relief, something familiar in all this overwhelming emotion. I kiss him like I always do and fall into his closeness. We both smell of sugar and vanilla, Christmastime and peace on earth.

When we break apart, Dawn claps and the crew cheers.

"What a lovely way to start the holiday!" she says and draws us into a hug.

The director calls for the cut, and the crew descends, cleaning up. Dawn breaks away. "Thank you for such a memorable moment on the show. I bet this becomes a classic."

"Happy to," Anthony says.

The sound tech unhooks us, and we head to the dressing room. Only when Anthony has left me so he can collect his things does the full weight of what we've done hit me.

I lift my hand, the diamond sparkling in the mirrored light.

To the entire world, I'm engaged.

I've just committed the biggest fraud of my life.

27

ANTHONY

The day before Thanksgiving, I take Magnolia to my dad's brownstone on the Upper West Side.

We haven't talked to them about our official relationship status. Magnolia slept in my room last night, but there was a strange quality to it. She seemed lost. Confused. Unlike herself.

Something is wrong, but when I ask, she waves it off, mentioning her sister. The holidays.

I understand that. Just walking up to my old front door infuses me with memories. Mom, turning to lead me up the steps, her arms laden with grocery bags. Unlocking the door, calling for Max to stop fooling around.

Glancing up with pride at her window boxes, teeming with red blooms. She loved bright pops of color. Life with her in it was always vivid and sharp.

I've only just begun to see those hues again, the world coming into focus since Magnolia arrived. I take her hand and head up the gray stairs. It's cold here, colder than Boulder even. Magnolia is angelic in the white puffy coat, made up like the show days even though we're done recording in New York. She spent a lot of time this morning doing it herself.

Grammy Alma opens the door. "Welcome, welcome!"

"What are you doing here?" I stamp the snow off my feet as we enter the small foyer.

"You're making me feed everyone at noon tomorrow. I have to start cooking today!"

"Is your deli covered?" Grammy has her own tiny counter-service walk-up in Brooklyn.

"Sunny's running it through lunch, then we're shut down until Monday."

"Nice break." I reach to take Magnolia's hand, then remember we haven't confessed. I take her coat instead and hang it in the closet by the door.

Dad is in the kitchen, his old familiar "Kiss the Cook" apron on. Mom gave it to him when we were young. My throat tightens.

"There you are!" he says. "Anthony, I could use a hand dicing the peppers. Magnolia, you're a guest, so you set your pretty self wherever looks comfortable."

Grammy heads to the fridge. "We have eggnog if you'd like some."

It feels like old times. I slide a set of peppers near me and pick up a knife. "When are the rest arriving?"

"Max and Camryn are on their flight," Dad says. "I've sent a car to fetch them. Jason and Nova will be later on."

"I'm so glad everyone's coming," Grammy says,

closing the fridge with her hip. Both hands hold sticks of butter. "They get to meet this one."

I glance over at Magnolia. She's not wearing the ring today. We agreed that until the show aired, it didn't matter.

"Oh, I saw something today," Dad says. He nudges his phone with his elbow. "It's queued up. Thought you and Magnolia might want to take a look."

I pick up his phone. His access code is the same, Mom's birthday. My throat tightens as I press the numbers. She would have been sixty in two weeks. No one's mentioned anything about honoring the day.

His phone serves up a video promo for *Kitchen Time with Dawn*.

"Look at this," I say to Magnolia. I press play.

The video shows a bit of bonus footage that was taken of me hiding the ring behind my back. The camera zooms in so that the pear-shaped diamond is in full view.

Magnolia busily rolls out cookie dough in the background.

An announcer says, "What famous couple will have a romantic surprise right on the show?"

Dawn's logo fills the frame.

I press stop. "Cool, right?" I say.

Magnolia nods. "A good ending to the season. This is the last one, right? We don't have anything else booked this year?"

"Charity has some leads, but only if we want to pursue them."

"You two ought to take a break," Grammy calls from the sink. "You've been traveling like mad."

"We have." I scroll through the comments. There are hundreds. A few of them are linking to the online store. Excellent.

"What is that?" Magnolia asks, and I pause.

There's a title on a comment that says, "THAT RING IS FAKE."

I shrug. "Probably some armchair gemologist."

"It's got almost a hundred replies," she says.

I open the comment thread to reassure her, then stop cold. I want to hide the phone, but Magnolia takes it from me.

"What?" Her voice has a high, frightened quality.

Dad and Grammy stop what they are doing to come close.

Magnolia reads the original comment, every word sharp, like an accusation. "I dated Anthony Pickle two years ago. He proposed to me, and this is NOT his family ring. He was VERY CLEAR that the woman who held his heart would wear his mother's ring. He gave that ring TO ME. I turned him down, but I know the right ring. AND THIS ISN'T IT. This relationship is a LIE. Listen to that recording where she admits it. THAT is the TRUTH. Magnolia and Anthony are only trying to sell you crappy food with a fake love story!"

Magnolia's hand is shaking, and I take the phone before she drops it. "Magnolia—"

"No." She shakes her head. "I've had enough. Enough. We've made good money. This has to stop."

She backs toward the door. "I can't take this. Fake kisses. Fake love story. Now a fake engagement?"

She runs into the door frame, then shifts so she can walk through it. "I'm going home, Anthony. My family needs me."

Then she hurries away.

I stand in shock for a moment, then glance at Dad. His lips are pressed tight. "Go get her, son. Try to make it right."

I sprint out of the kitchen.

Magnolia has pulled her coat out of the closet and heads for the door.

"Magnolia, wait."

She doesn't stop. "I'm getting a cab to the hotel. Please ask Charity to reinstate my old ticket for tonight. I want to go home."

She pulls open the door. "I'll leave the ring in the safe for you. We can talk business after the holiday."

I start to follow her, but she holds up a hand. "I've had enough, Anthony! Back off!"

So I stop on the top step.

She hurries down the sidewalk. Her arm lifts as she flags down a cab driving slowly along the curb.

Dad comes up beside me. "Aren't you going to go?"

I shake my head. "She's stubborn. We'll catch up again in Boulder."

He puts his hand on my shoulder. "So, what really is happening between you two?"

I shrug. I don't even know. "We were getting along."

"Is it true you proposed to that other girl? You never told us."

"I did. She said no. There was nothing to tell."

"Were you broken up about it?"

"Yes and no. I guess I knew she wasn't the one, but I was tired of looking."

He squeezes my shoulder.

We head back inside.

"I need to call Charity to get Magnolia's flight square."

"You do that." He steps away. "For what it's worth, I think you two will figure it out."

I nod and head to my old bedroom to make the call.

I'm no good at this. I never see what's coming.

All I can do is try to make the inevitable ending go easy.

Dad's house feels empty once Magnolia is gone.

Charity confirms that Magnolia used her ticket for Boulder.

The smells of cooking waft up to my childhood bedroom, still festooned with Mets pennants and high school memorabilia.

Max and Camryn arrive, and the hush that follows their boisterous entrance tells me that quiet conversations about me are happening elsewhere in the house.

When no one knocks on my door, I head to the desk and dig around until I find the lockbox hidden in the back.

I turn the three sliders until it opens. Inside is a worn blue velvet box.

My dad gave it to me shortly after I graduated culinary school. Opening it now, I can only picture the princess cut diamond flanked with blue baguettes on my mother's finger. Every time she brushed back my hair after a fall or showed me how to stir a proper batch of fudge, it winked on her hand.

I know exactly who wrote that comment on the site. Calinda Foster. I dated her while we were both in culinary school. But when I opened the deli, she made clear that her skills were for Michelin-starred restaurants, not counter service delis. She berated my choices.

Still, I proposed. I was prepared to abandon Boulder Pickle for her. Fly to France. Learn any cuisine.

But that wasn't enough. It turned out it was me after all. She handed back my mother's ring with a grimace. I regretted my heartfelt spiel. I brought the ring back to New York to get it out of sight.

And I made a mistake this time too. A big one.

In the car when we decided to buy a ring, Dad asked if I wanted to go somewhere else instead. He was asking about this ring. If we should fetch it.

And I had said no.

I said no.

I could have stopped this whole thing by coming for it. Using it instead.

But I hadn't. I didn't want to make a fool of myself a second time.

Now it's too late.

The front door opens and closes, a sound I could always hear from my room, as I'm directly above the entry. Jason's voice calls out, and the happy sound of my family gathering rises again.

I should go down there. Be a part of things.

But I can't stop looking at the ring. What would Mom tell me to do? I told Magnolia I loved her on the show. That was a mistake. She won't believe it if I tell her again. She'll assume it's all part of the ruse.

A rap on the door startles me. "Anthony?"

It's Max. He's always the one who reaches out. He'd flown all the way to France to fetch Jason once.

I pop the box closed and stick it in the drawer. "Yeah?"

He opens the door. "The gang's all here."

"I'm sure the whole block heard."

He laughs. "Subtle, we are not." He sits on the bed. "You want to talk about it?"

I shrug. "As usual, the youngest is making life difficult for everyone."

"No, bro. You never do that. You're the only one who's had your head screwed on right from the beginning. It's why you were Mom's favorite."

"Mom didn't have favorites."

"*Au contraire.* We don't begrudge you. You were the cutest kid." He reaches over and rubs my head with his knuckles. "Which is why we treated you the worst."

I duck away from his hand. "Well, I've screwed the pooch this time. Nothing's gone right since I went on that stupid show. I wish I'd never invented that spicy pickle."

The doorway darkens. It's Jason. "Now that's a sack

of bull if I've ever heard one," he says. "You went viral. You're famous."

"And look where it got me." I fall back on the bed and stare at the ceiling. It's the same swirl of paint with zero answers for me since I was born.

"So, do you like this girl or not?" Jason asks. "Nobody's clear."

"Yeah," I say. "I do."

Max elbows my ribs. "Then why the hell did you let her get away?"

"Like I could stop her!"

Max and Jason exchange glances.

They say the same thing simultaneously, "She's a Packwood."

I sit back up. "Hardly."

Jason slugs my shoulder. "We're not saying it's going to be a smooth ride."

Max punches my gut. "It never is."

"You two beating up on me isn't going to solve anything."

They both laugh.

"We're shifting your pain around," Jason says.

The two of them head to the hallway.

Max has a parting shot. "It's going to work out. Just don't quit on her. Say something. Even the wrong thing. Just keep talking."

Their footsteps disappear down the hall.

So I should say something.

Like what?

Sorry I proposed with the wrong ring? We've only *not* hated each other for a month.

I snatch up my phone from the desk. I'm not good at this.

But then, probably neither were my brothers, and they managed to snag their perfect match.

She's a Packwood. Were they right?

I start and delete a dozen sentences. Finally, I only text her this: *I'll be back in Boulder on Saturday. Hope to see you.*

But I'm not going to hold my breath.

28

MAGNOLIA

Despite the comment from Anthony's ex, the word about the fake engagement doesn't seem to gain any traction. Charity thinks that since nobody's seen the proposal yet, they are reserving judgment.

She has the show delete the comment, and Anthony's ex doesn't pursue it any further.

On Thanksgiving Day, as we all pitch in to cook the meal, I tell my parents about the upcoming fake proposal on Dawn's show to undo Shane's recording. It's a relief to tell someone the truth.

"I'm sorry I ever trusted that boy," Dad says. "Dan was particularly broken up. He'd taken Shane under his wing. He was like a son to him."

"I hope I never see him again," Mom says. "I can't believe he called me *Mom* like he had any claim to our family."

We've finished dinner and the dishes are drying on the rack when Havannah takes me aside. "I think this is as good a time as any, don't you think?"

"You're going to tell them you're pregnant?"

She nods.

She's done more research to make sure the baby doesn't belong to one of the other guys. Based on her positive pregnancy test date, it's impossible to have been anyone else. A pregnancy from either of the later men could not have given her a plus sign that early.

Psycho band dude has pled guilty to assault and will probably serve about a year. In the follow-up stories we've read, other women he's injured have come forward, so new charges are being filed. He's toast. We don't want him.

Havannah's decided single motherhood is going to be her lot. She doesn't want to think about the father and has decided she won't entertain any questions about him from anyone, not even Mom or Dad. She and I will be the only ones who ever know, at least as long as the man is in jail, and until the baby is old enough to ask about it.

I hold her hand as we walk to the living room, where Dad watches a football game from his recliner. Mom is knitting a green cap on the sofa, and Grandmama rocks in her favorite chair.

We wait for a commercial. Dad glances up. "Since you girls are on your feet, can somebody get me some iced tea?"

Havannah nods. "In a second. I have an announcement first." She picks up the remote and mutes the sound.

She draws in an unsteady breath. "Mom. Dad.

Grandmama. I'm having a baby in June. By myself. No father. I'm excited and I hope you'll support me."

Mom drops her knitting. Grandmama stops rocking. Dad looks at the floor a moment. Then, as if he suddenly realizes exactly what Havannah has said, he lunges out of the chair. "You are *what?*"

"Pregnant," Havannah says. "Due in June. I won't find out the gender for a while yet." She grips my hand like a vise.

"I'm going to help," I say. "We might get a larger place. It will probably be okay for a while. We've started rearranging Havannah's room to make space for a bassinet."

"I demand to know who the father is," Dad says. His face is bright red.

"Your demand will not be met," Havannah answers. I admire her calm. "I'm to be a single mother, and I will need my family."

Mom sets aside her knitting. "That's ridiculous, Havannah. The boy needs to step up."

"He won't," she says, but her voice has a shake in it. "And I don't want him to. If that is all you have to say, Magnolia and I will head on home."

"That's enough," Grandmama says. "It's a family holiday. We should spend it together." Her eyes shoot daggers at her son. "Sit down, John Paul. You're going to be a grandfather. It's not the end of the world."

Dad drops back into his chair, his hands gripping the armrests.

"Havannah, my love, sit over here," Grandmama

says. "How are you feeling? I had the worst morning sickness with your father."

Havannah lets out a tiny whimper of relief and releases my hand to sit near the rocker. "I've been terribly sick. Only crackers and ginger ale seem to help."

Grandmama begins to rock again. "Let a little Sprite go flat and sip that when you first wake up. That's what did it for me."

Havannah nods.

I lean against the wall, relieved that the moment of shock is over.

Mom resumes her knitting. "I found plain saltines were better than butter crackers. And it was all done by the time I was three months."

"Same here. How far along are you?" Grandmama asks.

"Ten weeks."

"So not much longer until you feel better."

I fetch the tea Dad requested. Now that the big news is out of the way, I'll compile our financials and take my idea to Dad about the new branch. We've planned it for years, but this is the first earnings quarter where it seemed like we could make it work.

The shipments from the online store will roll out in two weeks, and the preorders are tremendous, six figures, just like Charity promised. The money from the orders will be dumped into our accounts before Christmas. It's amazing.

With so much new business, we can expand, introducing new dishes regularly with an eye toward a brighter, fresher second store that will appeal to a younger crowd. Even without Anthony generating new ideas, we have Dan. He's a trained chef, too, and brilliant with food.

The original store can remain the same or adopt the most successful of the new items. That will be up to Dad. We'll leave Sakura to manage the old store, but maybe Dan could move to ours. The most expensive position would be covered if Havannah and I manage it ourselves. We'd only need a crew.

My personal plan is to throw myself into the work. When the proposal airs next week, we will have a new rush of business. I probably should have kept the ring. People might come in and ask.

But of course, I don't work the front room. I hide in the back. So once the initial publicity has passed, it won't matter.

My relationship with Anthony has run its course. I don't have to fake anything. We never saw each other in Boulder anyway, outside of tasting the new deli items and going on the local show.

Our affair was all about the publicity and the travel. Of course it happened. Temptation was so close, with so much fake romance and hotel rooms all to ourselves.

It was fun. Hot. Amazing.

But the shows are over.

And so are we.

Kitchen Time with Dawn airs the week after Thanksgiving. I half hope they'll cut the proposal, but it runs as expected.

I watch the show as Havannah gets ready for chef Dan's annual Christmas party. I've already declined. I never want to leave home again.

Havannah pauses by the TV, fastening long swirly earrings. She's got a tiny baby bump, but in the swish of her flowy dress, you can't see it. She's not planning to announce her pregnancy more widely until January.

"He sure looks earnest," she says as Anthony gets down on one knee.

I don't answer, wishing for ice cream to shovel in my gullet. I'm getting unexpectedly teary. I'd turn it off, but Havannah sits next to me to watch.

"What does he say right there?" she asks as Anthony leans close to my ear.

"I love you," I say.

"Shut the front door!" Havannah shouts. "He said he loved you?"

"It was for the show," I say. Now I really want that ice cream.

"If it was for the show, why isn't it loud enough for the mics to pick it up?"

I shrug. "He probably didn't know it wouldn't."

"I don't think so! You two have done a million shows at this point. He knows what a mic can pick up!"

"Whatever it was, it's over now."

"Did you sleep with him?"

I never told anybody, not even Havannah. "Maybe once or twice."

A day.

"Magnolia! Why didn't you say anything?"

"You are going through something much bigger. And it didn't matter. It was just a hotel room fling while we were traveling."

Anthony and I start kissing on screen. I can't stand it any longer, so I shut off the TV. "I'm glad you're feeling well enough to go to the party after all. Does Dan know you're coming?"

Havannah watches me a moment. "That's all we're going to say about this?"

I drag the blanket up on my lap. "Yep, that's it."

She pulls on my arm. "I understand where you are. But please come to the party. It might be important if we want Dan to come to our branch."

"No way." I scoot away from her on the sofa. "Let me sit here and wallow."

"All right. I suppose you let me do that." She stands up. "I understand about wallowing."

"Get me some ice cream from the freezer?"

Havannah tosses a *really?* expression my way, but heads to the kitchen.

I pick up my phone and check my messages out of habit. Anthony has written once a day, usually around dinner time. Easy stuff. *Did you see the labels? The stock just hit the warehouse. So proud of what we've done here.*

It'll be an hour until his daily message. Sometimes I write back. Sometimes I don't. They're not personal anymore, not since the Thanksgiving one when he hoped he'd see me.

I guess he's done too.

Havannah returns with my pint of Chunky Monkey and a spoon. "Knock yourself out," she says before disappearing down the hall.

We're back to Boudreaux status quo. Havannah is the elegant sister heading to a party. I'm the wallflower binging ice cream on a Saturday night.

My phone pings. Anthony's daily message must be early today. Maybe he just watched Dawn's show, too.

But it's Charity.

Milton must have seen the comment about the ring and prepared a social media blitz for the airing of the show. He's interviewed the woman and launched an offense we'll have to handle.

The other woman. Anthony's first proposal.

I don't even want to know about it.

More messages ping. Links. Something comes through from Anthony. It's a group chat. I fling my phone to the table, half hoping it breaks.

I'm going to be humiliated. Milton will say the other proposal was real and mine was fake. I was never *the one*. Anthony's one true love was that other woman.

It's horrible. I never should have played the fame game.

I set the uneaten ice cream on the table and fall face-first onto the sofa.

Havannah returns. "Uh oh. What's going on?"

The sofa squeaks as she sits next to me. "Mags?"

My phone *dings, dings, dings,* and I wave my hand in its direction.

Havannah picks it up. She can't unlock it, but she can read the previews of the notifications. "Mags, you have to deal with this. People are suggesting everyone cancel their preorders of your and Anthony's stuff."

That makes me sit up. "What?"

"Charity is saying you two need an appearance together — now."

"Oh, God."

The phone rings.

"Don't answer that," I insist.

Havannah ignores me and takes the call. "This is Magnolia's sister."

She nods. "Uh huh. Yes, we're headed to a Christmas party. Will that work?"

What does she mean *we*?

I paw at her thigh, but she bats my hand away. "I'll text Anthony the address."

Anthony?

"Make sure he has the ring. Yes, the one from the show. What's the story about why it's a new one?" Havannah nods, ignoring my slashing motion in the air. "I'll make sure some of our friends record it and upload to social media. Is there a hashtag? Right. Boudrickle. Got it. No problem."

She hangs up. "Come with me, Mags. You're getting dressed and headed to a party."

"No!"

She stares me down. "Do you think you're sitting here mooning over Anthony Pickle because of some hotel fling?"

I shrug.

"You realize he loves you, right?"

I'm not sure about that, but I'm not positive she's wrong either.

"And you sitting here like a lovesick fool isn't going to fix anything!"

I cross my arms over my chest like a five-year-old. "I don't care."

"Come on. I'm going to get you looking like yourself." She shakes her head. "Somebody has to make you two see what's right in front of your eyes."

She takes my arm and drags me off the sofa to the bathroom.

And I'm right back to where we started three months ago, my sister prettying me up to put on a show.

29

ANTHONY

I wait in my car for Magnolia and her sister to arrive. We have to walk into this party together.

The engagement ring from Dawn's show is too small for any of my fingers, so I twirl it on the end of my pinky. This is what I wanted, to see Magnolia again. But our entire plan is on the brink of collapse.

We have to save it.

Snow falls softly, quickly obscuring the windshield. I flip on the accessory switch, and the wipers *swoosh* it away. Colored lights twinkle along the street. It should be beautiful and calm. But I'm unsure of what Magnolia will be like. Apparently, her sister has forced her to come. The last thing I feel is peace.

Magnolia's car pulls up beside mine. Her sister is driving. She reverses and parks along the curb behind me. I shut off the car and fist my hand to avoid losing the ring.

Havannah is the spitting image of Magnolia, but with softer edges. Her long blond hair spills out of a sparkly knit cap. "Anthony!" she calls. "We finally meet!" She envelops me in a hug and whispers, "She's missed you. You've got this."

My heart hammers. She has? I do?

Magnolia crunches through the snow in red boots. She wears the black coat I remember from New York.

I hurry to her side. "Here's the ring," I say, and hold it out.

She takes it and shoves it on her finger. "Thanks."

I grasp her hand. "We'll make this happen."

"Did you see all the links? Five separate videos attacking us."

"Charity is on the defense. We have a plan."

Havannah leads us along the sidewalk. "Isn't it a beautiful night?" She turns in circles, like she's thrilled to be alive.

Magnolia is perfection, her hair in curls again, her red lips a temptation I know I should resist. But there will be mistletoe and, surely, we should kiss for the posts. We have to prove Milton wrong, show him to be the malicious jerk he is for bringing up my past to break us up.

Havannah knocks on the door, then pushes it open. "Come on, love birds!" she calls. "You're the life of the party!"

A roar goes up when we enter. The house is packed with people in bright colors. A lady takes our coats, and my breath catches when I see Magnolia is wearing the dress from New York, our first date.

I turn her in a circle and the dress flares. When I pull her to me, cameras raise. Perfect.

She forces a smile, and it's convincing. Only because I know her so well do I recognize the fake. I squeeze her hand. I want to make her happy again, to find that place we were at in Los Angeles.

Havannah works the room, asking to see images. She says if they use the hashtag, it might go viral. People are excited.

I make a big show of giving her a small package. "A gift for my lady!"

Magnolia tilts her head. "Really?"

Everyone lifts their cell phones again, jostling for a good angle.

She takes the small box and unties the string. When she lifts the lid, her gasp has to be real. I know her.

She glances up. "Anthony? How?"

"What is it?" people murmur.

Magnolia lifts an earring, and its cascade of rubies catches the light.

Photos snap. I take it from her and slip it through the hole in her ear. "The woman in New York, the night of our first date, said you admired these."

"I couldn't afford them," she says, a catch in her voice. There's no fakery there.

I take the second one and place it in her ear. "She said you said they were the most beautiful earrings you'd ever seen."

Magnolia nods. "I did."

"So they belong on the most beautiful woman in the world."

The room lets out a sigh.

Her eyes glisten. When I lean in to kiss her, she's lost her tough stance. She's my Magnolia again.

When we break apart, everyone claps.

"Excellent, Anthony," Havannah says brightly. She leans in. "Uploads are hitting everywhere."

So that's done.

A tall man with a gray beard walks up. "Magnolia!" His face shifts to concern. "I thought you weren't coming!"

Magnolia tenses beside me. "Surprise?"

Havannah steps in. "We wouldn't miss a chance to sample your incredible cooking. Right, Mags?"

This must be Dan, the host. And something's up. I see it in his expression. But he gives the sisters a smile. "Of course."

Dan leads us to a dizzying array of food on a long table shoved against the wall. Shallots in cream sauce. Puff pastries. Hand-stuffed ravioli. Dips. Paté. This man is a connoisseur. A real talent. I want to eat everything.

"This looks wonderful," I say.

His brow furrows again as he takes me in. "I don't believe we've met. I'm Dan Teagan, the head chef for the Tasty Pepper."

I shake his hand. "I'm Anthony."

"Oh, I know who *you* are!" His gaze crosses the room. "It's such a surprise! A surprise and an honor."

I cast a furtive glance at Magnolia. She's watching Dan with great interest. So she sees it, too. Something's off.

Dan's eyes go wide, and Havannah turns from the

table, a cheese-covered cracker in her hand. She also spots Dan's panic. He's petrified.

Havannah turns to look where Dan is gaping. She gasps. "Dan. You didn't."

I have no idea what anyone is talking about.

Magnolia follows her gaze, and her grip on my elbow threatens my blood supply. "Dan. No."

They are upset.

Dan's face has gone pale. "I'm sorry, girls. No one from the family RSVP'd. And he's like a son to me. I couldn't leave him out."

I turn to see a lanky young man with blond curls staring at us, his expression hard. I have no idea why he's causing such a commotion.

"Who is he?" I ask.

Magnolia's voice is cold. "That's Shane. The ex-employee who recorded me and released it."

"I can ask him to leave," Dan says. "I understand completely."

Havannah's expression to Magnolia is pained.

When I turn back to Shane, he appears to be trying to leave. Behind him, a young woman follows. Something about her tickles my memory.

"Let them leave," Havannah whispers.

Magnolia's jaw is tight, but she nods.

"Who's that girl with him?" I ask.

"I don't know," Magnolia says.

"Me neither." Havannah crunches a cracker as we watch.

I let go of Magnolia to get a better look. Shane and

the woman are headed for the front door. No one is paying attention to them.

It's killing me that I can't remember her. She's throwing on her coat when I catch up. "Have we met?" I ask her.

Her eyes widen with fear.

Shane pulls her beside him. "She's my friend. Back off, asshole."

I hold up my hands. "I just was curious how I know her."

"She sure as hell doesn't eat at your lame restaurant." Shane shoves the woman in front of him, and they head out the front door.

I stand in the open doorway, watching them retreat down the sidewalk. It's not her face I recognize so much as the green streak in her hair. Where did I see it?

Magnolia comes up beside me. "Good riddance," she says.

"I know that woman," I say.

"Her hair is unique. Shouldn't be hard to ask around."

We return to Havannah, who is still talking to Dan.

"Who's the woman with Shane?" Magnolia asks. "Anthony thinks he's met her."

Dan runs his hands down his apron nervously. "Some college friend of his. Talia, I believe. She's studying performing arts."

"Are they dating?" Havannah asks.

"No," Dan says. "They've been friends for a long time."

My memory snaps into place. "Does Talia work in lighting? In the theater?"

"Maybe?" Dan looks like he wants to escape. "Can I interest you in some wine? I'll go open a fresh bottle." He hurries to the kitchen.

Magnolia sidles close. "You think she was at Milton's filming? They had theater student volunteers."

I pull Magnolia away to a corner. "I'm positive she was. During rehearsal, they were setting up the lights. She was there."

Magnolia's gaze meets mine. "What are the chances that Shane had Talia doctor the pickles?"

"High. Do you think he wanted to make you look bad?"

She shakes her head. "No. He wanted to ask me out. I think he wanted to impress me. He wanted to make *you* look bad."

"Do you have his number?"

"Not in my phone. But Dan would."

We turn back to the party, which has been oblivious to the drama. Havannah remains by the food table. Dan is opening a bottle of wine in the kitchen.

I take Magnolia's arm. "Let's go."

Dan doesn't seem pleased that we're back, but he plasters a smile on. "Thoughts about that wine?"

Magnolia's voice is all business when she says, "Dan, I'm not here to put your employment at risk. You're a great chef and a strategic part of our expansion, should we get that opportunity."

Dan's hand stills on the bottle. "That's good."

"But I need you to text Shane."

The older man's throat bobs as he swallows. "Is this about the recording? I'll have you know that I fired him myself. When your father told me about that terrible breach of trust——"

"It's more," Magnolia says.

"More?" Dan's hands fall to his sides.

"We think he doctored the pickles on Milton's show. Or he had Talia do it. She had access to the set."

Dan sags onto a stool near the oven. "I worried about this."

"You did?" I ask.

The man nods, his fingers pulling at his short beard. "He asked me what would make pickles too horrible to eat, too hot for anybody."

Magnolia steals a glance at me. "What did you tell him?"

"To use capsaicin."

"Like pepper spray," I say. "That explains why it burned."

"It's a food product," Dan says. "It won't poison you."

Magnolia draws in a deep breath. "But it will incapacitate your mouth."

I try to control my anger. "And you didn't think to tell Magnolia about this at any point?"

Dan drops his gaze to the floor. "Magnolia had already talked to me about altering the pickles, and I told her about the tomatillo. I assumed Shane was just continuing the line of thought. He was with me at work when the show was recorded. I didn't see any way it could have been him."

"But it was her," Magnolia says. "Talia."

Dan nods. "I'm guessing so."

"Text him," I say. "You know we need a screenshot."

He pulls out his phone to send a message. After a moment, it chimes, and he types frantically, his mouth twisting at each response.

Finally, he turns the screen to us. "It's done."

I take it and angle it so Magnolia and I can read.

Dan: Does Talia work in theater arts?

Shane: Who wants to know?

Dan: Me.

Shane: Sure. She's done the lighting in the theater all semester.

Dan: What about Milton's show? That was a big one.

Shane: She was there.

Dan: So she had access to the pickles?

Shane: What are you saying?

Dan: Shane, did Talia put the capsaicin I told you about in the pickles on Milton's show?

Shane's response is exactly what we wanted.

Of course she did. And I'd do it again to ruin that asshole.

We have him.

30

MAGNOLIA

After the text exchange, Anthony and I dance a few songs and take selfies with the guests to make sure everyone sees us.

Then we escape to his car.

Charity answers our call on the first ring. "Lots of good party posts, you two!" she says merrily. "Did you leave?"

Anthony doesn't want to mess around. "We know who doctored the pickles. Sending you a screenshot."

We hear the ping. "Excellent. Time to put this to rest." Keys tap on her end, then she says, "Can you get to Vegas by seven a.m. tomorrow?"

Anthony looks up at me. "It's a twelve-hour drive. We only have nine hours."

"Hmm. Let me check flights." More tapping.

Anthony and I sit quietly in the dark. The snow has completely shrouded his car. We could be alone anywhere. Parts of me tingle at the thought.

Charity finally asks, "Can you get to the Denver airport by eleven?"

"Should be able to," Anthony says. "It's less than an hour drive. We have ninety minutes."

"I'm booking you on a flight to Vegas. Don't worry about clothes. I'll have something at the hotel when you get there."

"Charity," I say, "what are we doing?"

"You are going to be on *Vegas Today*, a morning show with national syndication."

My voice is admittedly a whine when I ask, "Another talk show?"

"You two will be surprise guests. I know the booking agent. He'll let you on."

"Why the rush?" Anthony asks.

"Because of the other guest tomorrow morning." Charity's voice sounds almost maniacal as she says. "Milton Creed."

We arrive at the hotel a little after one a.m. We have only four hours until we have to get dressed and made up for the show.

"Should we bother sleeping?" I ask as I open the suitcase that was already in the living room of our suite. It contains a vibrant green dress for me, and a pair of khakis for Anthony along with a matching green shirt and plaid Christmas tie.

"I'm feeling wired. Should we push through?" He kicks off his shoes.

"Maybe." Two bedrooms open off the living room. "Are we only here for tonight?"

"No clue. But we could stay another night." He hesitates. "If you want."

Do I?

Anthony sits on the sofa, elbows braced on his knees. He watches me quietly. "We haven't talked about what happened in New York."

I sink onto the rug in a puddle of red skirt. I can feel the beautiful earrings swinging. "Maybe I overreacted."

"I don't think so. We were dealing with a lot. Shane's recording. The decision to do the engagement. Then Calinda's comment."

"That's her name? Calinda?"

"Yes."

"You...loved her? Wanted to marry her?"

"I thought so at the time."

I unzip my boots and kick them off. I guess I should know everything. "So, what happened?"

"She turned me down. She wasn't that into me."

"And the ring?"

"I stuck it at Dad's house so I wouldn't be so stupid again."

"And that's why you bought a new one?"

At first, he stares at the floor, and I think—well, this is it. The admission that there was no way he'd ever think of me that way. We were a fling. A temporary bit of fun.

Relationships just don't happen for me.

Finally, he says, "I didn't want to use it on something that wasn't real."

So, there it is. We aren't real.

I stand up. "I understand completely. I'd feel the same about a treasured family heirloom. You have to be careful who you give it to."

I move toward my room, but Anthony leaps up and takes my arm. "Magnolia, wait."

I jerk it away. "It's fine, Anthony. We've had fun. The engagement made it messy. That's why I had to stop it. It was confusing me. Some kisses were fake, others weren't. This engagement was fake, but Calinda's proposal wasn't."

"I shouldn't have let you leave in New York."

I turn away from him to stare at my bedroom door. "You didn't have a choice. I took off."

"I didn't want you to." His voice is plaintive. My heart unclenches.

"I'm so confused." It's the truth.

He wraps his arms around me from behind, his mouth near my ear. "I've missed you so much. I wish we could have met any other way."

My laugh sticks in my throat. "I wouldn't have given you the time of day. You know it."

"I was the enemy. But we're a team now. A damn good team."

I turn around in his arms. "We are. And we solved the mystery."

"Together." His eyes search my face. "Can we be? Together?"

"I don't know. I'm not sure what's real."

He lifts my hand and opens my fingers. "This is what's real to me."

He extracts something from his pocket and lays it in my palm. The chain is long and unfolds from his fingers to my skin. At the end, lying on top, is another ring. This diamond is square cut with blue stones on either side.

My throat constricts. "What is this?"

"My mother's engagement ring. The one I should have given to you. I know it's not time for us to get engaged for real. It's only been three months, and we were at each other's throats for most of it. But I put it on a chain for you to wear. A secret for me and you while we continue this engagement for our fans. Do you believe that's what I want?"

I do believe him. I lift the chain. It's long enough to go over my head, the ring slipping beneath the neckline of my dress.

"Is it a good length to stay hidden?" he asks.

My gaze lifts to his smoky eyes. I've missed him. Everything about him. The real kisses, the touch. The way we've been behind closed doors. I press the dress over my chest, feeling where the ring falls low in my cleavage.

"Why don't you look and see for yourself?"

His kiss tears into me, our mouths hot. Fire licks through me instantly, heating the core of my body.

His hands slip behind me to unzip the dress. It falls to the floor, revealing the black bra and panties beneath.

Anthony bends down, kissing my skin beneath the chain, dipping his tongue between my breasts. He unfastens the bra, and it falls.

Warm lips close over my breast, and his hands slide

down my body. I'm back where I was meant to be, in his arms, naked and wet.

His fingers tease me along the narrow edge of the panties before shifting them down.

He kneels and lifts my knee over his shoulder. His mouth finds me, his tongue slipping inside. I grasp his hair, holding on, my back against the door.

He remembers everything, suckling the clit, and pleasure flares out like a sunburst. I close my eyes. How could I have walked away from this? He knows me. He pays attention. We fit.

Fingers slip inside me, reaching into the space already slick with need. He works them, sucking harder, and I'm lost. My head bangs the door as my chin lifts, the orgasm pulsing outward. My standing leg threatens to buckle, but Anthony grasps me firmly. He holds me in place, drawing the pleasure out, until I sink against the door, breaking his hold.

"I love you," he says, pulling me against his chest. "I said it in New York, and I'll say it now."

So it hadn't been for the cameras. The mic wasn't supposed to pick it up.

I wrap my arms around him. "I'm sorry I didn't have more faith."

He stands, lifting me with him. "I'm sorry I ever gave you cause to doubt."

He opens the knob and walks us to the bedroom.

We only have hours until we must prepare for the show, but there is no need to set the alarm.

We have no intention of sleeping.

31

ANTHONY

We end up taking about an hour nap, jump out of bed at six and get ready in panic mode.

None of the staff is expecting us, so we won't have stylists or help on the set. The only people who know we're coming are the show host and our handler.

It's gonna be a shocker.

Magnolia does her makeup in the car. Fortunately, we're only ten minutes from the news station where the talk show is held.

We wander through the front door, and the woman at the desk gets saucer-eyed when she sees us. "We're looking for Dante," I tell her.

She touches her headset. "Dante, you have people."

I give her a nod. "We're a secret, so remember, we weren't here."

A heavy-set black man rounds the corner. "This way. Quick. We don't want you seen." He motions for us to dart down a back hallway.

We pause inside a storage closet for a moment.

"They're moving Milton," he says. "Sorry. I'm Dante. We don't usually have secret guests. There's no protocol." He grins. "This is going to be great."

"What is Milton doing on the show?" Magnolia asks.

"Glazing a ham," Dante says. "Alicia says you can run with all the pig jokes you can stand."

"Happy to," Magnolia says.

"Damn, this is cool," he says. "All right, time to move."

We head down the hall. As we approach a set of double doors with the red *On Air* light above it, he slows us down. "I'm waiting on the go-ahead."

"Will we have mics?" Anthony asks.

"Yes. A sound tech is inside. They'll wire you, and we'll wait for Alicia to say she has a surprise for him."

He nods to a voice we can't hear, then opens one of the doors.

The backstage area is dim with red safety lights marking the path. Dante stops us right inside the doors, and a man with a tiny flashlight in his mouth clicks a mic to my collar and expertly slides the wire to a pack. I turn to watch as he does the same to Magnolia.

"Move it, move it," Dante whispers, his foot tapping.

His anxiety sends mine up a notch. We haven't rehearsed what we're going to say. Charity said to stick to the facts. She sent the screenshot in case Alicia wants to use it.

Dante leads us to the edge of the sound stage. A small audience sits in a smattering of rows. Milton stands behind a rolling counter, demonstrating his glazing technique. It's messy. I'm not sure why he's doing it. Any hack could pour honey on a ham as well as he is.

Alicia stands opposite him, facing our direction. She's a head taller than him, graceful in a gold-toned suit that sets off her dark skin. She sees us, or at least Dante, and turns to Milton. "While you finish, Milton," she says, "we have a little surprise for you."

Milton glances up, his gloved hands dripping honey. "Is that so?" His face is pancaked as usual. Alicia hasn't given him a step to stand on, so he looks puny, pale, and pathetic.

I'm feeling very fine.

Alicia motions us out. "Everyone, put your hands together for Milton's arch-nemesis chefs, Anthony Pickle and Magnolia Boudreaux!"

Milton's jaw drops as we walk out on stage, our joined hands swinging between us.

"Hi, Milton!" Magnolia says. She rushes up to him and squeezes his shoulders, pressing her cheek to his. I marvel at how different she can be on stage. Her over-the-top friendliness is like the first time I met her. I can't stop grinning.

"Whaaaa?" Milton seems speechless.

Alicia's smile is huge. "Milton, I invited the newly engaged couple on the show because they have a huge announcement to make in the wake of your campaign to discredit their love story. Anthony, Magnolia, who's going to do the honors?"

"You?" I say to Magnolia, right as she says, "You?" to me.

We laugh and she releases Milton to give me a kiss.

"We figured it out together," Magnolia tells Alicia. "Milton decided to use one of Anthony's ex-girlfriends to drive us apart." She turns to me. "Which obviously didn't work. But it made me start thinking about who from my past might have it out for *me*."

She squeezes my hand, so I take up the story.

"At a party last night, we ran into the guy who released that old recording." I give her a bright smile. "And it turns out the woman he was with just so happened to be a volunteer on the set of *America's Spiciest Chef* the day we were there."

Milton attempts to peel off his honey-covered gloves, his face contorted in rage. "Who? What's her name?"

"We can divulge that later," Magnolia says easily. "But suffice it to say, the whole pickle debacle was simply a case of a butt-hurt man." She beams at me. "But I'm grateful, because his pickle prank is what brought us together."

I switch places with Magnolia to put myself between her and Milton. "So you can stop with your ugly campaign. If you're not careful, this pig will look good compared to your career." I grab the butcher knife, wing it into the air, then neatly catch it and shove it into the top of the ham.

The audience goes crazy. Alicia claps her hands and waits until they quiet. "I love it. So tell us, Anthony, why did you switch engagement rings?"

Magnolia steps forward and pulls the long chain from her dress. "I have it. It's my something old." She glances back at me. "From Anthony's lovely mother who died twelve years ago."

The audience lets out a long *awwww*.

"It also has something blue." She holds the ring out to Alicia, who examines it.

Then she lifts her left hand to the audience, knowing at least one camera will zoom in on the ring I gave her weeks ago. "And something new. Alicia, we're almost all set for a wedding."

Alicia pulls a gold bracelet from her arm and slides it onto Magnolia's. "Girl, here's your something borrowed. I think I speak for everyone when I say—congratulations. We can't wait to see your wedding."

Magnolia raises the arm with the new bracelet to her chest. "Thank you, Alicia."

She's brilliant. Magnolia, my Magnolia. I grasp her hand and spin her into me. The icy blue dress twirls out. It's our signature move.

And I kiss her. Because she's come back to me. We've solved the puzzle and shamed the asshole trying to bring us down.

The audience cheers, and I hold her close. We're laughing and almost-crying, both of us. No shame in that. I'm the third Pickle brother, the baby. I'm allowed to cry.

Now, all that's left for us is to live this dream, pickles and all.

32

MAGNOLIA

I hold Anthony's hand as we follow Dad, Havannah, and the real estate agent into the old Salad Junction I used to go to as a kid. The long-time owners decided to retire, and when their lease ran out last month, it went on the market.

Dad found it first. He called Kirsty and asked if we could see it before it was stripped. He wanted to get an idea of how many tables it could hold, where a sandwich line might go, and how much kitchen space it had.

Kirsty unlocks the front door. The tables are still inside, chairs stacked on top. Dad takes one down and examines it. "Is Jenkins willing to sell us these?" he asks.

The stout woman adjusts her bag on her shoulder. "I can check. I'd imagine so."

"They're good," Dad says to Havannah. "That's a big cost we could delay if we can get a good deal."

She nods.

The self-serve salad bar sits along the side wall. It's a

good indication of how much space we'd have for the sandwich line. It's plenty.

"The drink station was back over here," Dad says. "It's been a while since I was in here, but I remember that."

I nod. "Definitely. And they had a small register set up by the door." I point to a discolored square on the floor.

We wander the space. Anthony stays quiet. In the back left corner is a short hall with a pair of bathrooms and a storage closet. It doesn't link to the kitchen, but Dad taps the wall. "This could come out. It's easier if we can come through this way as well as near the line."

Our group moves to the kitchen.

"It's smaller than the Tasty Pepper," Havannah says.

The sinks are on the back wall, which is unfortunate, but workable.

"It was a salad place, so there's plenty of cutting counters but not enough stove." Dad pulls a measuring tape from his pocket and sizes up the space next to the existing stove. "We'll need ovens for bread baking."

Anthony finally speaks up. "You could always bake at one location and deliver, at least at first. We had to do that for a while in New York."

Dad glances up at Anthony, as if surprised he has an opinion. "That's a fact. Keep costs low at first. Use what we've got. Spare you the early crew too. Keep labor down."

I smile at Anthony. He squeezes my hand.

Dad puts his hands on his hips and looks around. "Is there an office?"

"Over here." Kirsty leads us to a door in the corner. It opens to a large space.

"That's bigger than Dad's," Havannah says with a giggle.

"Harrumph," Dad says, but he's smiling.

We wander back to the dining room.

"I hate the colors," Havannah says. "It will need a paint job and a new floor."

"You'd have to do that anywhere you went," Kirsty says. "But this one is in the area of town you liked best."

She's right about that. Dad and I poured over maps, triangulating the existing competition and looking for spaces where younger clients would find us.

"There's plenty of parking," Kirsty adds. "That's not easy in this neighborhood."

Havannah sets her bag on one of the tables and rubs her belly. She's growing fast now that the second trimester is well underway. We're hoping to open before she delivers, since she has the most opinions on how the new branch should look.

"Why am I always hungry?" she asks.

"You've got a healthy Boudreaux in there," Dad says. "I can run down the street to the take-out Chinese place if you need."

Havannah waves him off. "I've got snacks. I'm not crazy." She pulls out a plastic bag filled with slices of mango.

I shake my head. "Our fridge is full of mango," I tell Anthony. "I swear it's the only thing she eats."

"Tell the baby," Havannah says. "The kid wants what the kid wants." She shoves a slice in her mouth, perhaps a little less gracefully than she would have before.

Kirsty approaches. "There's the other property to see. It's only a mile from here. A tad smaller, but it might have more ovens."

Havannah glances around. The tall windows in the front shine bright winter sun onto the interior. "No. This is good. Lots of light. Already painted white so it's easy to cover it in color." She holds out her hand. "I see pale blue and sherbert orange."

"It's the mango talking," I say.

"It's on the color wheel," she says. "Trust me. Paint a wavy line along the wall, about a third of the way up. It will be perfect." She has that look in her eye when she's envisioning something great.

I don't have that look. I only know the numbers on the page.

"It's in our price range. And we can lock-in three years," I say.

"Let's do it," Havannah says.

"Excellent," Kirsty says. "I'll have the paperwork drawn up."

Dad rubs his hands together. "The Tasty Pepper Two. It's a big step."

"Mmmm. No," Havannah interjects. "The Tasty Pepper Two sounds gross."

"What are you going to call it then?" Dad asks.

I glance over at Anthony, who shrugs. "Don't look at me. We're terribly unoriginal with Boulder Pickle, Austin Pickle, and L.A. Pickle."

"It should be something else tasty," Havannah says. "Tasty Sandwich. Tasty Bread. Tasty Relish."

She bites into her slice of mango.

The three of us think of it at the same time.

"The Tasty Mango!"

Havannah dissolves into laughter.

"Isn't that a little racy?" Dad asks. "Mangos are another name for, you know…" He holds his hands out in front of his chest.

"Dad! Stop it!" Havannah laughs so hard, I worry she's going to pee herself.

It's happened. Don't ask how I know.

"I think it's perfect," Anthony says. "You're going for the young market. They'll think it's a great joke."

"And it's all about baby Boudreaux," Havannah says, resting her hand on her belly. "We'll definitely use the mango craving as the reason in interviews."

Dad nods. "You have time to decide. Let's get back to the deli." He shakes hands with Kirsty. "Let me know when you're ready for us to go over the lease."

"Will do!" Kirsty says.

We follow her out onto the pavement. While she locks the door, I stare up at the old Salad Junction sign. Soon, this place will be ours.

Anthony wraps his arms around me. "It's a great choice. And I'm happy to loan you bread baking space if you need it, at least until you can afford new ovens. I'm closer than your other branch."

I kiss his cheek. "Thank you."

He lifts my hand to press his lips on the back. It's bare.

Since the publicity has died down, I haven't felt the need to wear the fake engagement ring anymore. Deli business is up. We introduce new dishes on their own merits.

Online sales are thriving. We haven't hit another viral pickle like the ghost pepper, and TikTok is on a feta cheese craze at the moment.

But we're good. Happy. And soon, the dream I started when I walked onto Milton Creed's show will be a reality.

And it's all thanks to a man I love, and his very spicy pickle.

Thank you all for cheering us on.

EPILOGUE: ANTHONY

I'm in charge of the giant scissors, and I've lost them.

Magnolia looks up from her spot near the prep counter as I move boxes around. The kitchen of the Tasty Mango is in chaos. All the employees are new except for Dan, and nobody's figured out where to store everything, especially on opening day. I shove aside a crate of potatoes.

Nothing.

"What's up, Anthony?" Magnolia asks.

I can't tell her I've lost the giant scissors. I made such a big deal about them. The ribbon on the door has to be cut with fanfare, not ordinary kitchen shears. I went to great trouble to locate the pair used on all three of the Pickle brothers' deli openings.

And now they're missing.

Magnolia's dad enters the kitchen. "We're all ready in the dining room. The sandwich line is set up. The crew is in place. We just need you girls to cut the ribbon."

Damn it. I slide another box aside. They were here yesterday.

"Is there anybody here to document it?" Magnolia asks.

Havannah breezes into the room, her impressive belly preceding her. "Hell yes, there is. Everybody wants to follow up on the deli love story of the century!" She spots me trying to casually shift a box with my foot. "Anthony, what are you doing?"

"There's a lot of boxes in here," I say, hoping to deflect.

She looks around. "I think we'll need another shelving unit," she says. "The stock closet isn't big enough." She kicks aside a box herself. "Well, what are we waiting for? Let's open this place!"

Both women head for the door in their matching mango aprons. Their dad starts to follow, then hesitates. "You've lost the scissors, haven't you?"

Damn it. "Yes."

He laughs. "I think a butcher knife works fine, don't you? Fits the theme."

He's right. I grab a large one off the knife block and take it with me.

When I make it to the dining room, Magnolia and Havannah stand near the windows looking out onto the parking lot, along with their mother and Grandmama. There's a good-sized crowd outside, including one news crew and several photographers.

I sidle next to her. She glances at my knife. "I thought you wanted the scissors."

I shrug. "I'm flexible."

She's about to take the knife when my family friend, Dell Brandt, turns around from where he's been watching the crowd.

And he's holding the scissors!

"Oh, there they are," Magnolia says. "You're so weird, Anthony Pickle."

I glance down at the knife. Maybe I am.

Dell and his younger brother, Donovan, stride closer. My dad sent them down to coach Magnolia and Havannah about best practices for opening a new business. It's the same series of lectures and planning sessions each of us brothers got when we opened ours.

Donovan's eyes alight on Havannah, and not for the first time. She's riotously happy, frequently doing a little boogie-woogie step and swaying her belly back and forth.

I slide the knife behind the sandwich counter. A fresh-faced teen flashes me a nervous smile. It's his first job. He's excited.

"Shall we?" Magnolia asks.

Donovan rushes to open the door for Havannah. Our entire party steps outside. An ornamental ribbon is set up across the porch between us and the bystanders. Most of us move off to the side as Havannah and Magnolia stand behind the center of the ribbon.

"Thank you all for coming!" Havannah says, the wind whipping her long blond hair. "We are so excited to cut the ribbon to open the doors to the new Boudreaux family deli—the Tasty Mango!" Her fist shoots into the air.

Her excitement is infectious and the crowd whoops.

"My sister and I grew up in our family deli across town, and we're so happy to strike out on our own. We couldn't have done it without our parents!" She gestures to her mom and dad. "We have the amazing Dell Brandt and Donovan McDonald here giving us advice." More applause.

"And of course, none of this would have been possible without your support of the new online store created by our culinary couple, my sister, Magnolia, and her fiancé Anthony Pickle!"

Magnolia waves to the crowd, then turns and gestures for me to join her. I walk over and press a quick kiss on her lips. The crowd whoops and flashes pop.

It's been a while since we were photographed.

Our relationship behind the scenes has gone perfectly the last six months. We planned the new store, mostly implementing Havannah's ideas. She's full of them.

Magnolia has expanded her culinary skills, since she'll be expected to do more kitchen work and not just the books. Dell Brandt recommended a financial person for them so they could focus on running logistics, at least until they could afford a manager.

Since we've mostly retired from public scrutiny, Magnolia rarely wears the engagement ring I bought. But she has it on today. It winks in the sun, and for the thousandth time, I wish I'd given her Mom's ring from the get-go. I can't undo it.

"Scissors?" Havannah calls and turns to Dell, who still holds them.

Donovan jerks them from his brother's hands so he

can walk them over to her. He's got stars in his eyes for Havannah. That's plain to see.

He passes them to her. She hasn't seemed to notice his attention. It's a big day.

Havannah and Magnolia wrangle the scissors into place. They cleanly snip the ribbon and it falls. We step aside to let the bystanders into the deli.

It's done.

When everyone has made their way inside, Magnolia hangs back. She grasps my hand. "Hey," she says.

The sun is warm. It's late spring and the weather in Boulder is fine. I shift her long blond hair over her shoulder. "What's up?"

She pulls me in front of the doors. No one's paying any attention to us, all waiting in line for the new mango-inspired line of relishes and salads Havannah has added to the traditional menu.

It's just us.

She takes my hand. "You remember when you gave me this?"

She slides the chain out of her cleavage.

"I do—" I halt abruptly when I see the chain no longer holds the ring.

The hand holding mine shifts, and she passes something to me. I glance down. It's Mom's ring.

She's giving it back? My heart falls. With the new deli open, is she ready to move on?

But her eyes say something different.

"Anthony Pickle," she says, "In the event that *your* deli hits hard times, I have the means to support us."

Her eyes are soft and shine in the morning light. "I will make sure you never want for anything. Will you marry me?"

What? She's proposing?

I couldn't smile any wider. "Yes. Yes, I will!"

She shifts the old engagement ring to her right hand so that I can place Mom's in its proper place.

I pull her close. "Now, that's some initiative, my love," I tell her.

"You were taking too long," she says, grinning up at me. "And besides, you've proposed to me before, not to mention that other woman."

When I frown, she presses her thumb to my lips. "I wanted something new for us both. A first." Her blue eyes watch me with wonder, as if I'm the best thing she's ever seen.

That's definitely how I feel about her.

"It's perfect," I say. "And the perfect day. The first day of your deli. The first day of our *real* engagement. We'll never forget it."

I lean down to kiss her. The sun beams down on us, bright and warm. The happy sounds of new customers filter from inside.

I think that maybe it could never get better than this, but then I remember—I get Magnolia from this day forward, as long as we both shall live.

And I know plenty more perfect days lie ahead.

We break the kiss and are simply smiling at each other when the front door bursts open.

It's Havannah, her face bright red. Her dad is on one arm, and Donovan of all people, is on the other.

"Baby on the way!" she calls out.

Her mother follows close behind. "I told you this was too much excitement so close to your due date."

We step aside. "Are you guys okay?" Magnolia asks.

Havannah shouts, "Magnolia, stop mugging in front of the store and get in there to run the deli. I'm having a baby!"

I squeeze Magnolia's hand. "I thought she wasn't due yet."

"Babies come when babies come," Magnolia says. "I was hoping to be with her." Her head tilts. "If this baby is early, could it be the doctors were wrong about her conception date?"

"I don't know anything about babies," I say.

We watch as they load Havannah into an SUV. Donovan backs away as the car takes off, John Paul at the wheel, her mom in the back with Havannah.

We wait while Donovan watches them leave, rubbing his head with his hand, then slowly turns to the front door.

"You okay?" I ask him.

"Sure. I guess she'll be all right, right?" His face is tight with concern.

Magnolia threads her arm through his. "Sure, she will. We can go see her later if you like. Want something to eat?"

He glances back at the retreating car and nods.

I open the door. Grandmama monitors the sandwich prep, making sure the new hires get the classic Boudreaux sandwiches right. Magnolia snags an apron from a hook and tosses it to me. "Make yourself useful, Pickle Boy," she says. "You're a Boudreaux now."

I tie on the mango apron. "But it doesn't go with my complexion!"

She shakes her head and pulls me behind the line. I guess I'm working here today. It's a good thing my own deli is in good shape with a full crew.

Because until Havannah's back in top form, it looks like I will be spending a lot of time at my deli's newest competitor, the Tasty Mango.

And I will love every minute of it.

Thank you for reading *Spicy Pickle*! I'm sure you can guess what book is coming next — TASTY MANGO!

Watch Havannah messily try to balance life with a new baby and a hot new relationship with one of Wall Street's rising stars — billionaire Donovan McDonald. Sign up here to be notified when it comes out!

While you wait, meet Dell and Donovan's family with Dell's billionaire romance Single Dad on Top. And don't forget to catch up on the Pickle family with Jason in Big Pickle and Max in Hot Pickle.

GHOST PEPPER PICKLE RECIPE AND TIKTOK CHALLENGE

Ready to try ghost pepper pickles yourself?

Here is Anthony's original recipe!

- 1 jar (I used an empty salsa jar — it shouldn't be too big)
- 1 cucumber
- 1 ghost pepper
- 1 clove of garlic
- 1 tablespoon sugar
- 2 teaspoons salt
- 1/2 cup of vinegar (Anthony does 1/4 cup of white vinegar and 1/4 cup of apple cider vinegar but you can do it any way you like — all white, or all apple cider to be sweeter)
- 1/2 cup of water

1. Heat the water, vinegar, salt, and sugar until it starts to boil.

2. Stir until the sugar and salt are dissolved. Turn off heat and wait five minutes.

3. While you wait, cut the cucumber into slices as thick or thin as you like.

4. For the ghost pepper, cut it into quarters and use however many pieces based on the heat level you want. 1/4 pepper = already too much for Magnolia. 1/2 pepper = will melt the makeup off Milton Creed. Whole pepper = just right for Anthony but might kill *you.*

5. Place the cucumber slices and ghost pepper into the jar. Pour the hot (but not boiling) vinegar mixture over them.

6. Close the lid and leave in your fridge for one week. Don't unscrew the lid until it's ready!

If you make a video prepping or eating your spicy pickle for the TikTok challenge, definitely tag @DeannaLRoy on Tiktok (JJ Knight is Deanna's pen name) and use the #spicypicklechallenge hashtag!

I can't wait to see what happens for you!

BOOKS BY JJ KNIGHT

Romantic Comedies

Big Pickle

Hot Pickle

Spicy Pickle

Single Dad on Top

The Accidental Harem

MMA Fighters

Uncaged Love Series

Fight for Her Series

Reckless Attraction

Get emails or texts from JJ about her new releases:

JJ Knight's list

ABOUT JJ KNIGHT

 JJ Knight is one of the pen names of six-time *USA Today* bestselling author Deanna Roy. She lives in Austin, Texas, with her family.

To choose your next read from one of her fifty books, visit the web site **Read Laugh Swoon** to pick by book boyfriend, story line, heat level and more!

facebook.com/jjknightauthor

twitter.com/deannaroy

instagram.com/deannaroyauthor

bookbub.com/profile/jj-knight